# Sistering

# *Sistering*

*a novel*

## JENNIFER QUIST

Cover design: Debbie Geltner
Author photo: Sara MacKenzie
Book design: WildElement.ca
Printed and bound in Canada.

**Library and Archives Canada Cataloguing in Publication**

Quist, Jennifer, author     Sistering / Jennifer Quist.

Issued in print and electronic formats.

ISBN 978-1-927535-70-7 (pbk.).--ISBN 978-1-927535-71-4 (epub).--

ISBN 978-1-927535-72-1 (mobi)—ISBN 978-1-927535-73-8 (pdf)

I. Title.

PS8633.U588S57 2015     C813'.6     C2015-901857-9
                                     C2015-901858-7

The publisher gratefully acknowledges the support of the Canada Council for the Arts for its publishing programme.

Linda Leith Publishing
P.O. Box 322, Victoria Station
Westmount QC H3Z 2V8 Canada
www.lindaleith.com

For Amy, Sara, Mary, and Emily,
all of whom inspired,
none of whom is depicted in this story.

# Suzanne [1]

She's something like a monster. That's what I'm thinking as I watch Heather—my barely-older-than-me sister—standing in a hospital elevator overseeing the lights on the control panel.

"That smell." She forces a gag. "You smell that, Suzanne? Maybe you're used to it by now, but that hospital smell still goes right through all my cell membranes and makes my perineum ache."

Everyone knows Heather can handle smells a lot worse than this. I smirk. "You mean you're glad no one's come here to see you do your thing this time."

"So glad."

The dirty metal doors slide open in front of us. Heather exaggerates a hop over the threshold, over the space where a black, empty crack drops four storeys that might as well be an oblivion beneath us.

We're in the hallway of this hospital's labour and delivery unit. I work as a nurse, but this isn't my hospital, this massive pink box visible from the Whitemud Freeway, marked with a crucifix that lights up and glows

1

at night in honour of the French-Canadian nuns who founded it. The Grey Nuns, the Sisters of Charity—out west, far from home, not at all related by blood.

Heather and I are related by blood, though we don't look alike. We have an uncle who's been joking all our lives that Heather must be adopted. Either we're too used to the joke to laugh or else it's never been funny. My genetic connection to Heather only makes sense when we're seen in a complete set of five, with our three other sisters. Then it's easy to trace Heather's wan, almost sickly features darkening, softening, becoming more robust as they shift through Meaghan to Tina to Ashley to me.

It's been a while since any of us have been inside the labour and delivery unit of the Grey Nuns Hospital—almost two entire years. The long walls are painted the same pale orange-pink colour, like the skin of most of the white people living in northern countries like this one. And Heather is right about the smell—the carts of disinfected white linens, the musty yellow mop buckets, the dread. Everything is exactly like it was the first time she was wheeled up here.

"Room number seven." Heather waves at a closed door. She's trotting down the hallway a step and a half ahead of me. "I know that room. That's where I had my first. Remember?"

I'm nodding. "Lucky seven."

Heather is all hair and noise in front of me, calling out landmarks like room seven, Tina's name jotted on the smeary whiteboard, the yellow vinyl chair that caught our brother-in-law when he passed out on his way to the coffee machine after being kept awake here for thirty hours.

There are other corridors in the hospital where the landmarks are different. They're not monuments to firsts but to lasts—not places where people have been born but places where they've died. We can't see them from this hallway, but they're a part of everything here. Heather and I, we sense it.

Don't get me wrong. I'm not morbid. I'm a nurse. The hospital's secrets are what they are, and they're known to me. Heather, on the other hand, doesn't have much to defend herself with when people accuse her of being morbid. She works as a funeral director—an embalmer, undertaker, a mortician licensed by the government to rinse out, wrap up, and send off the dead.

"Hey Suze, remember how you came here to see me while I was in labour that first time? And you brought Tina along?" Heather says. "She came into the room and stood right up against the outside of the curtain but wouldn't come any further. All I saw of her were shoes and socks—like she was that flattened witch sticking out from underneath the crashed house in *The Wizard of Oz*."

Of course I remember. Back then, none of my sisters had a baby yet. Heather was living out her privilege as the oldest of us, her curse of going first—our howling, flailing vanguard. At the time, I was only halfway through nursing school. I'd already attended to other labouring women—strangers. I had a nurse's face and I wore it for Heather, for me, for everyone when I came to see her.

She wouldn't have it. "What is with you, Suzanne?" she asked through the morphine cobwebs she swiped at but couldn't clear away from her cheeks and chin. "What's with your face? And your voice? They're all plastic and clean."

Our younger sister, Tina, was here that day without any face but her own. She was just out of high school. It was all too much for her.

And now, from behind a closed door, someone cries out in that Tarzan voice of the transition phase of childbirth. I glance around the hallway's fleshy walls. Maybe it's still too much, for all of us. Maybe it's worse and worse every time.

At the sound of the voice, there's a flinch in Heather's shoulders. "There goes all the cortisol squirting out of my adrenal glands. You feel that, Suze?"

Heather, me, Tina, our younger sister Ashley—we've each given birth to at least one baby in this hospital. Ashley laboured here, but her babies weren't actually born in any of the rooms branching off this hallway. She was taken downstairs to an operating suite instead.

"They strapped me down and gutted me like a fish," she told us when they finally let us see her and her enormous baby girl. I worried Ashley would've been sad or ashamed about not having a "natural" delivery. But that kind of fuss looked like nonsense to her after a day and a half of labour.

She came back from the operating room glorying in it, proud to be the first one of us to have a Caesarean section. Ashley is the fourth-born of our five member sister

4

group, and she hardly ever gets the honour of being the first one of us to do anything. Someone had forgotten to take the green operating room hairnet off her head before they sent her back to the maternity floor. When we saw her, she was still wearing it, like laurel leaves.

There won't be anything as radical as Ashley's surgical births happening when we find Tina here today. Babies come to Tina with all the gore and horror they're supposed to and no more. That's how it is for me too. I'd say more about my childbirth career, but no one wants to hear it. I know that. If they do, the Internet is full of blog after pink-ity blog of birth stories complete with every bit of mucus and vomit and meconium and whatever else we never find out until it's too late.

Meaghan is the only one of us never to have had a baby here. She's the youngest sister, number five, and she hasn't had a baby anywhere yet, not really.

"There's got to be a reason why I get that weird, traumatized post-abortion vibe wafting off Meaghan every once in a while. Don't you ever sense that, Suzanne?" Heather has asked me about it at least a dozen times. I don't know anything for certain. And I won't settle it by asking Meaghan. Neither will Heather. Still, the theory rings a little truer every time I hear it. Maybe this is what makes Heather so monstrous—the way her sick little hunches are usually right, terribly right.

Meaghan won't be coming to the hospital until later —until after. Ashley is already in Tina's room when we arrive, looking like a younger, prettier, slightly shrunken version of me—high, clean brows and long, dark hair.

Heather says her kids are too lazy to learn to tell me and Ashley apart without looking at which of their uncles we're married to. They're just kids, so it's hard to be snippy about it. My husband is Uncle Troy, a tall, splendid man, a dentist who likes golf and essential oils. The only thing he has in common with Ashley's husband, Uncle Durk, is his taste in female beauty.

Durk is an old teenager who likes cannabis and chakras. Today, he's been left alone to manage the fireplace store he and Ashley own.

We find my younger sisters in a birthing room near the end of the hall. Ashley is sitting in a chair pulled to the foot of the bed, texting Durk, a bit frantic from the waist up. Below her waist, her shoes are off, her legs folded into a lotus pose. On the bed, Tina is propped up by the mattress cranked and bent into a steep angle behind her. The little footstool that's supposed to be kept on the floor is set right on top of the bed, across Tina's thighs like she's about to be served breakfast. She's leaning forward, onto the rubberized black stepping surface of the footstool, resting her weight on the points of both of her elbows. I've seen it before.

"Where is Martin?" It's the first thing Heather says as we step into the room.

Martin is Tina's husband, the man known in the hospital today as a "new father" even though he has been a father for ages. I have secret theories sometimes too, and one of mine is that Martin has an attention deficit dis-

6

order, the kind no one diagnosed back in the seventies when he was the silliest, most jittery kid in his swanky school with the crested blazer uniforms. I think his disorder is what makes Tina have all these babies. She's flagging down Martin's attention by adding interest to their family. Believe it or not, this not-quite-born baby is their sixth child.

Tina doesn't answer Heather's question herself. Instead, Ashley uncoils and stands up to speak for Tina. "Martin's at the nursing station," Ashley says. "One of the ladies out there went to school with him back in the day."

Heather grits her teeth. "How heartwarming."

"Should I get him?" I offer.

Tina moans. Her verbal answer is spoken through Ashley's mouth. "Not yet," Ashley says.

"How're you progressing? What was your cervix at the last time they checked you?" I'm speaking through my hospital face, the warm clean plastic.

Again, it's Ashley who answers. "They say she's dilated to seven centimetres."

Heather throws her purse into Ashley's empty chair. "Seven? Her last three centimetres go from seven to a full ten in about twenty minutes—every time. Do they know that?"

Ashley turns up both her hands, empty. "That's what I told them. They acted like they understood me."

It's not the same as acting like they believed her.

On the bed, Tina surges into a sob.

"Where are her drugs?" Heather wants to know.

Ashley shakes her head. "They say they ordered them half an hour ago. But someone's got appendicitis downstairs, and they can't do an epidural for Tina until the on-call anaesthesiologist gets out of surgery."

"Well, there isn't going to be time for that."

"Honey?" I'm saying to Tina. "Honey, can you still talk?"

We hear Tina's voice, but there are no words. It's the sign. We all know it. It's the end.

"I'll get the doctor." Ashley is on her feet and out the door.

"Quick and shallow," I'm saying to Tina, panting, nodding. "Hee-hee-hee."

In other moments we've agreed fancy breathing techniques during labour are vain conceits left over from another, sillier generation. But right now we need something.

"He-haaa," Tina bellows back at me.

Ashley has returned with a man and a woman in green medical scrubs topped with white coats like smoking jackets at a sleazy adult pyjama party. The man's neck is long and skinny and spotty, the look of a smart kid in an accelerated high school math class. The woman is fully grown but young and quite short.

"These are Tina's doctors?" I ask.

"Yeah. She's a resident. She's brand new at it but she's still pretty much a real doctor. Right?" Ashley is moving behind them to close the door they've left open. "And he's Byron. He's a medical student."

8

We all gape at each other.

"So what can we do for you?" the resident asks.

"You need to check her," I tell the doctors. "She's close."

"She's only at seven," the resident insists. "We just checked her. And the attending doctor's not ready. He's not even here."

"Look, sorry, I'm a nurse," I say. "I hate to be pushy but this is my sister's sixth baby. She's not like other patients you've seen today. She's a multiparous woman with a history of precipitous labour. So, I'm sorry, but—"

The resident is nodding and nodding.

It's Martin himself opening the door just as Ashley gets it shut. He slides into the room right before Byron moves the footstool off the bed and the resident draws back the sheets.

The resident is the only one of us who gasps at the sight of a black-haired pate crowning between Tina's quaking white thighs. "Don't push," she calls toward the head of the bed.

In a corner, Martin is asking Byron how he's enjoying medical school.

On the bed, Tina pinches her eyelids closed and a tear falls from the outside corner of each of her eyes, moving in tandem over the pale, pink skin of her temples. More than any of us, Tina looks like our mother. I knew our mother when she was the age Tina is right now. Not all my sisters can remember back that far. Tina's face, my mother's—the familiarity makes everything strange.

Am I still in the Grey Nuns Hospital with my sisters? Maybe I've gone. Maybe I'm somewhere else—sometime else, watching as one of us is born.

"Don't—don't push," the resident says again, desperate and undoctor-ly. The sliver of the baby's head is getting wider and rounder. Tina's flesh is opening like a terrible red eye. "Don't!"

We're all talking at once.

"She isn't pushing."

"It's not like she can help it."

"It's too late. She can't hold it back."

Even Byron and Martin know it's true. The baby is being born without any consent or assistance from the rest of us. We can't let that happen, so we reach for our repertoire of hollow medical and maternal rituals.

Martin has come to the place in his typical birth script where he accepts his Platinum Card and his old-money family name have no power here. For a moment, he will be just like the rest of us. He has tucked his silk necktie into his monogrammed dress shirt. He's holding one of Tina's legs, bending it at the knee the way we've always told him to do it. Next to her flesh, a diamond-crusted cufflink glitters at Martin's wrist—cheap and obscene in this place.

Ashley is holding Tina's other leg. I am standing between the resident and the stainless steel tray of instruments Byron managed to uncover. I am here—not only a sister but a medical automaton ready to pass the resident whatever she thinks she needs and maybe a few things she won't think of at all. I don't always like Nurse Suzanne. She stands in for me—my face, my voice, my dead steady hands—when things are hard and harrowing. She shoulders past my real soul, the one that falters and suffers and loves, and takes its place.

Someday, I worry, there may be consequences. For now, Nurse Suzanne snaps sterile gloves over the resident's outstretched hands.

Tina's baby is coming so fast Heather misses one of her classic lines—the one where she crows at the squeamish males in the room to, "Get up there. Trust me: it feels way worse than it looks. Really, it just looks a lot like a slick, red sock turning itself inside out."

Instead of upbraiding anyone, Heather is bent low, her face close to Tina's ear, talking. "It's okay, sweetheart. You're never stronger than right now."

Tina's voice is mounting again.

At the sound, the glass over my medical automaton eyes cracks. Nurse Suzanne is giving way, forced aside. I can almost see him—Tina's baby—a tiny bird wheeling and wheeling through the air over my sister's body, coming close and then veering away, moving on a current none of us can sense, making himself ready to fold up his wings and alight on the earth.

We're watching when the baby sucks in his first breath. Even green Byron remembers to step forward and see, right at the end.

Tina is smiling against the pillow, holding the baby, able to talk again. She's bossing Ashley, telling her where to find the fancy camera with the autofocus low light capable zoom lens. It's engineered especially for taking photos of babies, and it cost as much as Tina's first car.

Heather steps away from the bedside. She accosts the resident in the mucky latex gloves and vocalizes what we all know. "This was your first solo delivery, wasn't it?"

The resident is grinning into her own chest, nodding.

Heather flings an arm around the woman's shoulders, jostles her like another younger sister, and tells her, "Well, you did great."

Kindness can be monstrous. It has power to devastate sometimes—now. We all look away as the new little doctor starts to cry.

In a restaurant half the city and half a month away from the Grey Nuns Hospital, Heather sits twisting an oversized topaz ring around and around on the middle finger of her right hand. Maybe the ring isn't over-sized. Maybe her hands are just too small. They'd look bigger if she'd grow her fingernails and get a manicure. She won't. Painted, bulbous nails are a sign of squandered resources and failed feminism. That's what Heather says.

She stops her twisting, looks at her wristwatch, and then at the four empty chairs at our table. So far, it's just the two of us sitting in the posh restaurant where Tina has booked a table for six in the middle of the afternoon.

"Come on, girls," Heather says.

I'm not impatient yet. Tina will be travelling with a two-week-old baby today, the perfect reason to be late.

"You want me to try calling them again?" I offer anyway.

Heather waves her hand. "There's no point. If Tina's not answering, it probably means her kids have washed her phone for her again. That nanny of theirs is a sham." She pushes her palms against the wintry static electricity of her hair, trying to get the flying yellow mass to stay behind her ears. She's laughing. "Look at that table full of lawyers over there. Could they be any less happy?"

I glance at the dour faces bent over menus on the other side of the dining room. They do look miserable, and it makes me want to defend the sad lawyers against my monster-sister. "That one guy doesn't seem too glum," I say, nodding toward the youngest man at the table.

Heather huffs. "He's not a lawyer. Look at him. He's just the poor working stiff they dragged out here to hold their coats."

But a nice place like this has a coat check. Whatever, I'll let Heather malign the lawyers all she wants. It's an oblique tactic of hers, meant to protect Ewan. That's Heather's husband. Ewan is always surrounded by lawyers. Most people assume he is one. It's a trick of his elegant vocabulary and the way he wears a suit so well. He's really a police officer.

"He is the deputy superintendent of police," Heather would insist. "Don't make it sound like he's some constable with his knee in a drunk's back, face down on Whyte Avenue."

Whatever Ewan is, the media love him. He's tall and smart and not afraid to stand in front of the crest mounted on the wall of the police station issuing official statements. "Integrity, courage, community"—those are the words on the crest. Ewan is a glorious caricature of all of them.

Reporters fix cameras and microphones on him while he speaks in sound bites about good and evil. And he doesn't embellish with those dumb police words like "utilize" and "indicated" and "subsequently." He talks in short Anglo-Saxon derived words, so people will understand, so they'll trust.

None of our husbands is here today. This afternoon, at the restaurant, it will be me, my four sisters, one newborn baby, and—as proof of what a special occasion this is—our mother. We're meeting for a baby shower luncheon. Our new-mom days of punch-bowl-party-game baby showers are long past, but we still celebrate together, quietly and bittersweetly. We meet in restaurants so none of us has to cook or clean up. Since Tina is the sister with the newborn this time, she has chosen the venue. It's one of the elite, upscale places Martin takes her when he's stuck in town.

Martin's family—Tina's family-in-law—are high society people with high society habits and tastes. This restaurant isn't the kind of place Heather, Ashley, Meaghan, or I should know exists. But lunch here is more casual than Tina and Martin's fancy dinner dates. None of the other patrons bother to deepen their scowls when Tina lumbers through the doors, still puffy with pregnancy fluid, an infant's car-seat banging against her shin. It's a classy car-seat, if there can be such a thing. She buys a brand new one for every baby. It's easier than cleaning the old one.

Meaghan comes ahead of her, holding the heavy wooden door as Tina passes.

"Ashley had better get here soon," Tina says, falling into the seat of a chintz covered chair. She flips the sheepskin cover off her sleeping newborn. "I've got forty-five minutes before he starts screaming and chomping again—tops."

I'm cooing at Tina's wrinkly red baby. I hold my hair so it won't drift down to tickle him awake. At his age, babies are anonymous enough that this little person looks like he could be one of my own. "I'll take him if he's bad," I promise. "I'll bundle him up and carry him right outside into the cold so he can sing for all the nice people walking down Jasper Avenue, if that's the way he wants it."

Tina smiles, slowly and sadly, with pale, unpainted lips and delicate post-partum melancholy. "Thank you, Suzanne."

Ashley arrives soon after we've each ordered a drink. She sails into this stuffy dining room with that careless, airy prettiness of hers, like she's flushed and windswept from a morning of surfing rather than from twenty minutes of looking for a parking space in cold, downtown streets.

Oh, and Mum has arrived too. She came along with Tina and Meaghan, walking in last, carrying a baby gift in a pastel paper bag with a satiny rope for a handle. Mum doesn't do anything she doesn't want to do anymore.

We're glad it suits her to be here with us now—at least, I hope everyone is glad.

We're sick of talking about Tina's new baby and our old babies. The newborn sleeps, strapped into his seat, under the tablecloth, while we talk about Meaghan's wedding. It's scheduled for a little less than a year from now, next March, when the city will be pitted with potholes and heaped in strata of grey, gritty snow.

"Lime green bridesmaid dresses?" Heather is saying. "Lime green, Meaghan? Seriously?"

The last time Meaghan was engaged, her bridesmaid dresses were coppery brown. I still have one hanging in my closet—brown as a not-so-subtle tribute to her old fiancé, an ecological sciences graduate student who specialized in soil analysis.

Ian—the man I've only just stopped thinking of as the "new" fiancé—works as a downtown corporate computer technician. And the dresses are now green.

"What? I've always loved bright greens. They're my signature colours. And they're just what we need for a spring wedding, right?" Meaghan's voice is pitched slightly higher than usual. Heather and Meaghan sound like mother and daughter when they disagree. Mum never argues with Meaghan, so someone has to be able to get her to sound that way.

Heather is twelve years older than Meaghan. Large families can't help but range widely through time. In the old days, people might have assumed Meaghan was actually Heather's biological daughter raised discreetly as her

16

sister. It's not true. Heather didn't start her period until four months after Meaghan was born. Everyone knows that. The fact is, if Meaghan was disingenuously raised as anyone's baby sister, it was as Mum's.

Heather fingers a lock of her own hair. "Green clothing brings out the green tones in my hair."

"Your hair is not green."

"All blond hair is a bit green. Check it out the next time I'm in fluorescent lighting. You pretty brunettes can all pull off lime green well enough. But I still say the only one of us who's going to look truly good in that dress is Suzanne, with those long legs."

It may be true, but it's burdensome. I try to crawl out from beneath it with, "Isn't it funny how they call it lime green? I mean, have the colour-naming people ever seen a lime in real life? They're dark green. They're not really that light, yellowy green at all. And they can't be talking about lime juice 'cause that's practically white. Right?"

Meaghan's shoulders sag away from the chintz at her back. "The dresses are pretty. You'll all look beautiful. That's why I picked them for you."

Ashley turns up her face and smiles. "I'll wear whatever you want, Meags. It's just one day."

Tina is moving on from the controversy of the green dresses, pushing all of us along. She does it as a reflex— like someone on a bicycle about to tip over who knows in her muscles and in the lowest parts of her brain that forward movement is what's needed to stay upright. Much of the peacekeeping in our family is no more than maintaining pace and momentum. No one stops for too long on anything awful. We propel ourselves forward with steady revolutions of patience and forgiveness, around and around, word by word. If we coast too far, we'll fall to the ground.

"You guys should totally have the wedding at the Hotel Macdonald," is what Tina says.

It's forward movement, but the direction is unfortunate. Someone makes a scoffing sound, quiet but audible to me. If Tina hears, she ignores it. "Wasn't it nice when Martin and I had our wedding at the Hotel Macdonald?" she says. "We got all those great photos on the terrace with the view of the river valley in the background. And remember those gorgeous sculpted ceilings in the ballroom?"

"Sculpted ceilings are a bit out of our price range," Meaghan says.

Ashley is laughing. "Remember the water-stained fibreglass tiles on the ceilings at my wedding reception?"

We've got to move on again.

"So what's in the bag, Mum?" I ask.

"Hm? Oh, just some baby stuff," is all Mum answers.

This is how she survives us—how our mother navigates the scary seismic energy of the family she's borne. She's not riding a complicated bicycle-built-for-five. Mum travels in a coracle, a tiny boat for one. She's rowed herself out onto the horizon—alone and adrift, buoyed up by the swells of the sea, high above the epicentres cracking and crashing on the surface of the earth miles below. From her distance, she can barely read the expressions on our faces or hear much meaning in our voices. We could be laughing or crying. Out at sea, she doesn't have to know.

I keep metaphors like these to myself or the girls will poke and laugh, telling each other how darling I am for never getting over that poetry contest I won back in high school.

I don't need metaphors to describe how our father gets around. He travels alone too, in a big white diesel pickup truck, driving through snow or mud from gas well site to gas well site. His solitude is literal, unequivocal. Maybe that's what makes it feel like it's not about us, and we can let it pass without hurting ourselves on it. And maybe that's not fair to Mum.

Heather leans into Tina. "How can you order the salmon and then not eat the roe that comes with it?"

Tina nudges her plate toward Heather. "This slimy black stuff? Help yourself."

Meaghan fakes a gag as Heather jabs her fork into Tina's meal. "Sick. It's meant to be garnish. You don't eat it."

"Sure I do. What's the matter with you guys? It's caviar. Don't think of them as fish embryos. Just imagine they're puffy, slippery salt crystals that burst in your mouth."

Tina laughs loudly enough to make the lawyers twitch over their table. "Yuck, Heather. You're such a freak!"

"Freak? You're the one who ordered it." Heather bumps her shoulder against Tina's arm, and they're laughing and shoving each other over a plate of fish eggs.

Ashley pushes ahead. "So where does Ian want to

have the reception?" she asks Meaghan. "I've seen him in that shiny purple dress shirt. He's one of those—what did they used to call them?—one of those metrosexual guys. He must have an opinion on everything to do with the wedding planning."

Meaghan gulps the food in her mouth. "Heh, yeah he does. It's actually Ian's mom who's got the reception figured out. She has this cute little country church hall in mind. It's got some traditional family significance."

"Aw, that's nice," I say. "A place special to Ian's mom."

"Ian's mom?" Ashley repeats. "Oh yeah. I forgot Meaghan's getting a mother-in-law along with a husband."

"A real live mother-in-law," Tina echoes. "How weird is that?"

My married sisters look across the table at each other, passing over me as they exchange smug grins.

Tina knows exactly how weird it is. We all do. Mothers-in-law are usually an unavoidable part of married life, at least for people our age, but I am the only one of my sisters to actually have one. My sisters are not very classy about their orphan-in-law status. For no reason at all, they've got all the mother-in-law rancour of girlie twenty-first century Fred Flintstones. And here they go again, bragging about how they get to live through marriage without any mothers-in-law.

Still, my sisters must envy me sometimes—like when my Troy shuts down the dental clinic for a week and we fly off to our timeshare in Hawaii, just the two of us.

Without any complaining, his mom comes into the city and stays with our kids while we're gone. We leave her in charge of our progeny and everything we own without worrying about a thing.

Our mum is different. When our mum—the lady on the far side of the table picking all the mushrooms out of the wild mushroom linguini she's ordered—comes across town to visit my house, she's greeted as an honoured guest and met with freshly cleaned bathrooms, tense grandchildren, and the best food I can cook.

Troy's mom, May, steps through the door of my house like a great, shining domestic angel from a 1960s marriage manual. She's "The Fascinating Mother-in-law." When we come home from our vacations, we find every item of Troy's clothing that's not still in his suitcase ironed and hanging in the closet. All the dishes have been taken out of the cupboards and washed by hand in scalding water because, as May says, mechanical dishwashers lack a proper human touch.

It sounds like I'm eulogizing my mother-in-law. She isn't dead, but I am a bit blue about her lately. May is going to leave us again. She'll be off on another one of her humanitarian service missions, cleaning teeth for poor people in Central America. She'll be gone for most of the year.

Don't misunderstand. Housekeeping and free goodies aren't the only things I love about my mother-in-law. The rest is difficult to explain. I'm afraid it demands metaphors. May is a screen, a living partition separating me from the flawed mess of people all around me.

My mother-in-law is an invisible wall—like the ones mimes pretend to stand behind, pressing their hands flat against it to make it real. And when I am seen through May's wall, miming my part, I am perfect—my movements, my form, all of me. It's perfection. I am not Sister Suzanne or Nurse Suzanne but Perfect Daughter-in-law Suzanne. May is the only person with the authority to call me that. And she did—spoke the words right into my ear as she hugged me goodbye one Christmas evening, ages ago.

None of my sisters is a daughter-in-law, perfect or otherwise. In this way, I am a singularity. I am one whole of something cherished by May rather than one fifth of something kept distant from my own mother. The math is tricky. I haven't solved the problem through to its end. But in my guts I know that as long as I have May in my life, I have a part of myself that exists without flaws, or ambivalence, or peers.

I am a daughter-in-law: the perfect daughter-in-law. None of my sisters can say the same. Not even Meaghan can say it. Sure, she's getting a living mother-in-law when she marries Ian, but perfection is not for everyone, especially not my sisters. There's nothing wrong with that. Poll any large family and they'll agree there can only be one sister recognized as the pretty one, or the smart one, or the crazy one. And there can be only one perfect sister. Our perfect sister has to be me. Don't mistake this for bragging. It's not an honour. I love it, but sometimes I hate it too. However I feel about it, I owe it to May. The sweetness, patience, compassion, decorum, fastidiousness—that's not an inheritance from my mother. It came from somewhere else. It must have come from May—things I learned from her and through her. All of my perfection, it depends on my mother-in-law.

Maybe I'm wrong, and mothers-in-law are more scarce than I know. Maybe it's not so strange that my sisters' mothers-in-law have vanished.

Ashley's husband, Durk, was born to a teenaged party-girl. Through a combination of headlong ignorance and wilful blindness, she didn't know for sure she was pregnant until it was almost time for him to be born. Naturally, she partied long into her pregnancy. Durk copes fairly well with the disadvantages his mother chemically engineered into his brain. But sometimes, when he's done some heavy self-medicating, and his clothes and hair are smelling particularly weedy, Durk will tell that story about being born in a public toilet during a high school football game. We all love Durk and want to believe him when he tells us anything, even this. But we can't believe it until he tells the story sober, at least once.

Durk's girl-mom swore she loved him. And she knew lots of nice teenaged moms who raised nice kids, so she figured it couldn't be too hard. They lived together until something awful happened. No one knows for sure what it was. All we know is what we see on the tops of each of Durk's hands. They're marked with stiff, flat spots without any lines or pores on them—white scar tissue that won't tan in the sun. They're the same size and shape as those cigarette burns we'd find in the grimy broadloom carpets of the old motels we stayed in when we were taken on vacations as kids.

By the time Durk was four years old, Ashley's first potential mother-in-law had turned him over to the state. There was a short interim where he lived in foster homes he says he doesn't remember before he was adopted by a woman old enough to be his grandmother. He got a legal mother through the adoption but not a father. The lady's husband wouldn't let the lawyers print his name on the court documents.

The lady who adopted Durk kept him warm and properly fed. He was fully vaccinated and safe, the way anyone would be with his own in-house social worker. When he turned eighteen, Durk stuffed his huge, smelly football equipment bag with everything he owned and fired her as his social worker, as his mom, as his daughters' grandmother, as Ashley's mother-in-law. None of us has ever met her.

Tina has never met her mother-in-law either. Martin's mother was one of the Socialite Suicides of the 1980s. Remember them? They were those sad, rich ladies—ones who acted out clichés like long black cigarette holders and martini lunches and pet peacocks. In another cliché, they became so crushed beneath their own ennui that six of them killed themselves within two years. Most of them took civilized overdoses of what people used to call "tranquilizers." Typically the socialites were found dead in their beds, Marilyn Monroe style.

Martin's mom liked luxury cars better than she liked movie stars. After her kids were in bed and the staff were finished for the night, she shut all four of the garage doors and turned on the ignition of her silver 1950 Bentley. Martin's father had given it to her the same winter she met his mistress in person. That night, Martin's mother sat in the dark of the garage and waited. The car ran out of gas after she was asphyxiated, and just before Martin and his brothers would have been sick from the carbon monoxide seeping into the house through the ceiling and walls. They were unharmed, but the paramedics rushed them to the hyperbaric chamber in Calgary anyway.

It's not like Martin's mother meant to annihilate her family. She was just never troubled by trifles.

The family sold the silver Bentley. Now it's an exhibit in one of those travelling auto shows. It's the Hope Diamond of death-cars—pristine and tragic and cursed.

The last time the auto show came through the city, Tina wrapped a silk scarf around her head, topped it with a big hat and sunglasses. She paid the gate admission and found her mother-in-law's Bentley. It was parked inside an arena, diagonal on a maroon carpet, rimmed with velvet ropes, the doors open. Tina ducked under the ropes, bent her body—pregnant belly and everything—through the driver's door. She sat behind the wheel, the tip of her pinky fingernail slid into the ignition's keyhole. If she turned her finger, the nail would have broken off, the ragged-edged sliver falling through the slot, disappearing into the machine. Tina tipped her head back, against the seat, crushing the brim of her hat, closing her eyes behind her sunglasses. And she stayed there, trying to sense— something. She didn't move until a guy with a walkie-talkie and a T-shirt marked STAFF politely asked her to step out of the car.

"Another overgrown Goth-girl," she heard the auto show guy report.

When they first got married, Tina believed it was dutiful and helpful to coax Martin to talk about the Socialite Suicides.

He was confused, genuinely bewildered. Martin's emotions are bizarre and inappropriate most of the time, but that doesn't mean they're always faked.

"Talk about it?" he'd said. "What do you want me to say?"

"Well, maybe you should start by telling me how your mom's death made you feel."

"Why? Anyone can imagine how it would make someone feel."

"Sure, but what if the feelings I imagine for you aren't the right ones?"

"Of course they're the right ones. Why wouldn't they be?"

That's how it always went. Tina hasn't broached the Socialite Suicides with Martin in years, not since she sat in the Bentley herself.

The story of the end of Heather's mother-in-law is the one we like least. Heather did meet her mother-in-law.

We all did. We called her Carol. Heather and her mother-in-law knew each other for over ten years before the end.

It was a difficult decade, as most people's final ten years usually are. During that time, Carol was poor, morbidly obese, and probably mentally ill. Her blood pressure, cholesterol, blood sugar—everything in every cell of her body was strained to breaking. Her first heart attack hurt. She couldn't breathe, and the violent diarrhoea that came with it—her body jettisoning cargo, desperate to do *something*—was a particularly rude surprise. No one tells people to expect these things. We talk about heart attacks in terms of a crushing but civilized sense of doom and pain above the waist, never a feral collapse of the lower works. We medical people are complicit in it. At the hospital, we quietly clean everyone up, and the secret stays safe.

Carol said bypass surgery and the recovery from it were worse than the heart attack itself. She's not the only person to think so. I hear it often from patients in the ICU still groggy from brushes with clinically controlled death, stapled shut and sore.

"I know what she's trying to do," Heather intoned to me over the telephone. It was the day Ewan had to drive his mom back to her house in the middle of a visit, the day Heather discovered Carol had been staying with them for three days without the blister pack of prescriptions she needed to stay well. "Carol knows there's more than one way to make sure she doesn't have to live through the recovery from another heart attack."

I don't know if Carol brought her pills with her the

last time she came to stay at Heather's house. It was midway through the morning, after Ewan and the kids had left for the day, when Heather carried a load of clean laundry into the bedroom where Carol was sleeping—only she wasn't sleeping.

When the ambulance didn't arrive the moment Heather ended her 911 call, she hopped onto the bed, kneeling beside her mother-in-law. Heather is a person who fixes things, not a person who waits for things. She knew just enough emergency first aid to believe she had better try to fix this too.

She stayed there, compressing Carol's chest with the heels of her hands, until the paramedics came. In all that time, with all that pressure, the skin on Carol's sternum never bruised. The fat beneath it was waxy like the untrimmed edge of a pork chop palpated through plastic wrap in a grocery store cooler. Between compressions, Heather stooped to blow breath after breath into Carol's throat, sealing the void with her own mouth.

I've seen death countless times in the hospital, as a professional. In intensive care units like mine, rolling out a green sterile carpet for death to strut in on is what we do. I've seen death happen, watched it dawning over everything. But Heather is one of the few people—maybe the only person I'll ever know—who can say what human death tastes like. And not "tasting death" in some ephemeral poetic sense, but in the real sense—lips and teeth. She tried to tell me about it once, not to shock me but to comfort me, as if she was afraid I might think it was worse than it had turned out to be.

"Everything is there, the whole planet—mucus membranes and saliva that's cold like something spat on the street. There're yellow plaques, un-brushed morning teeth, wet dental metal, all the sugar and salt that's never quite swallowed away. It's cold but it tastes," she said, "like anyone would taste when you get too close."

Two months after Carol was buried, Heather began an apprenticeship as a mortician, working a few days a week in a pastel stucco funeral home. She told us it was inevitable. She told us it was only a sign of bad high school guidance counselling that she hadn't known to choose a career in the funeral industry instead of mucking around at university getting that criminology degree. She told us to ignore the timing, that her new job was a long time in coming and hadn't begun with her mother-in-law's death.

Maybe it begins in the same place for everyone who does Heather's work—someplace defiant, near the need to reject the secrecy meant to protect us, hiding death away from us so we can live. A funeral—an embalming or a cremation—is an interruption of decay, a re-routing, a hijacking. In that way, Heather devastates devastation every day. Death has a thousand yellow-grey faces she can know, features for her to set in peaceful poses. My sister takes death by its hands, lifts it, turns it, drains it, and fills it. She's mortal as anything, but she's moving through the ends of all those worlds, upright, alert, warm and alive, taking everything apart.

# Meaghan [2]

There's a broad, flat television screen flashing from the rafters. And there must be something wrong with me, because I'm standing underneath it, here at my local video game store, again. The store is usually deserted this late in the evening, after all the commuters have cleared out of the downtown. I have no idea how they make any money. But tonight there's a small, surly crowd gathered behind me. They're teenaged geek-boys who may never be mature enough to know how to approach something as feminine as me. They're watching over my shoulder, scowling at my thumbs swivelling and tapping at the plastic game controller moulded into the shape of mushy, damp man-hands much bigger than my own.

"Die, already," the snotty short-guy of the group mutters. He's their fearless leader. And on the Openly-Perturbed-by-Females index, he's moved well beyond being intimidated by me and on to being infuriated.

*No fear, Meaghan. Don't look back at them.*

I stand here, fighting to stay aloof and statuesque, resisting the twitches and flinches my stupid nervous system involuntarily synchronizes with the lights on the screen.

The angry geek-boy blows out a loud sigh. The sound is directed toward the counter, where a grownup geek-man is usually sitting on a high stool, one hand cupped around his bearded chin, the other hand flipping pages of a gaming magazine written mostly in Italian.

"Dude," the boy calls to him, "she's been stuck on this level for fifteen minutes."

There's movement in my peripheral vision. The man behind the counter has raised his head to glance at me. That's all.

The boy tries again. "Come on, man. Don't you have, like, a store policy on time limits for game demos?"

"Nope," the man says into the magazine.

I want to look at him properly, this man who refuses to take control of me even though I'm in his space, even though another guy is calling on him to do it. But I don't look. Even something as small as that look would be giving up ground.

Petulant leader-boy huffs. "There's no way you'd let any one of us stand here and demo a game for this long while paying customers were waiting to try it. You know what this is, man? It's sexism—reverse sexism."

I love that gag. I laugh out loud without looking away from the screen.

The man behind the counter closes the magazine. "Look, bro, you're welcome to buy the game and take it home."

"Yeah? Well, she can buy the game and take it home

too." There's shuffling behind me as the boy widens his stance even though it will make him shorter. "I am not spending any money on this until I get a firsthand sense of the game play."

I toss the game controller back onto the display's stand. "Its game play is pretty ballistic," I say. "Good for noobs. You'll be fine."

I walk away, all swag, like I'm an actor in a movie about myself. I move toward a rack of magazines with names like *Game-ista* and *PlayProX* and flick one of them open, flattening it against the glass countertop.

From the opposite end of the counter, the store clerk glances at me again. I'm bent over at the waist in my turquoise, seaweed-cloth yoga pants, scanning pages full of gun barrels and undead minions. I hope stupid gravity isn't making me look misshapen. I'm the curvy sister— too curvy, if you ask me. Ashley says not to worry about it. She calls me "voluptuous" even though the last traces of her childhood speech impediment make the word an almost impossible mouthful for her. That's Ashley: she'll happily grapple with "voluptuous" if there's a chance it'll make me happy.

Whatever anyone calls my figure, I'm getting sick of it. I've been seriously considering doing something crazy like eliminating all hard cheeses from my diet, at least until after my wedding.

The clerk behind the counter shifts to look at his T-shirt rumpled beneath his cardigan. It's printed with a picture of a fierce panda bear. It must give him courage.

He speaks to me. "Hey, I definitely don't want you to take this the wrong way, but are you ever going to, you know, buy anything here?"

I look up from the magazine. I'd prefer to seem poised and cool right now, but when I'm not all noble with indignation, I can't deadpan anything. I'm like a little kid that way, painfully earnest, and I hate it. He probably notices my tiny smile as I answer, "Someday, maybe."

Despite my dumb, accidental warmth, he swallows like his mouth has gone dry as he says, "So if you're not exactly a customer, how come you're here?"

I let a long breath out my nose. I know what I need to get through this: Heather. If I can't be tough and curt, I can at least be Heather. I can say whatever I want.

"Alright. I had it out with my boyfriend on Sunday night, okay. He's been getting all huffy because of the 'inappropriate' amount of time I spend gaming. So every night since then, I've been telling him I'm going to the gym. But then I come here instead so we don't have to argue about it. That's what you call a successful relationship, my friend, one where everyone is sufficiently sheltered from their own unhappiness."

It's far more information than he asked for, and something about it must feel like a gift. He takes more courage and says, "It's not that I mind the foot traffic in the store or anything, but, I mean, why don't you tell your boyfriend you're headed back to your own place and go play at home?"

I laugh. "He's at my home. We live together. We're

engaged."

He looks sceptical.

"What?" I demand.

"Engaged?" He seems the right age to have lots of engaged friends. "Chronically engaged or, like, seriously engaged?"

I don't know him, but I shove him with one hand anyway. I've slipped from being Heather into acting more like Tina—not just mouthy but sparking with impulsive aggression. "Seriously engaged," I say. "We have a wedding date and everything: March 15th. And you can spare me the Ides of March remarks. It was the only day that month we could book the church hall his mom wanted."

He's squinting at the hand that's just shoved him. "Engaged with no ring?"

"It's the twenty-first century," is all I say as I lean back, jamming my hands into the tight, undersized pockets on the front of my hoodie. I do have an engagement ring—a classic, brilliant cut white diamond like the one on the luxury tax square of a Monopoly game. I made Ian promise he'd buy one mined out of a pit in the far north of our own country, where I can be sure it's never been smuggled in someone's colon. I don't wear it because the band is a little too tight. By the end of the day it makes my finger swell like links of cartoon sausage. Ian offered to have it resized, but I told him to leave it. The bad fit is good motivation for losing some of my cuddly, engaged-girl weight.

There's something inside my pocket. My fingers recognize it and pull it into the open to vindicate me. It's a small swatch of satin fabric cut with pinked edges. The card stapled to it identifies its colour as lime green, no matter what Suzanne says.

"This," I say to the clerk. "See this? It's a fabric sample for my bridesmaid dresses. We already ordered them."

He raises both his hands. "Okay, okay. You're seriously engaged."

I nod. "That's right. And that's my story."

"Great."

"Want me to tell you your story?" I curl the green fabric around my finger as I step closer to the counter. "Let me guess your story. I'm good at this. You can't be solid cliché. It'd be way too easy if you were one of those video game store clerk tropes. You know, a guy in a panda T-shirt who's got three quarters of the credits he needs to finish his physics degree, but will probably never make it back to school. One of those people who doesn't have a girlfriend though he's starting to wonder about maybe meeting that chick from his favourite message board in person, hoping she doesn't turn out to be another bored twenty-something guy. And, of course, in the video game store cliché, he'd have to live at home, in the suburbs with his mom. That couldn't possibly be you, right?"

His laugh isn't genuine. His head droops and his shoulders rise, like he's slightly suffocated. "Uh—no. Solid cliché—no. Mostly, no," he says. "It's an unfinished creative writing degree, actually. And my mom—she's dead."

Behind my glasses, I raise one eyebrow. "Your mom

is dead? For real?"

He shifts his weight from foot to foot. "Yeah, for real. People die all the time. It should be normal, though it never is."

I'm not Heather or Tina anymore. I'm humble, regretful me—which looks sort of like Suzanne.

"I am so sorry," I say. We stand on either side of the counter, looking down as if we're both reading the same ad for the upcoming release of Mech-Commandos 4 taped to the underside of the glass. I can't help but smile again, but I manage to keep it from spreading further than just one half of my mouth. I'm raising my head, saying, "Awkward is something else I'm good at."

He snorts a quiet but real laugh. "Don't worry about it."

I pluck my phone out of my waistband to check the time. "Look, it's nine o'clock now. Throw these kids out, lock up, and let's go somewhere."

He blinks. "Go somewhere? Like where?"

I shrug. "Nowhere special. But for taking a slam on your deceased mother so gracefully, you've earned a coffee, on me. Let me buy it for you. I won't make you talk to me anymore if you don't want to. If it's more civilized, we can just sit and text each other."

He laughs with his voice this time, but he's still hesitating.

I jab my left hand into his face, though I'm still not wearing my diamond. "I'm engaged. Remember? I'm safe. You won't end up having to date me or anything. And even if I hadn't been a jerk about your mother, I'd still owe you something for letting me loiter in your store all week."

He reaches under the counter to shut off all the television screens from one central switch. The geek-boys grumble but don't make much of a complaint when their games power down. No matter what they say online, most geeks have a dark, secret love for unilateral authority.

I get the video game store clerk to jaywalk across the avenue to a boutique coffee shop, the kind staffed by girls Tina calls my clones. She's silly. The coffee-girls don't look exactly like me. But they might look more like my twins than any of my real sisters ever will.

Unlike me, my coffee-clones can draw animal shapes with creamer on the tops of lattes. Tonight, my coffee animal looks like a llama. The video game store clerk, who says his name is Riker, has a brontosaurus floating in his cup.

I'm pretending to be Heather again, all deathly business, when I ask, "So how did you handle your mom's remains? Burial or cremation?"

He ducks like he's about to hide inside his cup.

I sit back in my tiny squeaking bistro chair. "Sorry, Riker. That was too much, wasn't it?"

He wipes his beard dry. "No, it's only natural you're curious."

I shake my ponytail. "Okay, forget the burial. Tell me how she died."

Riker coughs into the crook of his elbow. "Heart attack."

"Right." I'm nodding. "Where was she when she—

37

you know?"

"Where was my mom when she died?"

"Yeah."

"Uh, in an ambulance on the way to the hospital. But she never made it."

I let out my breath, relieved. I am the girl who can't stop hating what happened to Heather the morning her mother-in-law died. I am the girl who can't stand the grim grey cast that's dimmed my sister's life ever since that moment, whether it now comes with a pay cheque or not. An ambulance—that's a proper, professional place to die.

"So how old was she?"

Riker swallows. "She was old for someone with her kind of heart condition."

I wrinkle my nose. "My mom is old. She was almost forty when I was born."

He makes an eager leap at the change in subject. "Wow. Why'd she wait so long to have kids? I thought people didn't do that back then."

I dip my fingertip into the latte-llama's long, creamy back. "She didn't wait. My oldest sister was born when Mum was in her twenties—perfectly normal reproductive schedule. But then it took them a while to reach me in the birth order. I am a failed boy, the last in a long line of failed boys, the youngest of five sisters."

Riker jolts in his seat. "Hey, just like the Dionne quintuplets."

"Huh?"

"The Dionne sisters, from Quintland. You know—

38

those five baby girls the government took away from their parents and made into a museum exhibit way back in the Depression era."

I start to nod again. This time it's like I'm Ashley and I'm cool and sweet enough to humour arcane dork-lore. "Yeah, okay. That's sure some obscure Canadian history trivia you got there."

Riker's face blanches for just an instant. He runs his hands through his beard as the colour returns beneath it. "Oh, come on. The Dionne quints! There was a documentary about them on the CBC a few years ago. They must have aired it five or six times by now. You know."

I shrug. "We have cable."

He whips his phone from the tabletop. "Look, I'll show you. Here." He's beckoning me closer, where I can see the screen. "One summer, more tourists came to see the quints than Niagara Falls. Look at the picture. That's not their dad in the back. It's some politician and those five babies in the front are quintuplet sisters. No fertility drugs, no in vitro technology, just a natural wonder."

I lean away from him. "A wonder, like my family."

"Exactly."

I smirk. "Exactly. Except we aren't multiple-borns. We came one at a time over the space of twelve years. And we are not now, nor have we ever been, part of a government sponsored freak show."

"Freak show? What? No, the quints were a national treasure, a sign of hope and growth during an economic cataclysm, an inspiration."

I'm laughing. "Making them even less like my sisters and me."

Riker sets his phone back on the table. "Still, five girls in a row—that's got to be unlikely."

I've heard it before. "Not really. In theory, every time a baby is conceived there's a fifty-fifty chance it will be born a girl. You wanna read up on the gambler's fallacy."

"Sure, it may be so in theory. But—"

"But here I am, a girl." I stand up. "And here I go."

I need to get home. The company Ian works for is installing new printers tomorrow, and he has to get there early. He'll go to bed moping if he doesn't see me again tonight. His job is running around an office tower calming down furious executives who mess up their computers. Most tech-support staff aren't happy in their jobs. There's nothing anyone can do about that. But Ian has more to be disappointed with than most, weighed down by a languishing degree in Romantic English poetry. That's his first education, the one he got before the computer training that actually pays his bills and funds his natty pastel wardrobe.

"Anyone ever tell you you're not like other English majors?" I ask Riker as he stands to leave the café with me, "As far as I can tell, all Ian uses his degree for now is keeping people like me in our place."

Here in Edmonton, at this point in the spring, it's cold as winter once the sun starts to set. Out in the street, I'm clutching my thin hoodie around myself, twisting my face into that betrayed snarl people get when they've underestimated the weather.

And then she sees me. Suzanne can't help but spot me through the windshield of her minivan as she drives past me in the street. I'm standing here in the turquoise yoga pants she doesn't believe I should ever wear out in public. That's Suzanne—and Troy too—preoccupied with the loveliness of everyone. It's innocent enough—some kind of scar tissue she's grown over the fact that everyone's always said Ashley is the pretty one. What kind of an idiot would say a thing like that? All kinds, apparently.

I must have some faint scarring, too. The thought of Ashley's supreme prettiness and Suzanne's supreme fussiness makes me bow my head and frown at my turquoise legs. Ashley is the only one of us who wears yoga pants to do yoga, out on her back lawn in the sunshine with yogi-thin Durk, his shirt off, neither of them wavering a millimetre as their kids teeter in and out of poses all around them.

I've heard Ashley say, "I'm sorry, but until people actually work out, all they've got are faux-ga pants."

The funny thing is, once Suzanne is paired with Troy, her pretty trophy husband, she gets prettier herself. As a couple, they add up to something more beautiful than the sum of their parts. They're like an old YouTube video of Donny and Marie Osmond—a Flowers-in-the-Attic version of Donny and Marie where they double up their matching DNA and spawn a bunch of gorgeous, eerily similar kids.

Suzanne must be leaving Troy's clinic after dry-mopping the laminate floors and refilling the paper dispensers afterhours. She's heading to the suburbs as I'm beginning to make my way back to Ian.

"Hey, Honey-girl," she calls, her minivan rolling alongside the curb, stopping in a tow-away zone. Through the open window, Riker and I can hear Joy Division playing on her car stereo, though, if you ask me, it's still too early in the day for it. "Hop in," she tells me.

At the sight and sound of our Suzanne, Riker takes a step that's more like a stagger backwards. I must be panicking slightly too, pitching my half-full paper coffee cup into a waste bin.

Over her car stereo's relentless bass-line, I'm not sure Suzanne hears me telling Riker, "This is quint number two."

She waves at him anyway, and the light in Riker's face changes, brightens. He's backing away, nodding so deeply he's nearly bowing, as if he's been blessed. He turns to leave and I join Suzanne in her van.

"What's with the gloomy tunes?" I ask her.

She steers into traffic as I slam her van's door. "Gloomy?"

"Gloomy. Listen to him, singing like that."

"What? He's okay. He's just thoughtful."

I turn toward her. "Hey, maybe something deep and troubled from your subconscious made you pick this sad music today. What is it, Suze? What's your darkest latent fear right at this minute?"

Suzanne gasps—loud and dramatic, like she's a voice

in a radio play. "It's my mother-in-law. Today this song is about May. She's heading back to Central America, and I always get so worried and sad when she goes."

How boring is that—boring and unlikely. Even with the gasp, Suzanne has failed to convince me. She mentioned May not because she's sad about the big trip, but because she loves talking about her mother-in-law—a lot. It's like she's obsessed with her and she wants all of us to keep thinking about May too. Strangely enough, it works. At any time, my sisters and I can converse fluently about May's business, even though we've seen her in real life less than half a dozen times—once at the wedding and once for each time Suzanne had a baby.

And I can't tell if it's messed up for Suzanne to be this way or not. Maybe every woman who has a mother-in-law is obsessed with her. For all I know, the obsession could go both ways. I mean, May might go around slipping Suzanne's name into conversations until everyone May knows feels like Suzanne is their own daughter-in-law.

Maybe someday I'll have to do it too. I'll learn to obsess over Ian's mom.

"So who's the beard?" Suzanne asks right when I've gone back to thinking about Ian.

I turn off her music and groan into my seatbelt. "Some guy from the video game store over there. I just said something totally offensive to him and I was trying to smooth it over with some coffee."

Suzanne is laughing before she's heard the rest of my

explanation. It's not her exaggerated actress laugh. It's a real one that lilts, sweet and a little delighted, like she thinks I'm still made of apple sauce and warm milk and my mistakes are all tiny and adorable. "Oh no, Sweetie. What did you say to him?"

I groan one more time. "I was channelling Heather or something and I made some lame mama's boy joke only to find out his mother is actually dead."

"Well, that's an honest mistake. At his age, he's got to be used to people assuming his mom is still around." It's a comically short car-ride down the avenue, and Suzanne is already parking underneath the awning of the big yellow high-rise where I live with Ian. "So is the video game store guy feeling okay now?"

"Hope so." My fingers are on the lever of the door handle, but I'm not letting myself out onto the sidewalk. I want to know something—something about Suzanne and her mother-in-law. It might be important. Of course, I can't just demand, "Hey, Suzanne, what's with your obsession with Troy's mom? Is that normal? Is that mandatory?"

No way. If you ask me, anyone who says she can talk to her sisters about anything must have a stinking, oozing, pus-crusted scab of a relationship with them. Talking about everything is stupid. It's rude. What some people like to spin as the virtue of honesty is really the vice of carelessness—thoughtlessness. What they're really saying is, "I can't be bothered to be discerning about what I force you to lug around in your head and heart."

People in decent relationships know to keep their

mouths shut sometimes—not that it works to hide much. The kindness, the mercy, is in the lack of telling, not the lack of knowing. Being close means soaking up and leaking out far more information than anyone would purposely know or make known. It's like my sisters and I are all sponges sopping in a single bucket. We've each got our own edges and pores, but we're squeezing out and sucking in the same mucky water.

Look at me, sitting next to Suzanne, thinking in metaphors—thinking like she does because it might be the best way to try to understand.

Instead of blurting whatever I want to ask about her mother-in-law, I turn to Suzanne in the front seat of her minivan and say, "Isn't it weird? Whoever that beard guy marries, she won't have a mother-in-law. She'll be like Heather and Tina and Ashley."

Suzanne clucks. "What a shame, huh?"

"Sure, but still. That guy's future wife—no mother-in-law."

"I guess."

"Yeah, I guess so." I'm opening the door.

Suzanne leans forward, YouTube Marie Osmond's thick, dark hair draping over the steering wheel. She's calling to me as I step onto the sidewalk. "Hey," she says, "don't forget to introduce Ian to your new orphan-friend."

Once more, I let her door bang shut.

# Tina                                    [3]

It was the screaming that woke me up. This time, it wasn't the baby screaming. He is capable of waking me up, but by baby number six, newborn crying is just funny, kind of pathetic, a nice try.

No, this time the screams in the night were mine.

I gave up reading pregnancy manuals when I realized I had the experience to write one of my own. Know what I'd include in my personal pregnancy manual? Something I've never read anywhere else. I'd write a section about the nightmares—those secret postpartum bad dreams. I can't remember exactly what I was dreaming when I woke up tonight. All I know is near the end of it I dreamed I sat up in bed screaming. And then I really was sitting up in bed screaming. Postpartum nightmares: no one writes anything to prepare us for those.

My dear Martin is out of town on business tonight. Yes, somehow he tore himself away from the bed where I bleed and sweat and come and go all night. He says if the new baby refuses to sleep unless he's in full sunlight, I should hire a night-nanny. Night-nanny—is that even a thing?

No, I'll stay up with the cute little cry-hole myself. I'll sit here with the lights off, fantasizing about propping a bottle in his mouth, desperate enough to lie down and take my chances with the nightmares. I'll keep sending menacing texts to Martin's five-star-hotel room in downtown Toronto, chronicling all of this in real time. And he'll keep responding with ridiculous non-solutions that all amount to writing another cheque.

The baby's not so bad—for a baby. I've had worse. So did my mother, the lady who must be the biggest bottle-propper there ever was. Frankly, I think my sisters are way too hard on Mum. None of them is raising a big family, not like me or Mum. I know better than any of us what she was up against—what she is up against. I may have one more baby than Mum but she didn't have a nanny for a single minute of the time she was caring for us, day or night—not even a lazy, dirty nanny like mine.

And that's not the only disadvantage Mum had. I don't know how she managed it, but she lived through her entire childrearing mess without sisters.

Yes, I'm still in the postpartum sappy phase. Symptoms include this crazy tenderness I've got for my sisters right now. Don't dismiss my feelings as hormonal chemical reactions. I'm still a person, not a physiology demonstration. And listen to how that kind of dismissal sounds. It's like saying a bullet isn't valid if it's propelled by a nuclear reaction instead of the usual flash of gunpowder. It's still a real bullet. It'll still tear right through anyone. In the end, it doesn't matter what sent it flying. My feelings

47

are just like that.

I sit here in the dark, shaking off nightmares, remembering my old life when I lived with my sisters, getting choked up over stuff I haven't thought about since the last time I was late night baby-meat. Who knows—if I didn't have my sisters, I might be mad at Mum. Whatever else she's done, Mum kept on giving me sisters.

It's not like Mum doesn't have a sister of her own. She does. But it's not the same for them as it is for us. We've never seen much of Mum's sister, our Aunt Beryl. She lives in British Columbia, on the other side of the Rocky Mountains, in the same weird old house where she and Mum were kids together. It's a house penned in by trees, too far from the coast for a glimpse of the ocean, but near enough that people who know the ocean well can say they're able to smell it from the yard. The house was our grandmother's before she died. Even though she's gone, the building still feels like an old person. Underneath the basement stairs the floor is dirt. There's a tiny milk door cut into the back wall. And the attic isn't just a hatch on the ceiling that no one ever opens but a real room with stairs and stuff stowed and forgotten in it like a room in a book, where the real story begins.

Once, when Dad's old job sent him to a convention in Bermuda for a whole week, Mum brought us to stay at Aunt Beryl's house so she wouldn't have to lock us in the car and roll it down the ravine into the river. During the days, Aunt Beryl kept us busy and outdoors. We pulled dandelions out of the lawn, shelled fresh peas, foraged for blackberries. When it was hot and muggy, we'd lie under cedar trees that wouldn't survive the winters back home, watching Heather and Suzanne learning to crochet doll dresses that would've been pretty slutty on real girls.

Ashley and I were so young we weren't considered human enough for crochet. And Meaghan, she was waiting, off in that place where the rest of us will go to wait for her someday when she's still alive here after our time has run out—assuming, as we always have, that's how all of this works.

What I remember best about the visit to Aunt Beryl's are the nights. Mum slept in the master bedroom while Aunt Beryl slept in our whiny boy cousin's room with him. The spare bedroom was for the rest of us. What looked like the closet door was actually the entrance to the attic. It was locked but still creepy. I didn't mind, because our instructions were to sleep together, under the same blankets—an exorcism that never failed me. Suzanne was assigned to sleep in the double bed with the glossy wooden frame that looked black in the dark. Ashley and I were supposed to snuggle in next to her. A little cot was brought down from the attic for Heather. As soon as we saw it, we knew the big girls would trade beds. Heather slept in the bed with us while Suzanne took the solo cot.

Look at me remembering details like these from one week out of my life when I was seven years old. We've all heard about repressed memories—about minds erasing things and editing out stories that hurt or scare us most. I'm not sure I believe in it. For me, the things that hurt and scare me, those are what I can't help but remember.

No one could have slept easily in quarters as close as those in Beryl's spare bedroom, especially when it was hot and the sun wouldn't go down until after nine o'clock. We stayed up, playing, keeping our footsteps from activating the creaks in the floorboards by pretending our beds were boats and the floor was covered in untouchable water. Heather's big bed was the mother ship and Suzanne's was the little row boat Heather sent out on adventures. Suzanne invented the game, complete with her role as Heather's lackey. It was brilliant, really, the way Suzanne would set Heather up as the boss lady. When there was trouble, Heather was presumed responsible for all of it and got the worst of Mum's moody, frazzled, slapping, ad hoc justice.

We were four little girls in the room at the foot of the attic stairs of a strange old house, wide awake hours after we'd been put to bed, jumping from mattress to mattress, convinced the women playing rummy in the parlour below were fooled into thinking we were asleep.

And then Mum opened the door. We hadn't realized how dark it had got in the spare bedroom until we were squinting in the light from the hall. The doorway framed Mum's shape in a blinding yellow rectangle. The doorknob in her hand was made of glass and warped the light moving through it, like a grimy jewel.

We stood stunned as a herd of does in the shadows of the spare room. Suzanne had a pair of sweatpants on her head, the legs hanging down her back like pink fleece ponytails, the waistband clamped over her real freshly pixie-cut hair. Ashley was caught with her nightgown completely tucked into her underpants. The effect was lumpy and goofy and would have been embarrassing if she hadn't been five years old and pretending to wear a bathing suit. Heather had a pillowcase draped over her head like she was part of a nativity play or a convent. The scene is a photograph shot with the lenses of my eyes so I, the photographer, am nowhere in sight.

"Girls, get to bed," Mum said. It wasn't her spanking voice. It was the tired, tired voice of Aunt Beryl's sister. "All of you, lie down. It's okay. You don't need to be scared to sleep in here just because it's the room where your grandmother died."

I started to speak. "Mum?"

"It's okay, Tina. Grammie was old and she was sick for a long time and died peacefully, sleeping in that big bed. Aunt Beryl saw the whole thing. It was okay. So don't make a huge deal out of it. Everyone dies someday. I will and so will all of you. There's nothing anyone can do. Just try to get some rest."

The door closed and the room went dark. Even though I could still see a little, I knew I'd never been anywhere darker. Of all the things Mum said—the awful things—the very worst were the ones that made us alone, words that called down dark grey desolation. For little girls, Mum was big enough, high enough to see the space around us. She knew we were hung in an empty infinity, our little fingers reaching for each other but not touching, never quite touching.

Suzanne pulled the pants off her head. She tossed them onto the ground and walked them like a plank, making her way toward the big bed where our grandmother died. Her hands were stretched out, one for me, one for Ashley. Suzanne was guiding us to her cot, away from the bed we could not sleep in anymore.

As she came toward me, I started to speak again. "Heather?"

Let me do the math. If I was seven that night, then Heather was eight, nine, ten years old. And she was brilliant.

She said, "Stop. Where are you going?"

On the cot, Suzanne lifted her blankets and Ashley crawled inside. "It's okay," Suzanne was saying to her. "We'll make my boat into a tent. And we'll be inside of it instead of inside this room. It'll be perfect. We won't even see the other boat."

Ashley burrowed inward. Suzanne waved to me. "Tina, come on."

"Hey, you guys, stop," Heather said. "Suzanne's bed is too small. And her tent will get too hot. You won't be able to breathe in there."

It was true. And even if we did cram into a tent on Suzanne's cot, Heather wouldn't come with us. She'd stay by herself, lost, folded into all those blankets.

I looked across the room to Heather, a white figure against the black headboard of the deathbed. Her new super-short haircut was just like mine, just like all my sisters', but she looked like a stranger, like someone who wasn't even a girl. Her hair was blond and cut close enough to make her look completely shorn in the dimness. The black wood behind her outlined her skull like a hood.

"Heather, you have to come with us," I said just before I would have been too scared to look at her anymore.

She stood up on the pillows, her foot slipping, nearly disappearing into the gap between the mattress and the headboard. "No, you guys come here," Heather said. "You too, Suzanne. I have a new game, a better one. Bring your blankets."

In those days, before the horror of her hospital job, Suzanne was not what I would have called a brave person. But she was an experimenter—a cold little scientist willing to prod and probe, the kind of kid who'd find a field mouse left dead on the sidewalk by a cat and flip the carcass over with a stick. Suzanne balled up her blankets, tossed them onto Heather's bed, and hopped after them. Ashley and I scrambled to follow.

"Now this," Heather began, walking the length of the bed, one hand dragging lightly across the wallpaper, "is not my boat anymore. You heard Mum. It's Grammie's boat."

Heather bunched Suzanne's blanket into a long roll and laid it against the footboard of the bed. "See? Here she is."

Heather bent to kiss one end of the rolled blanket, as if it was Grammie's face. She sculpted and fluffed it until I could imagine arms, legs, belly.

"She's dead so she can't sit up," Heather went on. "We're alive so we have to drive the boat for her. But she tells us where to go and what to do. As long as she's with us, we can go anywhere she can go and see whatever she sees."

I got it. "It's Grammie!" I said. I threw one arm around the roll of blankets like I never would have done to the real, frail grandmother I didn't actually remember. "Long time no see, Grammie. Where are you taking us tonight?"

"To the sun," Suzanne joined in. "Grammie says we can go to the sun. She goes there all the time, no problem. Dead people can't be hurt by anything. They're the strongest things ever."

Ashley laughed and jumped hard on the bed, landing on her knees in the place where our dead grandmother's ribcage would have been.

"Ashley, no," Heather scolded. "You have to be nice. She's strong but you still have to be good to Grammie or we can't play the game."

Looking back, I think Heather owed a lot of her travels with a ghostly spirit buddy story to Charles Dickens—or at least to the *Mr. Magoo's Christmas Carol* we'd seen on television a few times by then.

We spent the week at Aunt Beryl's sleeping all together in the deathbed, each of us careful not to kick at the roll of blankets laid out at the end of the mattress. We didn't smooth out the roll when we made the bed for the day. We preserved its shape, protected it. Ashley and I would watch our older sisters reverently and ceremoniously lift it—Heather at the head, Suzanne at the feet—and slide it underneath the bed every morning.

"Good-bye, Grammie," Heather would whisper as we closed the door behind us. "Rest in peace until tonight."

I'd like to say I was cured of being afraid to be in the bedroom where my grandmother died. Most of the time, it was true. Allying with her on the boat gave us power over fear and the dark and maybe over our mother's lonely universe too.

Brazen with my portion of that power, I sneaked away from dandelion-picking one afternoon, my digging fork still in my hand, and went into the house by myself. I climbed the stairs and walked the hall. I laid my free hand on the glass jewel of a doorknob and turned it, heard the iron grinding in the old latch. And then I stopped. This was not a place I could be alone.

Tonight, in my living room with my sixth baby, this moment of my childhood is what I am remembering. I'm shivering again, like I was in the hallway of Aunt Beryl's house, like I was minutes ago when I awakened from my nightmare here in Martin's house.

I remember the word in my throat, the one I used in both places to wrench myself free. I could have called any of their names. But what I shouted was, "Heather!"

# Suzanne [4]

My Troy is not a trophy husband. Yes, he is pretty and shiny. He is the kind of husband I would have had made to order when I was twenty-two years old. He's the kind of husband I would have clipped out of the Sears catalogue and played with as a paper doll when I was seven years old—tall and clear-eyed, charismatic and authoritative, though he's still fresh and young, exactly like the Sears models in their twenty-dollar, cotton-poly dress shirts.

Here in his dental clinic, a decade and a half into our marriage, Troy is dressed in white, a medical mask hanging slack around his neck. He looks as capable and impeccable as an actor playing a doctor in a soap opera. Maybe that's the reason there are always plenty of lady-patients in his waiting room. The women seated along the walls watch as I carry a box through the clinic's foyer. I don't pause to ask permission to come aboard, as I smile at the receptionist—the doughy, middle-aged lady I hired myself. I indulge in the intimacy of letting myself into Doctor Troy's inner office.

And he is a doctor: a doctor of dental surgery. That's

real. I don't know why the medical world cordons off the mouth and refuses to consider doctors who specialize in caring for it *real* doctors. Dental school was a tough programme. The students had to dissect cadavers and everything. And Troy didn't go there as some kind of second rate, plan B career option. His undergraduate grades were great. His MCAT score was perfectly respectable. He could have got into medical school and been a full-body doctor but—never mind, I'm sick of going over it.

Doctor Troy joins me in his office, wiping his damp hands on a paper towel left brown to show it's recycled. "Suzanne? You brought the new footbath down already?"

I pat the top flap of the box I've picked up from the courier depot. "Yep."

He steps forward, flexing his fingers. The box contains an ionizing footbath. I know—a footbath in a dental clinic. Dentistry is actually quite competitive in the city. Lots of clinics have started offering enhanced services, which I'm trying hard not to call "gimmicks." Troy's specialty is dental detoxification. It started as a comfort for people fretting about their old mercury fillings. Troy drills them out and then uses natural health treatments— essential oils, acupressure, these footbaths—to care for people convinced they've been exposed to toxins in every bite of food they've eaten and every mouthful of spit they've swallowed since they got their first fillings as kids.

I know how it sounds. I'm a nurse, a scientist. Troy is a scientist too. But this is how his patients want to be treated. They demand it. And so what? No matter what ghastly conventional dental treatments Troy does in their mouths, everyone leaves the clinic happy and smelling like eucalyptus. They might be a bit hypochondriac, but that doesn't mean Troy is a fraud.

These new footbaths are simply tubs of warm, swirling water. They're painless and soothing and, by the end of the treatments, their water is brown or orange or green or some other sickly colour. Sometimes dark flakes or chunks of foam are left floating in them, like the gunk washing up on beaches where no one wants to swim. According to the box insert, its biological mechanism is "ionization." The new machine I've brought to the clinic today is identical to the one already in use here.

"Did you try it out already?" Troy asks.

"No. But it should work just as well as its twin, right?"

Troy shakes his head. "Think, Suzanne. We can't just turn a new machine on patients without having someone we trust test it first."

"Okay. Fine, I'll take it home for a trial. But I won't be able to bring it back today. I've got to go over to Ashley's shop. She's been calling all morning. She won't say why, but she wants to see me in person."

He's skimming paperwork stacked on his desk as he says, "Intriguing."

I slump against the top of the box. "I'd rather be home straightening things up before your mom gets here tonight. There's still a huge pile of laundry."

Troy waves his hand, keeps skimming. "Save the laundry for Mom. She wants to do the laundry for you. She wants to do everything for you."

"Yeah, but I like to have everything perfect for May. I'm happy when I'm getting everything right. May and I are the same that way."

He smirks. "Just carve off a little slice of your precious domestic paradise and let Mom have it. Be the perfect daughter-in-law by easing up on perfection for a few days."

I smooth a ridge of sealing tape that's lifting off the edge of the box. "Irony is so stupid."

"Come on," Troy says, "It won't kill you to spare some outstanding feat of housework for Mom to do as soon as she hits the ground."

I flinch. "Troy, do you have to say it like that?"

"What?"

"Do you have to talk about your mother using violent expressions?"

He stops reading, creases surfacing on his face, making him look his true age for a moment. "You mean, 'won't kill you?' That's the opposite of violent."

"No, not that."

"'Hits the ground?'"

"Yeah."

"That's not violent either, Sue. It's a cute reference to World War II paratroopers. Right?"

I try to laugh. "Is it?"

Troy drops his paperwork, advancing on me, moving to finger the acupressure point between my eyes—the magic spot that's supposed to keep me from overreacting to his charm. "You've got lighten up about Mom. She's safe and she's fine. No one takes better care of people than Mom does, and that includes taking good care of herself. If you need to worry, it'll have to be about someone else."

I nod my forehead against his fingertips.

# Ashley                                    [5]

They each take their sweet time getting here for today's
emergency sisters' meeting in the back of Dash Fireplace
and Monument. That's the name Durk and I gave our masonry shop. Durk and Ashley—Dash. Get it? It's perfect.
"Dashley" was a little too right on. And my sisters said
"Ashurk" made us sound like a couple of ancient Meso-
potamian warlords.

The "Monument" part of the name sounds impres-
sive, but all it really means is we'll install or repair gravestones for money. I don't mind the work, but Durk would
rather we didn't spend so much time in cemeteries. He's
not scared. Don't get me wrong. He agrees when I say if
the people buried in any of the city's cemeteries were all
to stand up at the same time they'd look like the crowd
from the mall: grandmas and grandpas, teenagers with
premature driver's licenses, party-guys who just got paid,
a few moms and babies.

It's not about ghosts—nothing supernatural. The effect the cemetery has on Durk is perfectly natural. It's
got this energy that upsets Durk's *chi,* rankles him right

down to the life force in his solar plexus, and ruins his day. I know. I can hear myself sounding like a poser Western loser. But there's no arguing with the way Durk has to pop a whole roll of antacids to fix his stomach after a gravestone job. He's sensitive, tuned in. I like it.

Heather got us into monuments through her funeral business connections back when we needed the contracts to keep the masonry shop a going concern. We can afford to be choosier about the work we do now, but "Monument" is already printed on all our cheques and stationery. So here we are.

I'm the one who called this meeting. It's one of the very worst kinds of emergency sisters' meetings: the kind where one person can't be invited. Today, Tina will be missing.

Durk is outside the office, in the rearmost bay of the shop, picking and stacking astoundingly heavy crates of bricks using the forklift. Thank God for the forklift. No really, I'm thankful, no sacrilege intended. For the first year we were in business, Durk shifted the crates with nothing but a hand truck and a cheap manual pallet jack. It was barely possible—probably took years off the lifespan of his spine. Troy took pity and gave us samples of minty essential oils from his clinic. I was supposed to rub them on Durk's back. We're all for organics and purity, but as far as we could tell, Troy's oils were nothing but fancy, teeny, pricey vials of the same Deep Cold ointment we could have bought at the drugstore in big, cheap handfuls.

Through the indoor window of my office, waiting for

the last of my sisters to arrive, I watch Durk standing on the edge of the forklift with his shirt off, driving the machine like it's a blip on our old Atari console. His back doesn't look injured from here. It looks fine—way more than fine, actually. Sometimes I sit at my desk and get stalled, stunned, a bit hypnotized watching my beautiful, half-broken cyborg working his smooth, mechanized, back-and-forth, pivot-lunge. Sometimes, but not right now.

Heather is waiting with me, tapping one finger against her own forehead, like a cranky metronome. She arrives on time for everything and exercises her right to get mad when anyone else is late.

Satisfying Heather is not why Suzanne arrived early today. I wasn't surprised to see her coming through the doors of our showroom while I was still busy signing off on today's shipment. Suzanne's Mary Poppins mother-in-law is arriving at her house this afternoon. She might be there already, for all I know. I'm decent enough to nod and hum along when Suzanne raves about how great it is to have her visiting. But if you ask me, one uptight perfectionist in a home is already too many. I have no idea how May and Suzanne function when there're two of them under the same roof, even if it is for just a few days.

Heather stops tapping when Meaghan finally arrives, closing my office door without looking up from her phone.

"Okay, this is all very dramatic, Ashley," Heather begins, scratching at the crown of her head. The part in her hair is dusted with heavy, white powder. It'd be kind of gross if I didn't know she's been sanding drywall over her head all morning. She left a project unfinished in order to be here. Maybe I shouldn't blame her for being impatient with all of this.

I can never make sense of the lifestyles of part-timers. It must be one of Heather's days off from the funeral home. The girl abhors relaxing. When she's home, she's renovating—ripping up carpet, refinishing cabinets, crawling around in the rafters stringing electrical wire like the son Dad never had, or something dumb like that.

Meaghan is still minding nothing but the screen in her palm. "Let's get going. I've got to be at work in half an hour," she says.

While Heather is shooting preservatives into people who are dead, and Suzanne is dripping IV fluids into people who aren't quite dead, and Tina is gestating babies who aren't quite alive, Meaghan is sticking labels onto prescription bottles in the back of a drugstore. She's a pharmacist's assistant though she's smart enough to be a pharmacist. Don't worry. I'm not about to go off on the tragedy of unfulfilled potential. I never went to university either, and I'm pretty sure I'm doing just fine without it. Meaghan's job is nothing worse than boring, and not everyone finds boredom unpleasant. It's exactly what some people want.

"Well, I'm sorry to bother everyone," I begin, not sorry, "but I don't know what to do about something— something big, something about Tina and Martin."

"Okay," Suzanne says, rushing through the pause I

tried to create.

I know this is weird, meeting to talk about Tina's husband. It's weird for me too. Most of the time, none of us thinks about Martin when he's not standing right in front of us.

"Okay," I repeat. "You guys remember the restaurant where we had Tina's baby shower lunch, right?'

Everyone's nodding.

"Well, we've got a contract there doing some brick work on this new wood-fired oven they have in the kitchen. So Durk's been down at the restaurant every day this week. And on Thursday," I pause again to look at each of their faces. Meaghan has gone back to watching her phone. "Meaghan."

"Sorry."

"On Thursday, Martin came to the restaurant for lunch with a pretty woman, just the two of them. They were eating at that really private table—the one set up inside the big old elevator car, away from everything else."

Heather rolls her eyes. "Well, it's not the best judgment. But it's still classic Martin behaviour."

"So did Durk go over and say 'hi' to them?" Suzanne asks.

She sounds so innocent and reasonable all the time. It can really bug me.

"No. He says he was going to but then he got creeped out after he saw Martin kiss this lady—right on the mouth."

This time the pause is theirs, not mine. None of my

sisters wants to ask the next inevitable question. There isn't a way to ask it without being offensive and risking escalating this into one of those sister meetings where everyone ends up crying. No one wants to ask me, "Is Durk *sure* that's what he saw?"

The fact is, my Durk has a history of—I don't know—having ideas come into his head when he's smoking up, taking them way too seriously, and coming down on the delusional end of reality. I know the girls still remember the Thanksgiving when Durk announced to their husbands that he'd dated every one of the sisters in our family before settling on me as the best one.

"The best one for me, bros. That's all I mean. They're all fine ladies."

It would have been a big problem if it was true, especially since Heather was already mother to two of Ewan's babies and Meaghan was still in junior high school when I first met Durk and brought him home. Everyone knows to act like he never said it.

Fine: so they tend to reserve judgment when it comes to Durk's stories. Uncorroborated eyewitness statements, Ewan and his police would call them. I know it and there's a little bit of me that hates my sisters for it. Then there's another bit of me that might hate Durk for it. And the worst part of all is the one that hates myself for it.

It's up to careful Suzanne to find the smoothest path out of this. And she would have if Heather hadn't started talking first.

"Someone saw Martin kissing a strange woman,"

Heather restates. "I hate to say it, Ash, but, 'So what?' We've all been kissed by Martin. Give him a glass of wine and we can hardly walk past him without him trying to kiss us. It's a high society thing. Kissing is their normal, accepted greeting ritual. Right?"

Meaghan agrees, bobbing her head, talking in some loud onomatopoeia. "Mwah, mwah. And sometimes, *mmmwah*!"

It's rough but it works. I can be crestfallen without being furious. "Okay, maybe," I say, "but who is this lady? She's not one of Martin's sisters-in-law."

"She could be anybody," Meaghan says. "Martin is well-known in the city. He gets around. I've seen it too. He knows and he paws everyone downtown: waitresses, janitors, lawyers, fellow CEOs, everyone."

This is also true. No one else is particularly spooked by Tina's husband's smoochy lunch in the elevator car with the unknown pretty woman. In a way, I get it. They would be concerned if it was anyone else's husband, but this is Martin. His money-driven moral code is kind of experimental, based mostly on trial and error and whether Tina throws a fit. He's like a corporation wrapped up in a human body and an Armani suit. And while I'm pretty sure he knows people generally don't like full-on adultery, the murky grey areas of what makes a terrible husband must be confusing for him. A secluded lunch for two, complete with casual kissing, might not mean to Martin what it would mean to other men.

Still, I can't leave this alone. If I go back to Durk and

tell him the girls don't really care what he saw in the restaurant's elevator car, it will stand between them—between my husband and my sisters. And I can't have that.

Heather couldn't sigh any louder. "What is it you
want us to do, Ashley? Spy on Martin ourselves? Play
stake-out? Follow him around snapping pictures?"

"Maybe," I say.

Meaghan is shaking her head, reaching for her phone
again. "Creepy."

"Yeah, it's too much," Suzanne agrees. "What else
could we do?"

I'm standing up. "Nothing. We'll do nothing. We'll
just sit here and let Martin fool around until he gives Tina
some disease."

"Ah, for crying out loud," Heather interrupts. "If we
stalk Martin we could wind up charged with criminal ha-
rassment."

"What? Following people is a crime?"

Heather rakes her fingers through her own hair and
a tiny squall of white dust snows from her scalp onto the
floor of my office. "It can be a crime. Ewan told me about
it the time that freaky old lady whose son was charged
with manslaughter followed us all around the grocery
store."

The meeting's crisis is drying up and shrinking away
from me. I fall into my seat. The wheeled chair creaks and
rolls backward, into the wall. Something about the sound
of it makes me want to cry. I can still see Durk through
the window. He's finished with the forklift and he's using

his hands to stack loose bricks into a perfect cube. He could toss them into a box and be done with it but he doesn't. He needs to see the bricks aligned, squared, set in order not as a reflection of an inner peace he has but as a wish for an inner peace I'm not sure he can ever have. I don't know. But any hope of finding real peace for Durk is impossible without me—without all of us.

I don't need to explain it to my sisters.

"Ash, honey," Suzanne says to me, "Troy's clinic is downtown, close to Martin's building. I'm in that neighbourhood just about every day. I can keep an eye on Martin without harassing him, okay? We all can. Tell Durk we'll be paying closer attention from now on. Go ahead and tell him we're worried about Tina too."

Her offer is patronizing—painful, but typical. At this end of the birth order, I'm used to slinking away with consolations. I can accept them as the tokens of love my sisters mean them to be.

# Meaghan [6]

"Marie-Reine."

That's Riker, talking to me, standing behind me. I've come to his store again to blast and roll my way through video games identical to the ones Ian and I have at home.

"Marie-Reine." He says it again. I guess this is how he begins conversations: with an announcement—short, without context, left suspended for someone to pick it up.

"What? Queen Mary?" I say. Like just about everyone in Canada, I know enough cereal box French to make clunky, literal translations all by myself.

"No, just Marie-Reine. That's the name of the fifth-born of the Dionne quintuplets. She'd be your quint avatar."

"Ya don't say."

I haven't bothered to wear my gym costume tonight. I'm here in my usual geek-bunny wear—irony from head to toe. Ian says this T-shirt is too small, but I'm wearing it anyway. It has the words "Frickin' Repent" written across the chest and is completely awesome. There's a pair of skinny jeans flexed over my curves, and I've got army green canvas ballet flats on my otherwise bare feet.

Believe me, I tried not to come here tonight. I even delayed it with a round of phone calls to my sisters. The only one available to talk was Suzanne. And frankly, Suzanne and I don't speak well on the phone. The call was desperate and we both knew it.

"So have you ever read *The Importance of Being Earnest*?" I asked Suzanne.

"Wha? No, I guess not."

"I just finished it. I liked it."

She hummed an answer.

"Yeah," I went on, "I don't think I've ever met anyone named Ernest in real life."

"At your age? Probably not," she agreed. It's the kind of dead-end reply Mum would make when trying to end a call.

Now, at the store, Riker is the person struggling to chat with me. Somehow, he knows to talk about the sister already on my mind. He's asking after Suzanne. "The sister I saw you driving away from the coffee shop with the other night—the second-born—she'd be called Annette back in Quintland."

I nod. "Cool. We call her Suzanne."

"Suzanne. Yeah." He waits for three beats and goes back to the beginning. "They say Marie-Reine was special among her sisters because the whorl in her hair spun clockwise when everyone else's went counter-clockwise."

I smirk at the screen. "So you've got the Dionne quints' Wikipedia page memorized?"

"Uh—sure, among other things."

"I'm touched." But I still won't turn around.

Riker starts all over with a new non-sequitur. "Cremated."

My thumb slams against the pause button. "Cremated?"

"Yeah. We had my mother cremated, after she died. You—you said you wanted to know."

"Cremated? Wow. My sister Heather cremated her mother-in-law. I mean, she paid a funeral home to cremate her mother-in-law," I clarify. "That was before Heather could actually do it herself. Now that she works in a funeral home, she'll cremate anyone's mother or father or kids or lonely neighbours."

Riker raises his eyebrows. "Seriously? Which sister is Heather?"

"She's the oldest."

He rubs his beard, as if this is important. "Heather, firstborn—in Quintland she'd be called Yvonne."

I snort. "Yvonne Dionne?"

He almost laughs. "Yeah, yeah it rhymes. It's a show-biz name, remember? She's the firstborn quintuplet, the headliner."

"Hey, can we go for coffee yet?"

He looks at the wall clock, the one shaped like a red, pixelated mushroom. "Now? It's still fifteen minutes until nine."

"Come on, Riker."

He ducks his head. "How can I refuse Marie-Reine? No one ever says no to Queen Mary."

72

I scoff because everyone—everyone—says no to me.

As I turn to tell him this, I see something through the plate glass window that makes me throw the game controller into Riker's chest. He doesn't catch projectiles easily and fumbles the controller between his hands before he gets hold of it.

"Is he coming in?" I hiss. I'm an idiot, raising my arm to hide my face.

"Is who coming in?" Riker is gaping around the empty store as if he's never been here before.

"Ian. My Ian."

Riker looks through the window, into the street. "You mean the guy in the purple shirt, on the sidewalk?"

"Yes."

Outside the store, Ian is extending his arm, reaching for the handle of the door.

"Yep. He's coming in."

I swear at my shoes as bells ring over the front door. Ian steps inside, scanning the shelves of games. He isn't looking at Riker and hasn't seen me, hunched and cringing, standing behind him.

Riker calls out a greeting. "Hey, there. You looking for something in particular?"

Ian laughs at himself. "Yeah, actually. I'm looking for a gift, for my girlfriend."

"Your girlfriend likes video games?"

Ian finally makes eye contact with Riker, smirking. "Yeah. How cool is that?"

I am totally stupid. "Hey, honey," I say, stepping into

Ian's view.

"Meaghan, what're you doing here?"

"Same as you. Getting a game."

Ian takes my hand. "Okay, here's what I'm thinking," he says. "Instead of you having to go out in the dark and the cold to the gym every night until the wedding, we could get one of those games that—you know—kind of tricks us into standing up and getting a good workout right at home."

He sounds like an infomercial. All I say is, "Yeah, great." I look at Riker like I don't know him. "You got anything like that?"

"Something dance-y?" Ian adds.

Riker is playing the obsequious salesman. It's masochism, and it's sadism too. He'll have manners so good, so self-effacing, so smarmy we will both be made miserable.

He claps his hands once. "Of course. Right over here, sir." He leads us to the rear wall of the store, the area farthest from the cash register. It's the sports section, the place least in need of surveillance because it's stocked with the kind of inventory video game consumers will be least tempted to steal.

Ian is talking to me as we follow Riker between the shelves. "I was pretty sure you were getting sick of me copying eighteenth century love poems onto the flyleafs of books of old poetry and passing them off as gifts. You're always saying the Romantics need to get over themselves, so—"

I make a faint protest, blushing.

"Sorry, Babe," Ian goes on. "It's just that I was raised to think girls were supposed to like that kind of sweet stuff, and it's a hard habit to break. But, well, who can blame you for rejecting my dumb, old-fashioned ideas about gendered artistic preferences, right?"

Riker claps again. "And here we are. These dance games are quite popular and so much fun you won't know you're exercising," he says, quoting from the script of Ian's infomercial. He picks out a game that uses some form of the word "hot" five times on its packaging.

Ian takes it. "Awesome."

When the transaction is over, and Riker has slid the game into a plastic bag with one final humiliating flourish, Ian dismisses him, the way any customer would, and turns to me. "You still shopping, Babe?"

I'm nodding. "Yeah, actually. I haven't found anything for my nephew's birthday yet."

"Really? Which nephew?" Ian asks.

The question grates. I probably roll my eyes as I snap, "One of Tina's kids. I'm not exactly sure which one, okay. I'll figure it out when we get to the party next weekend. They all love video games, so it doesn't matter."

"Wow, already? I can't believe it's time for another one of those kids to have a birthday."

"Well, it is." I'm scowling. "Ian, I'll be home in a little while. Just go. I'll meet you there."

Ian goes. He always goes—no questioning, no sulking, just going.

The door closes behind him. Riker is standing at the

counter, mute, nearly motionless, like scenery. He moves, bouncing the palm of his hand against the countertop. "Meaghan, you had me thinking your boyfriend was some kind of hyper-critical control-freak jerk."

"Yeah. Sorry."

He steps from behind the cash register, jostling past me, moving toward the door. "He lets you play all the video games you want. He uses poetry to kiss up to you, not to put you down. And he obediently trots off home as soon as you tell him to leave."

I bow my head. "Sorry."

"Meaghan, he seems fine."

"He is fine."

Riker is stepping further away from me, backing himself against the door of the store. "So then it's not him that chases you out of your apartment and down here to my store every night?"

"Not really," I say into the end of my ponytail.

Riker speaks to his feet. "Then what is it, Meaghan?"

I toss my ponytail over my shoulder. Ian is not what's troubling our relationship. Riker is right. Ian is a good guy—clingy and sissy, but good. What's ruining everything is someone else, someone completely hapless who would be shocked to hear it, someone who isn't Riker either.

"Ian's mom," I begin. "She's amazing. She runs marathons and grows her own organic food and doesn't eat meat except at Christmas. She is going to live forever."

Riker is listening. But I can't go on, not yet.

"Look, it's past nine o'clock now." I try to redirect him. "We can leave the store and go for coffee without upsetting the owners."

"You mean, we can go for coffee so we can talk about how I cremated my mother, while your fiancé waits for you at home, by himself?"

"Don't make it sound—"

"You know," Riker says, pulling his keys from where they hang on a lanyard around his neck. "I'm not all that thirsty."

"Thirsty? What's that got to do with coffee?"

"You'd better go home, Meaghan." He pulls the front door open. A tiny tornado of dust twists inside, spinning into the store from the long, dirty avenue outside. "Go home to your perfectly fine fiancé and your immortal mother-in-law and try to learn some hot new dance moves."

I'm stepping toward the door. Riker holds it open with his arm stretched out. It's a mistake. As I leave, I'll have to walk right through him.

I stop in front of Riker in the doorway. If he dropped his arm, it'd fall around my shoulders. I can smell soap on him—flowery and lady-like, Yardley's lavender maybe.

"I am sorry," I say. And I touch his face, dragging my fingertips across his cheekbone, next to his eye and his nose, one of the few bare places where his beard doesn't grow.

# Heather                                    [7]

Someone is screaming in our backyard. It's nothing. It's typical. It's me.

If my sisters were left to tell our stories alone, the ones about me would always sound like monster movies—lots of screaming. Maybe that's fair.

Even if the neighbours weren't used to it, my noise isn't the kind that would make someone call the police, except maybe to complain about a disturbance. The energy and tone of my voice—it's not fear, it's not suffering, it's—I don't know—laughter.

Don't sneer at us. Some people are just happy. My husband Ewan and I, we're happy. Or, at least, we don't realize we should want anything more than what we have here.

We're in our backyard, a large, triangular piece of land at the end of a cul-de-sac in one of the city's new neighbourhoods. The field behind our yard is slated to be crammed with thirty-two new houses in the next three years—hundreds of eyes forced to see us whenever they look out their windows. I'm miserable thinking about it. Here's hoping the saplings we planted along the fence will grow tall and full quickly enough to give us some privacy. For now, our young willows and chokecherries and tower poplar trees look like leafy twigs stuck into the ground. We are doomed to become fully exposed once the pocket gophers and bees and wild canola are cleared to make way for people behind our house.

"You cannot fly a kite on a day like today," Ewan is calling to me from across the yard.

I toss my hair into a gust of wind to clear it from my face. "You say that every time I want to fly a kite for the kids."

"The kids?" Ewan scans the yard. "Where are the kids, anyway?"

"They went back inside because you won't help us."

"They went back inside because it's way too windy to fly a kite."

"Ewan, you are the only person I know who uses an abundance of wind as an excuse not to fly a kite."

"Why would I want an excuse? I love flying kites."

"Do you even know what makes kites fly? It's wind." I fling my arms apart, throw my head back, letting the air rush through my hair until my face is engulfed. "Nothing but wind!"

Through the tangles, I hear him laugh. "Fine, give me that mangled kite."

Indulgence: this is how things usually begin with us.

I take the spool of kite string, and we walk backwards, away from each other. Ewan stops, holding the ratty, dingy kite by its light, wooden frame. There's a sun-bleached blue and red superhero grinning from the nylon sail, but Ewan looks sceptical anyway.

He's waiting for a suitable stream of air. "It is too windy." He tries one last time.

"Do it!"

He jumps, throwing the kite into the air at his fullest height. I tug the string and the wind snags the kite in a tight, wild spiral. It never gets more than twice Ewan's height from the ground. The kite is circling closer and closer to the earth with each rotation. It isn't flying or gliding. It's whirling fast, like it's caught on the tip of a spinning power drill.

Mishap: this is also how things usually progress with us.

I scream. "Look out!"

Ewan looks but it doesn't help. The kite spirals into his forehead. He yells as the end of its centre dowel careens into his eyebrow. Staggering, he lets himself fall onto the lawn, spread out and helpless like a gigantic starfish marooned on the grass. He's quiet, staring glassy-eyed into the sky.

I scream again, tossing away the spool of string. The wind tumbles the kite against the fence in an irretrievably snarled mass of knots. I run to Ewan.

"I'm sorry, I'm sorry," I say, high and fast, taking his head in my hands. "You were right. It's a terrible day for kites. I'm sorry." I kiss his forehead from one temple to the other. "I'm so horrible. I'm so wrong. Are you okay? Did it hit your eye? Ewan?"

He moans like an extra in a zombie movie.

"Ewan?"

He's throwing one arm and then his other arm around me like they're dead weights on the ends of his shoulders. Their heaviness traps me as he rolls over, on top of me.

This: this is how things always end with us.

I'm screaming again. See, I'm nothing like the monster everyone else knows me to be, not with Ewan. This thing with him—maybe it's what keeps monstrosity from overtaking me.

I'm laugh-screaming a set of numbers now, over and over again. "Two-seventy-one, two-seventy-one!" It's the number of the Criminal Code assigned to the section on sexual assault law. I've known it for a long time. Don't tell me it's not funny. This is my marriage, safe, with its own code.

There's another voice, calling over mine, from across the yard. "Hey, you guys."

It's Suzanne, singing out a greeting as she starts down the porch steps. To strangers—to our phantom future neighbours who are not yet afflicted with our family drama constantly unfolding in front of them—our sweet Suzanne might look menacing, closing in on my husband and me with a plastic bag and a sharp knife.

Honestly, I can't vouch for her state of mind right now. May, Suzanne's legendarily perfect mother-in-law, has been staying at their house for two full days. Suzanne claims she loves it when May comes. She won't shut up about it. It's like bad, relentless propaganda.

The rest of our sisters might accept it without question, but I remember visitations from a mother-in-law of my own. No matter how sweet May is, she is set in an opposing corner of a love triangle topped by Suzanne's husband. Or, at least, she should be. If they had a more normal relationship, that's how they'd be aligned—Suzanne and May each tugging at Troy. That's how it was for Carol and Ewan and me. It's not nice but it's the way things are supposed to be. The shape drawn between Suzanne, Troy, and May is strange—oblong, bladelike.

I'm not the only one who'd say things between May and Suzanne are—well, they're not right. I studied classic in-law love triangles in a sociology course required for my criminology degree. My mouldy old criminology degree—it's not much help with the work I eventually ended up doing at the funeral home, but it does apply to my family life with a frequency that's a little disturbing.

"May's rhubarb!" I gasp and spring away from where Ewan and I have been lying on the grass. "I completely forgot about it until I saw you standing there."

"Don't worry. I can cut it myself," Suzanne says. "As you were, you guys."

I snort and give Ewan a parting shove. "Nah, we are so done."

I skip ahead of Suzanne, leading her to a spider-webbed corner between the shed and the house. This is where my electric clothes dryer vents out of the wall into open air. It's also where the rhubarb is growing. We dug it up and moved it to a better spot once, but a few tiny rhizomes slipped through the transplant and the rhubarb grew right back.

May has finished cleaning every part of Suzanne's already clean house she can reach and now she's sent Suzanne to harvest our early rhubarb. "Harvest" is a nicer expression than "clear-cut," which is what we're really doing by hacking it out of my yard today. Since the patch won't go away, it needs to be pared early, before the rhubarb grows rampant, thickening into broad, stringy stalks and huge, toxic leaves large enough to fan a Pharaoh on a barge.

"Make sure you wash it well," I warn Suzanne, as we bundle the rhubarb into her bag. "It gets linty back here, and it might make everything taste like fabric softener. So what's May got planned for all this anyways?"

She shrugs. "Who knows? Rhubarb cobbler, pancakes, slushies, wallpaper paste."

Ewan has me in such a good mood, I'm finding Suzanne funny, and I laugh as I wipe pink juice from the blade of Suzanne's knife against my thigh.

I crush and fold severed rhubarb leaves into our composter, jabbing them into the cube of rotting plants with the end of a broomstick. It's paranoia, but I'd be an irresponsible big sister if I didn't cut the toxic leaves off the stalks before I let Suzanne take them away. The truth is I've been a person longer than any of my sisters. It means, for now, that I see farther than they can. So I worry.

I tell Suzanne, "I don't want to be sitting here, fretting about your mother-in-law poisoning you with rhubarb leaves I grew myself. What's the name of the chemical in them again?" I call to Ewan.

"Oxalic acid."

"Right."

Suzanne almost scoffs. "Don't be silly, Heather. My sweet May is not exactly bloodthirsty."

No one out-scoffs me. "I didn't say she'd poison you on purpose. I just can't risk any accidents. The worst things in the world, Suzanne—most of the time, they're just accidents."

# Suzanne                              [8]

I've finished the rhubarb harvest, and it's time to leave Heather and go home, back to where May is not plotting to poison me with oxalic acid-enriched baked goods. I'm much more likely to go home and find her apologizing for having taken so long to pull the refrigerator away from the wall and wash the floor underneath it, where the juice pools whenever the kids spill it.

It's bittersweet, this time with May, as she makes one final, loving tribute to us before she goes to Guatemala for the rest of the year. Ever since she retired, she's been travelling, exercising that practical dental hygiene compassion of hers. May's savings—padded by the settlement Troy's dad surrendered before he fled to live on a sailboat with that suntanned woman from the Internet—pay for it all.

On the drive home from Heather's house, I'm stopped at a level railroad crossing. Another badly scheduled heavy freight train is grinding its way through the city's rush-hour traffic. May will have dinner on the table, early as usual, but I am late. Troy will be late too. The golf courses have just opened for the season, and he's got a tee time this evening.

I've heard policeman Ewan say it contravenes the law prohibiting texting and driving to look at my phone even when I'm idling at a full stop, but I still reach into my purse when the ringtone peeps. Troy is texting me. He mistakenly left his good shoes at the clinic when he bolted for the golf course and now he wants me to fetch them.

I don't sigh. Dinner—a lukewarm plate of May's boiled potatoes and chicken legs made with love and a painfully old-fashioned culinary aesthetic—is already ruined anyway. I steer into an alley, away from the train crossing, veering north, toward downtown.

Most of the rush hour traffic has emptied out of the city centre by the time I arrive at the clinic. I'm driving away with Troy's shoes when I'm stopped at a red light, right in front of the tall building housing Martin's company. This is where my brother-in-law spins his family's old money into new money—the place where no one has ever seen him wearing anything but a great suit, where everyone laughs at his jokes, brings him coffee, and calls him Mister. I'm not exactly sure what kind of work they do—something about oil field contracting.

This is the building Ashley wanted us to stake out and surveil. Looking up at it from the avenue is the closest I will get to doing that. At least I'll be able to tell Ashley I was here. Martin's upper floors are dark. It's strange. This hour would be late for most people to be leaving work. But Martin's company is his true love, his real mistress. He never leaves it before eight o'clock. Tina says, if he had to,

Martin would work here for free just for the pleasure of it, kind of like Troy when it comes to aromatherapy.

On its ground floor, the building is clad in sheets of mirrored glass lit with yellow light. And in the yellow light, on the paving stones of the building's patio, I see Martin himself in a long cashmere overcoat. He is striding toward the sidewalk when he stops, swaying like he's overcome with something strong and sweet. A woman is coming toward him. She looks fairly ordinary—dark-haired and thin, closer to Heather's age than to Tina's. At the sight of Martin, she skips to meet him, taking him by both hands.

My heart thuds. The traffic light is still red. My phone is on the passenger seat. Honestly, I don't want to be stalking or harassing Martin. Maybe I'm still patronizing Ashley. Whatever I'm doing, I've taken hold of my phone. I'm framing Martin and the woman inside the screen, through the camera lens. The woman is tilting her head to kiss his face, close to his mouth. The fake shutter sound snaps as I take a picture of them, just as her face is closest to his.

There's a heavy steel rectangle filling the road behind me now, a bus indignant that I'm stopped in its designated lane after the light has turned green. I crank the steering wheel and move out of its way. When it roars past and I glance over my shoulder, toward the patio, Martin and the woman are gone.

And I drive away.

Durk didn't invent this. I glance at the screen of my phone as I drive. The picture remains. Martin kissed a strange woman right in front of me. I saw it. Of course I did. This is me—the eyes of the family, the watcher, the haunter, the ghost that will see everything but probably won't do anything.

"Martin," I say out loud as the road bends on to a dirty black bridge. Of all the men we've brought into our family, the cheating one is Martin.

With May in town, there's no need to rush home to put the kids to bed. This is for the best since things never move quickly in the place I'm going now: Ashley's house.

I ring my sister's doorbell and wait. I finish texting my profuse apologies to May and still no one's come to answer the door. There's usually a delay while Durk tucks away whatever he needs to hide. It takes time for Ashley to throw the windows open and douse the house in that Roasted Vanilla Bean Fantasy air freshener. Everyone knows what's going on while we wait—even law-and-order Ewan knows it. No one ever says a word.

"Martin," I announce when Ashley answers the door and the wave of vanilla bean hits me. "I was coming home from the clinic just now and I saw Martin. He was with somebody."

She yanks the phone out of my hand. "I knew it." She's scrolling through the pictures, gasping. "You got them together—and kissing. I can't believe you got them kissing."

"It wasn't a long, mushy kiss," I say, leaning to see the picture again. It looks far worse crowded onto my screen than it did in real life. It's like one of those grocery store tabloid cover photos, capturing a split-second and holding it down until it becomes something torrid.

"I don't know, Suze. They look pretty close."

"They were close," I admit. "But there could be an explanation other than—"

Ashley is already opening the door to the basement, shouting down the stairs for Durk. There's a shuffle of slow feet, and then he appears—shirtless, as usual, in a pair of long hemp-cloth shorts that sag around his waist. In my peripheral vision, he looks like a teenager—all lean and dishevelled. The effect disappears as he steps into focus.

He's rubbing his eyes, red and lazy. And he's looking over Ashley's shoulder, into the screen of my phone. "Yeah, there she is. Martin's sexy lady friend."

Troy is still out with his golf buddies when I get back to our house. I haven't been home all evening, but the jumble of sparkly shoes my girls usually leave in front of the door is neatly stacked inside the hall closet. The baseboards running along the walls—the ones Troy took pains to stain exactly the same colour as the hardwood of our floors and stairs—have been dusted and rubbed with lemon oil. In the morning, I will rave my thanks to May for all the work she's done. I will rave and rave until we're both exhausted.

She and the kids are on the same early-to-bed-early-to-rise schedule. The house is dark and quiet. In the fridge, there's a bowl of muffin mix covered in cellophane, waiting for the bundle of rhubarb I've left in the van. If I were a less than perfect daughter-in-law, I'd ignore it, make myself a cup of Troy's purifying serenity herbal tea, and go upstairs to bed.

But perfection is not like that. It's inconvenient—difficult. Perfection demands I go back to the garage and retrieve the rhubarb. It requires me to turn on the lights and stand at the sink washing away the lint and the laundry perfume. It will keep me awake on my feet, chopping stringy stalks until my fingertips are stained red.

# Heather [9]

This must be the swankiest Italian restaurant in the entire downtown core. It happens to be just a few doors south of the pebbly, brown, hollow block of concrete and misery that serves as the city's courthouse. That's the only reason Ewan and I would ever come here.

He's sitting over a plate of fancy ravioli garnished with flakes of grated black truffle. As the cream in his meal is cooling into something slimy and not at all swanky, I reach across the burgundy table cloth to squeeze his wrist. "Hey, are you okay yet? You're still not looking at me."

He nearly smiles. "Sorry. Looking at you is an emotional experience. And I can't handle feeling anything right now."

Ewan is sweetest when he's saddest. It kills me. I tighten my fingers around his wrist—strong and quick—like a pulse.

It's been a terrible day in court. A drunken nineteen-year-old, who is referred to in the legal system as a fully grown man, ran a stop sign at four in the morning last New Year's Eve. He killed a sober single mom driving home from her shift as a taxi dispatcher. Today, he's pleading guilty. Ewan is attending the sentencing hearing as a representative of the police department.

The hearing is a madhouse. The anti-drinking-and-driving movement has been railing on the courthouse stairs for days, waving signs, burning candles, slapping stickers on lampposts, calling out the penitent, despondent driver as if he's an Anti-Christ. The words on their placards are old, standard slogans, smeared in drippy red paint, like fake stage blood.

"It's not an accident. It's murder."

"But it isn't murder," Ewan told me again last night at home, standing in the doorway of our walk-in closet, unthreading his belt through its loops.

I sat on the bed and nodded at him. "Yeah, there's no real murder without *mens rea*. There has to be criminal intent for it to be murder. Everybody knows that." I laced my fingers together, holding them down, purposely breaking my loathsome habit of sniffing the tips of my fingers for signs of the stench of my rubber work gloves.

"Right," he agreed. "This collision was a tragedy. It was a crime. But it's a crime of negligence known in the Criminal Code of this country as impaired driving causing death. That's exactly what we charged him with, and that's exactly what he's pleading guilty to. Everyone hates us but we've done everything *right*."

It's a discussion we've been having daily, like catechism, for weeks.

In court today, the judge sentenced the driver to

two-and-a-half years in jail. The prosecutors say they're going to appeal and ask for a little more time. It sounds like a slow remedy—remote and desperate. No amount of criminal charges or prosecutions would have yielded the public flogging or life sentence or exile to Jupiter the protesters demand.

For now, Ewan's name is in the city's yellowest newspaper, under a headline reading, "Brought to Justice?"

He hasn't seen the headline yet.

On days of big unpopular trials like this one, if there's no funeral for me to run, I come to the courthouse to sit in the gallery. I sit on the groom's side near the accused, away from Ewan. He thinks I'll be safer that way. During breaks, he meets me in the parking lot, in the car, and we talk about the proceedings. It's not just because I have my own degree in criminology and can follow along in court. Ewan needs to see me when he's caught up in something like this. It's as if my perspective is a strong current in the stream of his own consciousness, and he'll be disoriented if he pretends it's not there.

We are in the street outside the Italian restaurant now. Ewan is taking my hand and trudging toward my car when I stop on the sidewalk, tugging backward. He stops, our arms stretching out between us. "What is it?"

"Look, there's a video game store right there, across the street," I say.

"You want to stop and buy the kids a new video game—right now?"

I don't answer the question. "Remember video

arcades? There used to be one in every shopping mall when we were kids, right beside the food courts. But you never see them anymore. Everyone just plays games at home now. You used to love arcades back in the day, didn't you?"

The right corner of his mouth twitches. "Yeah."

"Amusement parks and these stores are all that's left of arcades. Look." There's a gap in the late evening traffic, and I'm pulling him across the street. "Come on. They let you try out new games for free on those TVs hanging from the ceiling. You can stand there and just play and play. No quarters to lose, no line-ups, no emotional experiences, nothing."

Inside the store, the guy behind the counter barely looks up as I tow Ewan through the jingling front door of the shop.

*More parents.* That's probably what he's thinking. It's okay. He's not wrong.

The game loaded in the television is called Mech-something—I don't care. There is nothing in this shop that either Ewan or I could possibly care about. That's why we've come.

Ewan's childhood muscle memory for buttons and joysticks means he's able to play the game as soon as his thumbs hit the controller. I, on the other hand, am terrible. I'm yelling as if it will help the soldier-lady I've walked face-first into a corner avoid getting shot in the back. Soldier-lady would look hilarious if she wasn't so sickening. Her figure is like Meaghan's, only tall and fatally cinched at the waist.

The store clerk sighs into the counter. He's starting to move. He's probably hoping if he asks us if we need any help we'll stop goofing around and buy something.

Before he finishes his approach, the door bangs open—jingle and clang—and someone stumbles into the store, just outside my field of vision.

The clerk speaks, but not to us. "You're back."

"Of course I'm back. We aren't finished. You can't be mad at me anymore, Riker," the newcomer says. "It's not natural. I need you to like me again."

"Meaghan?" My sister is here, stomping around acting bossy in a place where she has no business being the boss. I recognize the sound of my own voice in hers. I spin away from the screen without pressing the pause button. The CPU shoots the guts out of the soldier-lady.

Meaghan flinches. "Heather? What are you guys doing here?"

Ewan squawks. "Whoa! Heather, you can't just—hey, how do I switch it to one-player mode?"

The clerk steps up to make the adjustment for him.

"We came in here so Ewan could unwind a little," I say. "Bad day in court."

Meaghan frowns. "Yeah, I heard about it on the radio."

I'm shaking my head, speaking without moving my lips. "Talk about something else."

What would be more fun for me than a re-telling of Ewan's bad day would be an explanation of the connection between my baby sister and this guy she says she wants to like her. He is clearly not Ian, my brother-in-law-to-be. He's retreated behind the counter where he's feigning disinterest in us.

It doesn't matter. I'm talking to him anyway. "Hi there. You're Meaghan's friend. Nice to meet you. I'm her big sister, Heather."

He startles—alarmed but eager, like I just mentioned his favourite fandom. "Yeah? Hi. Nice to meet you too."

Meaghan is stepping behind the counter as if the whole store belongs to her. She says, "This is Riker."

I open my mouth and laugh at him. "Cool! Your parents are sci-fi fans?"

He grins. "Yeah."

"Meaghan loves sci-fi too, right Sweetie? Her boyfriend is a huge fan-boy too. You know Ian, don't you, Riker?"

He nods. "Yeah."

They won't encourage me, but I keep talking anyway. "Well, at least your parents had some nerve, unlike people who choked and named their daughters Heather in the 1970s."

I laugh at myself until he joins in—painfully, like plaster falling off a ceiling.

It's beginning to be uncomfortable even for me. I turn and circle my arms around Ewan's torso. "You ready to go home, honey?"

He sets the game controller back onto the stand below the television. "Yeah, sure. Thanks." He nods at Riker. "Come on, Meags. We'll drive you home."

Obediently, she follows Ewan and me into the street. Ewan has been a part of our family since Meaghan was nine years old. With Dad's crazy work schedule, she probably saw as much of Ewan as she did of her own father while she was growing up. He's different from the other brothers-in-law who came into the family later, when Meaghan was no longer a child. He's more of a brother, more in, more like the law.

We're on the sidewalk when I thread my arm through Meaghan's, laughing with enough force to bend my body at the waist. "Riker? Riker? Come on, that is *not* that guy's real name."

Meaghan's shoulder collides with mine, knocking me sideways as we walk. "Shh! It is so."

"What? I missed it. What does he say his name is?" Ewan asks.

"It's Riker," Meaghan says. "R-I-K-E-R. And it's totally believable. He was born in 1987, the same year Jonathan Frakes got his big break on television. And Riker's mom loved *Star Trek* way back in the sixties, so—"

It is utterly scoff-worthy. "He says his mom is a Trekkie?"

Meaghan knocks me sideways again. "Don't you start on his mom. She's dead."

In full monster mode, I laugh louder than I have yet. "No. His mother is not dead."

Meaghan stops walking and pries her arm out of mine. "Of course she's dead. Don't act like you don't know people die, Heather. You, of all people."

I'm still laughing. "I know—"

"Martin's mom is dead. Ewan's mom is dead too and you don't think that's funny, do you? Honestly, Heather, what is the matter with you?"

I stand up straight and push my hair out of my face. "That boy is not bereaved. I can sense bereavement like it's a tiny pea left under a big stack of mattresses. I bet Riker's mom is at home bleaching his whites right now."

"What a thing to say. You are depraved. Ewan, tell her she's nuts."

It's a foolish move. Ewan makes his career in a field where all kinds of people stand up on their hind legs and tell him lies, day in and day out. He's primed to hear lies everywhere. He hums. "I don't know, Meags. You seen any proof of it? And what's his excuse for working in a store at his age?"

"Oh. He's on hiatus from school. But he's earned most of a creative writing degree already."

As she says it, Meaghan hears herself—hears herself as if she's one of us, one of her own sisters, cringing at the sound.

# Suzanne [10]

My mother-in-law's last batch of rhubarb muffins is in the oven when I step into the kitchen the final morning of her visit. May herself is upstairs, packing her suitcase, getting ready to leave for another epic Central American odyssey. I'll drive her to the airport after the kids leave for school. People with perfect daughters-in-law have no need to ride in taxis.

I sniff at the fruity, cinnamon smell. I still hate rhubarb. Being a picky eater is a secret shame of mine. It isn't easy to hide. I wish I could cheerfully eat anything, the way Troy can. Cantaloupe, raisins, hotdogs—my life would be better if I liked these things. It's a good thing May doesn't mean for this batch of muffins to be eaten but frozen, stored in the deep freeze with the homemade elk sausage a patient gave Troy as a gift and the bags of shredded zucchini from my organic gardening phase. That suits me fine.

In the living room, I turn off the cartoons my kids abandoned when I sent them upstairs to get dressed for school. That's when I find Durk. He's passed out on the sofa still wearing a jacket and shoes. I can't see his face, just a mass of stringy brown hair and a scar. His right hand lies palm-down beside his head.

He's done it again.

I slide the heavy curtain aside to check the patio door and, as it always is when I find Durk like this, the pane of sliding glass is out of its track and leaning against the wall outside.

I text Ashley to let her know Durk is here. She doesn't reply. It's easier this way.

I toss an afghan over him—the pink and blue one May crocheted for us when we got married. I hope she hasn't noticed my brother-in-law lying here face down on the furniture, breathing nosefuls of our dust-mites.

Durk is fathoms below sleep. I step closer to the couch, near enough to brave a long, unembarrassed look at the smooth, pale scar on his hand.

Alcohol vapour putrefies the air around his body. I sway away from him, as if it's insect repellent and I'm a big bug. On sunny afternoons when we find him dozing in the grass at family picnics, we can tell ourselves Durk's habits are benign trappings of an alternative lifestyle—that he's a mystic who's transcended nuisances like dependence and domestic turmoil. We ignore this dark side as long as we can—right up until it forces its way through our backdoor and collapses in a noxious cloud on the couch.

The kids are leaving for school, bleating about mateless shoes and overdue library books. I remind them to run upstairs to hug Grandma May goodbye. She won't be here when they get back.

The house falls into its strange, sudden, childless stillness as I close the front door behind them. It's quiet enough for me to hear May's footsteps on the floor above my head, as if she's invisible and walking upside down on the kitchen ceiling. Actually, her feet are pacing triangles between our spare bed, the closet, the bathroom. She moves quickly. Spry, is what our dad would call her.

May is about to come down the stairs. There's the sound of her suitcase castors rolling across the rug laid over the hardwood planks at the top of the stairwell. In a moment I'll see her feet and legs through the metal rails of the banister. I'm already starting to compose a smile and some sort of explanation for the man passed out in the living room.

And then everything—everything—breaks apart.

It begins with noise in the stairwell—spinning suitcase wheels, thuds and cracks against varnished hardwood and metal spindles, and May's voice, not loud but wordless and terrified, like a sound she might have made in childbirth, only clipped short.

I run, skidding into the entryway. At the bottom of the stairs, I find my mother-in-law. She is lying on her front, her neck twisted far enough to her left for me to expect her to be lying on her side. Her legs extend up the stairs; her head is on the floor at my feet, eyes open—shocked but desolate. One hand is still cupped around the handle of her suitcase.

"May!" I gasp.

I call after her even though she can't be here anymore.

I am a nurse but there's no one who could fail to recognize her current medical condition. May is dead. She broke her neck falling down our stairs. The impact has ruined not just the bones that hold up her head but the cord of nerves that tells her to breathe and live. She has died, in a flash, in an instant, here on the same stairs my bouncy, supple little kids fall down several times a year without any injuries worse than bruises. It shouldn't be possible. It can't be denied.

"Aw, no. No. May—"

I kneel to examine her, but I don't touch anything. It's not that I'm squeamish. It's still May lying here. And after all my hospital shifts, it's not like I go through life without touching dead people—newly dead people just like May is newly dead. She's exactly like a hospital body, only out of pyjamas, out of bed, upside down.

I don't touch her because I can't fix this. I won't try—won't unwind her and press my mouth to hers and beat against her sternum until someone drags me away. There is nothing to be done.

Calling 911 is the next step in the death rites prescribed by my faint-hearted culture—the culture wailing at me to hide at the sight of my own dead. As it requires, I will call for strangers—uniformed, registered strangers in ambulances and police cars. I will call even though there is nothing anyone can do for May except pack her up and take her where we can't see her.

On my knees, I crawl to the kitchen, groping the countertop for the cordless phone. My grasp is weak and shaken with a tremor. And while I tremble, looking at the keypad, trying to remember the number for 911, the phone lights up and rings.

"Hello?"

"Tell him not to bother coming in to the shop today." It's Ashley, calling to frighten Durk.

Normally, I'd keep her on the phone, try to cheer her up, tug her forward, past her frustration. "Sure," is all I say to Ashley the morning my mother-in-law is lying in my stairwell.

"Sure?"

"Yeah, I'll tell him. Oh, and Durk is really sorry he forgot to call home when he decided to stay here last night."

Ashley scoffs. "He broke in through your patio doors while you were sleeping, Suzanne. And he's not even awake yet."

There's a beep on the line. Another call is coming in. "Hang on a minute," I say.

The other call is from Heather. "How come I was the last one to find out you had a picture of Martin with his girlfriend?"

"What? You were not."

"Yes, I was. Even Meaghan knew about it before me."

I can't think. "Look, Heather, I'm busy right at this second." I glance at the stairs. "May is—she's still here."

"Fine. Bye."

I flick back to Ashley's line. She's too mad to wait and she's gone.

I sit with the quiet telephone cradled in my hand. As I

wait, my tremor is abating. My grip is strengthening. I am waiting, maybe it's for Meaghan or Tina to ring the phone and complete—something.

It's time to alert official personnel about this rapidly cooling emergency. The ambulances and police cars won't have their sirens on when they arrive here. Maybe they'll use their lights. They'll clog up my cul-de-sac and spook the neighbours.

May is dead and sliding, crumpling into a heap at the bottom of the stairs. She's going away, leaving me. My mime act is exposed. I'm not standing behind an invisible wall, measuring out its length and breadth with the palms of my hands anymore. I am standing in the open, unsheltered, imperfect.

I make a noise like a sob—just once, all voice, no tears. "Don't go. You can't go."

She's leaving anyway. My mother-in-law is dead, like Heather's and Tina's and maybe even Ashley's, for all we know. When the ambulances and police cars leave here today, I'll be in the no-mothers-in-law club right along with all my sisters. I'll be there with Heather, the spoiled monster, punished and punished by our mother. I'll sink to the level of Tina, the ignored and betrayed. I'll be in line with Ashley, who is more like a probation officer than a wife on mornings like this. Maybe I'll even be more like Meaghan, the girl so traumatized by a botched brush with motherhood she's convinced no one can love her properly—not any of her fiancés, not any of her sisters.

In a few hours, everyone will know. It's time to begin

telling them. I've got the phone in my hand. The act of making the call that will begin the processing of May's death is all that keeps me from a passing away of my own. It is the death of myself as a daughter-in-law. It is the death of what little perfection I have. Daughter-in-law Suzanne—the one aspect of my being that was flawless— she dies with May.

Maybe I'll wait a little longer.

Maybe I'll get up off my knees, go into the kitchen, finally drink a cup of Troy's purifying serenity herbal tea, eat a piece of toast, cherish the dying moments of the perfect daughter-in-law.

May won't mind the wait. Take care of myself before worrying about her—wasn't that what she always wanted? She'd eat standing at the counter so other people could sit down at the dinner table; she'd ride sitting on the parking brake, squeezed between the front seats of an overcrowded car so someone else could be safe in a seatbelt. If May could tell me to take a moment for myself to calm down and think, I know she would.

The dark brown, overcooked rhubarb muffins are out of the oven, the kettle is boiling, and the toaster is making a dangerous, burning smell as it cooks my breakfast. The kids must have accidentally torn off a bread crust and left it caught inside the toaster elements again. It smells like it's about to catch fire.

Is May about to catch fire? Heather is always proseletyzing cremation to everyone. She loves it, like real fireworks. Her mother-in-law was cremated, of course. Everyone knows that. I can't remember whether May has told us how she wants her body dispatched in the end. Knowing May, there's a sensible will written somewhere. The funeral is probably pre-arranged and paid for and everything.

Tina's mother-in-law is buried in the antique part of the graveyard with the rest of her dead, old-money family. We've seen pictures of the grave in Tina's family album. She takes her kids to visit it every year on her mother-in-law's birthday—takes photos of them standing next to it holding bouquets: tea roses for the girls, lilies for the boys, yellow pollen smeared on their white shirts. The gravestone itself is so fancy Ashley whistles every time she sees a picture of it.

No one's ever told me how long Tina's mother-in-law stayed in the garage, in her Bentley, before anyone found her. I asked Heather once how long Carol, her mother-in-law, had been lying dead in bed before she found her there. Hard-faced lab technologists can pinpoint times of death to the minute on television crime shows.

"That kind of forensics is fiction," Heather said. "After the first few hours, once the rigor comes and goes and the blood settles to the low spots, it's all muddled and confounded. It's fiction, Suzanne. And the truth is, when it comes to old people with pre-existing health conditions, the police seldom ask."

I pressed her anyway. "But they still need a death date—something they can write down. What do they write when they're not sure what day someone died?"

The official date, she told me, the one on death certificates and gravestones and everything, is the date when a body is discovered. It's the date the police and the medical examiners and the undertakers and the government use in spite of everyone knowing it's wrong.

It's a sham, but I can see why they do it. Once a life ends, what matters are the perceptions of the people still alive—what we know and feel and see. My sisters' mothers-in-law weren't dead—not really, not fully—until someone else discovered them, wrote it down, took them away, and planted a stone over them.

Maybe there's no meaning in dying when no one's looking. If a tree falls in the forest—we all knows how that goes.

The toast pops in my face, black, smoky, and shrunken.

I know what will happen next.


First, I'll wake Durk.

He is still sleeping on the couch. My shadow darkens his profile as I lean over him. In this dimness, the dark circles and tiny lines around his eyes are obscured. He looks like a photo of a rock 'n' roll angel in a magazine—our family's very own Kurt Cobain surviving to have a bunch of kids and his own masonry shop.

Where on his body should I take hold of him to shake him awake? There's his foot, still in its untied sneaker. A disturbance at his foot, so far from his central nervous system, might not be compelling enough on a morning after a night like the one he's had. Maybe I should shake him by the hand. I could finally press my thumb against that scar and see if there's any heat left in it. Instead, I grab his shoulder, pushing and pulling until his arm rolls in its socket.

"Durk," I say. "Durk, you need to wake up now."

His eye, the one that isn't mashed into the cushions, squeezes tightly closed before it opens, looking into my living room without any recognition.

"Get up, Durk," I say. "You're at Suzanne's house, mostly passed out on the couch."

He rubs his eye with the heel of his hand as he pushes himself to sitting. "Suzanne's?"

We've got to stop talking about me in the third person. "Yeah, you're on my couch. And I think you're still partied out," I say. "Let me get you some tea."

"Tea," he repeats as I walk to the kitchen. "Ashley."

"She called already," I tell him over the whistle of the kettle. "She'll be too mad to see you for a while."

"But work—"

"She says just to stay away for today."

Durk hangs his head and swears at my shiny walnut floor. "It's worse than I thought."

I glance into the stairwell as I approach the couch again. "Oh, it could get worse. Take your tea, Durk. It's lemon with cinnamon, Doctor Troy's own blend."

He shudders. "That means there's fish oil in it."

I try to laugh. "Maybe a little. That's okay. You look like you could use some detoxifying."

Durk sighs and stands to collect his teacup. I rush to meet him in front of the couch. I move too quickly, and a wave of hot, yellow water surges over the rim of the cup and scalds my hand. I don't react. If I pause, I won't reach Durk in time to stop him from seeing what's in the stairwell.

I'm stepping into him like a bad dance partner, forcing him backward with my movement and the hot liquid I hold in front of myself, keeping him in the living room. "Sit down."

He takes his tea and slumps into the cushions. "Thanks," he says. "You guys are always so good about this."

"Well," I begin, "it is kind of a bad time for you to crash here, actually. M-May is in the house."

"Troy's mom."

"Yeah. She's been staying here. She was supposed to be leaving for Guatemala today but there's been a glitch."

"Yeah?" he says, not bothering to seem interested.

My throat ripples as I swallow. "Durk," I say. It's all I say before I start to move toward him again, advancing in slow steps, faintly rocking, side-to-side, like a cobra.

He looks up from his tea. "Suzanne?"

It's like a movie—a stupid, sleazy, sickening movie. I do love Durk. Don't misunderstand. I can't fail to love one of the few adults in my family who never begins a sentence with the words, "Think, Suzanne ..." But this is the part of the movie where I have to press myself as close to Durk as I can. I am about to step further into his space than I've ever been, saying something creepy about the powerful connection that has always existed between us.

Is it even real?

It doesn't matter. As I stand here, I can't bring myself to say anything like it. I can only speak his name again, lower and slower. "Durk."

"Uh, yeah?"

*Ashley*, I tell myself, *look at him the way Ashley looks at him.*

The next time I speak, my voice sounds exactly like my sister's. That's the real secret of imitating a voice: don't mimic only by trying to sound like someone else. Begin the imitation by trying to look like someone else. Ashley—I open my eyes wider, turn out my lips to make them a little fuller, thrust out my jaw the slightest bit further.

"Durk."

Of all the sisters, Ashley and I are the ones who look most alike. It's the shape of our faces, the colour of our hair, our brow bones, the way our legs are attached to our hips—something. It's always made me feel weird about Durk—like we have some unintended carnal kinship, like he might have a pretty good idea what I really look like all over, if you know what I mean. It's funny, but I've never wondered if Ashley feels the same way about my Troy.

I never wanted this connection to Durk. But it's here. And right now, I need it.

"There's been an accident," I tell him, right out of the sleazy movie script.

Durk looks around the room. "Huh? Is everyone okay?"

"No." I touch him. I mean to smooth his early morning hair the way Ashley might if she saw him looking like this. But when I try to be her now, I'm Ashley taking care of a child, and I sweep Durk's hair into place deftly and quickly, nothing like a lover. But the voice is still working. "The accident involves my mother-in-law. She fell down the stairs."

"Dude."

I sit beside him on the couch, setting my hand next to his thigh. "She fell all the way down the stairs, with her suitcase in her hand and everything."

Durk looks around the room one more time. "Where is she now? Is she taking it easy in bed?"

"No." I move my fingers and they graze the fabric of his jeans. "I need your help Durk. There's trouble. But it's not like I've done anything wrong."

This is where most anyone else in my life would have bolted. Durk, however, waits—wide open as ever. "What exactly's going on?" is all he says, as he sets his teacup on the coffee table.

"May fell—on her neck—and it killed her."

"No way."

"Yes." I take his hand as I stand. "She's dead. Come here. I'll show you. She's stuck in the stairwell."

He yanks himself out of my grip, raises both of his hands in front of his face, palms turned toward me, as if he's deflecting something I've thrown at him. "No. I can't. I don't want to see."

"I need you to see. You can't help me if you won't see."

111

"No." He's moving away from me, off the couch and onto the floor with his head between his knees. "I'm not like you guys. I don't play with dead people. I don't like them. I don't look at them, not even at funerals."

"They're just people."

"Not anymore they're not."

I kneel next to him on the floor. "I can't have May die. Not right now. I'm not ready. I'm scared. I need to stay a daughter-in-law. It holds me together. It holds everything together."

He hasn't stopped shaking his head. "Then call the ambulance and maybe they'll be able to help her."

"No. She's been dead for a while now. Right from the start, no one could have helped her. I wish there was some kind of mistake but I've worked in a hospital way too long to be wrong about this."

He wants me to be wrong badly enough to get to his feet and takes four brave steps. It's enough to bring him to where he can see May lying upside down on the stairs. He gags, doubling over, pivoting back into the kitchen.

"Her face—"

He's bent in half and I can see the stairs over the hump of his spine.

"Yes," I say. "It's okay. All her blood is settling into her face and head because it's the lowest point on her right now. That's just gravity doing its thing. It's normal. But it is kind of gross. So we should move her before it gets any worse."

"Call the cops," he pleads. "Get Ewan and his cops

over here. Get Heather—get anybody."

"But then everyone will know she's dead and—and it's too soon for that. I can't do it. It'll wreck me. I need May alive or I'll—I don't know what I'll be but I won't be me anymore. Me—this Suzanne, right here—I'll be gone too. And I can't face what might take my place—not yet."

Durk is shaking from his ankles to his head, his back pressed against my kitchen wall.

I'm leaning into him, talking. "Now that she's dead we have to think about ourselves, right? It's okay. May would understand. She always thought of me before herself, always." My silky coolness is flaring into desperation. This isn't the way to convince him. The strongest hold I have on Durk—the only thing close to strong enough—is Ashley. I revert to it.

He's slid down the wall and is sitting on the floor again, turned away from where May lies. His face is shiny with sweat. I sit on the floor, holding Durk's cold, slick face between my hands, his jaws cradled in my palms. My own face is as close to Ashley's as I can make it.

I hold Ashley's look, pausing, remembering one of the nights we made an emergency trip to Tina's after Martin stormed off. He was cooling down in a posh hotel lounge somewhere, after breaking plates and screaming at Tina in spittle like an overwrought Shakespearean actor.

"This is not how we fight," Ashley said as she swept shards of bone china across the marble-tiled kitchen floor. "Durk and me, we fight close and quiet. He winds his arms around me, I thread my fingers into his hair, and we whisper vicious things into each other's necks. If anyone found us fighting, they'd think they'd caught us making out."

In my kitchen, over Durk's upturned face, I brace myself and come closer to him. "Last night," I say in Ashley's voice, "you were wasted and you tried to hide it. We hate that."

He chokes, like he's about to cry.

"But it's okay," I say. "Everything is going to be okay. You're not bad. You're going to help Suzanne. And we're going to forgive you. We won't be mad anymore. We'll understand everything."

He's looking at me, our noses almost touching, so close our images are blurred in each other's eyes. There's a kaleidoscope of feelings tumbling through his face—surprise, relief, terror, joy, horror, disbelief—they're all there, whirling and changing, turning inside out, over and over again. "We?"

"We."

He's looking at me, not blinking as a glaze forms over his corneas. "Ashley."

"Ash-ley." I sound like a stage hypnotist. I know it and I don't care. It's working. Durk's mind is wide open. His mysticism, his transcendence, his hangover, his desperate unworthy love of Ashley—I've marshalled all of it against him. For the moment, Durk may not be sure which sister I am.

I tip my face into his neck and whisper his name.

Durk's hand is moving toward my head, into the

depths of my hair. "Ashley."

"Yes. We know," I say. "We know you got sick and you couldn't make it home safely so you stayed at Suzanne's all night. We understand."

Durk exhales against my skin. He closes his eyes and his hand sinks deeper into my hair. Rough, brick-abraded fingertips move across my scalp.

"We'll help you," I say into his ear. "But you need to help us first, Durk. You need to help us move May out of here. We need to make this go away."

He's bending his neck to look at my face—at Ashley's face.

I take his head in my hands again and draw it into the side of my neck, his chin on my collar bone, as I wrap my arms around his shoulders. "Yes. We'll forgive you." I turn and kiss his forehead. "All of us."

I call Ashley's cell phone, lying, telling her Durk has a fever. "He got sick and dozed off watching the game with Troy last night so we let him sleep. You hung up without giving me a chance to finish explaining."

Ashley scoffs. "I didn't give you a chance? You were the one who put me on hold."

"Yeah, sorry. Heather was calling about the Martin thing."

Ashley hums.

"Anyway," I say, "Durk is here, and he's safe, and his temperature is starting to come down."

She hums again, more like a grating sound. But she

says, "Don't give him any aspirin. He can't take it. His stomach lining freaks out."

In truth, Durk is in my garage pulling a yellow foam camping mattress out of the rafters. When I hang up the phone, he's standing in the doorway that connects the garage to the rest of the house. "Good. You found it," I say.

He pushes the mattress through the jambs. As long as there's a chance he might see May again, he won't come into the house.

I accept his unspoken terms and the mattress. It smells like sawdust and wood smoke from last season's campfires. It's just the thing for our purposes.

The sheet of camping foam is unrolled and spread on the floor at the bottom of the stairs like a crash mat.

"Okay. Just like at the hospital," I say to myself, breathing deeply, gathering strength. Those harrowing acts of noble professional compassion, each and every shift, all over the hospital—this isn't very different from any of those, right?

I step over May's body, tip-toeing onto the treads of the stairs through the gaps between her limbs and the banisters. Through her clothes she feels cold as I lay my hands on her and start to rock and slide her down the rest of the stairs, toward the mattress-shroud. Touching her now that she's dead is strange but not exactly unpleasant—until her head moves on its broken stalk as her weight bears down on it.

"Aw, May."

With some rather gruesome rolling and shoving and

with gravity pulling along with me, I get my mother-in-law's corpse off my shiny hardwood stairs and onto the mattress. Her body hasn't stiffened yet. There's time for me to arrange her arms and legs so she won't be any more unwieldy for us to move than six feet of well-fed human tissue has to be. I roll the foam around her and bind it with the elastic tie-down cords Troy uses to strap camping gear to the top of the van. When I've finished, the ends of the yellow foam bundle make it look like a dirty, nasty, oversized cinnamon roll.

I call into the garage. "We're ready."

Durk is slow to come into the house. He's a little quicker when he sees the bulging, fake cinnamon roll lying in May's place. I move to one end of it and he stands at the other.

"It's going to be heavy," I warn. "She's built like a female Troy."

"Which end do I have here?" Durk asks.

"Uh, the top."

"You mean her head?

"Yes."

"Trade me."

"Durk, it doesn't matter."

"Then trade me."

"Fine."

When we lift her, she's even heavier than I expect. I walk backwards, moving through the door, to the garage, and into the minivan. The rear seats have been removed, and there's a flat, open space for her. Durk has already packed a gas can, a shovel, a barbecue lighter, and a sturdy, plastic picnic cooler.

"What's that for?" I ask.

"The cooler? It's to carry back whatever's—left." In the years we've been family to each other, I haven't seen much of this practical Durk. He's useful but I might have liked him better when he was hypnotized, or whatever it was I did to get him to agree to this. "Don't forget to bring her suitcase," he adds.

I was going to forget May's suitcase. I take it and her purse and set them in the van. Everything is packed and braced so she won't roll around as we drive. We close the rear door of the van and stand at the bumper.

"So where to?" Durk asks.

I know exactly where. "To the sun."


I've backed my minivan into the deserted mid-morning suburban street and started out of the cul-de-sac. "Now," I say to Durk, "we drive like we're going on a normal camping trip."

He shakes his head. "This early in the spring, on a Wednesday morning."

"Right. So look up an address for a quiet campsite." I say, handing him my phone. "Like, really, really quiet."

He pushes my phone away. He says, "Make a left at the lights."

I follow Durk's directions and we move along the freeway until he tells me to exit left again. The new road gets narrower until it turns steeply west. We travel along a township road I've never seen before. Soon its pavement turns to hard-packed, oiled clay strewn with loose brown gravel. In the rear-view mirror, the Edmonton skyline is hazy and faint, like a set painting in a play.

"Right there," Durk says, pointing across the windshield to the south.

We leave the road, steering into the mouth of a rutted track overgrown with quack grass from below and with new, green aspen branches from above. The opening between the foliage is spanned by a rusty metal gate clamped shut over the road. I brake to a stop.

"It's a bluff. It's never locked."

That's what Durk says as he bails out of the van and ducks to run along the road, beneath the trees. For a moment, I'm afraid he's abandoned me, until he stops and lifts one end of the gate out of its clasp. In a wide arc, he walks it open while I follow in the van. The branches bend and scrape against the roof and windows. It's too late to worry if they'll leave marks on the paint for Troy to see.

Troy—he'll be okay. His mother is not really dead until someone openly acknowledges it. I'm not concealing. I'm just postponing. I'm like the life support equipment in the Intensive Care Unit, managing appearances and formalities, technicalities, while the family of the body arranges to end everything on their own terms.

The trees clawing at my van are just a rim of vegetation growing around a vast open space where the soil has been scraped away, down to the rock beneath. The rough road leads out of the trees and becomes a rougher trail, dipping into the lowest point in the landscape. The trail is meant for motor bikes and all-terrain vehicles, not minivans. But I'm all trust and desperation and I follow Durk. He's descending a slope into a ragged, grey-brown bowl. In its centre is a scorched black smudge, like the crash site of a space ship.

I park and step onto the hard ground, scanning the low cliffs cut into the earth around us. "What is this?"

"You are in the gravel pit." Durk answers, as if I'll say, "Oh yes—*the* gravel pit. At last."

The scorched spot is the remains of hundreds of bonfires. In the soot, there are crushed beer cans and the shards of broken liquor bottles that will never burn away. This place isn't a working excavation, not anymore. It's an illicit party hideout. Durk shouldn't know it, but he does. There's too much sunlight for a party right now. There's just us.

Durk strides to a pile of old wooden shipping pallets dumped here, jumbled to one side of the fire site. It seems party people are not without foresight, not in ultrapractical Alberta, anyways. The wood is light and dry. He grabs two pallets, one in each hand, and tosses them into the dusty black centre. He stomps the thin boards with the sole of his foot and they splinter and snap.

I douse the pile of broken wood, trying hard but not successfully to keep from splashing gasoline on my clothes. When I'm done, Durk touches the fuel with the barbecue lighter and leaps out of the way. There's a roar as everything ignites, hot and yellow. I toss May's vinyl suitcase and her purse into it. In the heat, they're instantly melting and toxic. Her passport, cell phone, health care card, the dollars and pesos in her wallet—they're gone for good.

This is no Boy Scout fire. It's more like fire I've only seen on television, on the news, burning in the streets of some faraway place where people are trying to kill their neighbours.

"Let's get it," Durk says.

But I can't move. "Are you sure the fire's hot enough? She's my mother-in-law. I—I don't want her to smell like a cook-out."

Durk's shoulders fall. "Hot enough? Suzanne, how should I know? The fire's as hot as we know how to make it."

I move. I open the rear hatch of the minivan and tug at the cinnamon roll. A piece of musty yellow foam tears in my hand, and I flick it away. Durk is beside me now, and together we drag May's bundle onto the ground.

"Juice it up," he says.

I pour gas over the thirsty foam until the mattress is soaked. "Take your end," I tell him.

The foam is a fuel-filled sponge. When I lift it my grip wrings gasoline out of it, onto my clothes and skin, beneath my fingernails. We move closer to the pyre anyway. I count to three, and we heave May onto the stack of burning pallets. The fire roars again as it swallows the mattress whole. We are falling back and away from the flash of heat and the light. I stumble, landing hard on my tailbone on the floor of the gravel pit. Durk is sprawled on the ground next to me, on his back, pushing himself to sitting with the palms of his hands.

In the fire, the foam shroud melts away as if it was never there. May's outline is exposed. Durk throws another pallet on the flaming heap. It helps her to burn, and it nearly hides her from view. But it's not good enough. Her head—the bobbed, white hair already seared away— I can see the shape of her head.

"No," I say. I'm reaching for the gas can. More fuel will make it all burn faster and hotter—get it closer to the point where everything will vanish. The red plastic handle is in my grip but I'm held back, kept away from the fire.

"Stay back," Durk is yelling into my ear as he pulls me to sit beside him in the dirt.

I yelp and punch at him as my tailbone hits the ground again.

"You can't go near it," he calls over my voice. He sits beside me, holding me in place, his hands closed on each of my arms. "Your shirt is soaked in gas. Feel it. Smell it, Suzanne. You'll set yourself on fire if you get any closer, tossing gas around."

My head sags toward my chest as I wail, "It's May. I can see her. God—May."

"Close your eyes," Durk says. "We can both close our eyes."

His hand palms the back of my skull, and he's turning my head, pushing my face into his shoulder. "There's nothing else you can do, and we can't take it back. Just—don't look."

We sit there for—I don't know how long. We sit on the rocky ground while my mother-in-law's body burns and burns. With my eyes closed, I don't see her. I hear crackling, like the burning of wood that's too wet for a campfire.

Durk's head droops and he rests his cheek against my hair. He says, "I still don't get it."

I open my eyes, looking no further than the grey dome of Durk's shoulder in his T-shirt, still pressed to my face. I'm tired and dizzy with gasoline. I answer slowly. "If no one knows what happened to her, then she's not fully dead—not really, not completely. Other people's minds are what finish us off. Right? We saved her—for Troy, and for my kids, and for my sisters. To them, May is alive somewhere. And I'm still a daughter-in-law. I still know exactly who I am. We saved all of that for a little bit longer."

"What the eye doesn't see, the heart doesn't grieve." Durk says it in a low monotone, distantly, as if these are not his words.

"What is that? Where'd you hear that?" I ask.

Durk's grip slackens enough for me to turn away from him. I tug against his hold and his arms fall away. He says, "It comes from a fake fiend quoting a fake saint, I'm pretty sure."

I've never heard Durk use the word "fiend" before.

He sits back, arms straight, palms against the ground.

"Troy and the girls haven't seen anything. But you've seen May dead. How are you going to stop seeing it, Suzanne? How am I going to stop seeing it?"

We tend the fire, building it up over and over again with junked wooden pallets. The sun is low when we let the flames sink into slow, woody smoke. The bonfire is now a bed of red embers, grey dust, and sooty sticks.

It's time to gather May's remains. I move to stand. Maybe it's the effects of the gasoline fumes, or maybe it's the weight of grief and guilt that presses me into the dirt when I try to rise. I fight against it, lurching to my feet. If I keep this confused, heartsick daughter-in-law persona, we will never conclude what we've started here. A perfect daughter-in-law is not equipped for this. It violates her. I need to dismiss Daughter-in-Law Suzanne, just for a little while, and be someone else.

Nurse Suzanne—that's who I need. I need my professional nurse's detachment, compassionate and capable but so far away. I close my eyes and remember that man they brought in—the one with third degree burns over eighty-five percent of his body. He was a twenty-year-old cook lighting the broiler at a steakhouse, right before lunch. The unburnt fifteen percent of him was his head. His face was unmarred—a tiny gold hoop in his earlobe, freshly trimmed goatee, a trace of lingering acne, his hair shorn close enough to bare his scalp between his follicles. He slept, eerily serene in a therapeutic coma, his consciousness stashed somewhere to stop his eyes from seeing what had happened to the rest of him. Another nurse came out of his room, shaken, too sad to inject his medication. So I did it. Nurse Suzanne saw to the living charcoal and did it.

"Intravenous cannulation—0.09% sodium chloride in water—NaCl—normal saline." In the gravel pit, away from Nurse Suzanne's hospital, I recite her reassurances, remembering familiar letters and numbers and signs printed on bags of IV fluids, comforting technical checks, clinical mutterings. I'm summoning Nurse Suzanne like I'm a medium at a séance. I don't always like her. But I need her, like my own Mephistopheles. I mouth the words until I sense her presence.

"Hand me the shovel," Nurse Suzanne tells Durk.

We scrape heaps of sandy dirt onto the embers of May's pyre, smothering the last of the dull red firelight into nothing. When the burning is over, we sift through the sand and ash. The long, inelegant shaft of the shovel is not a good conductor for the gentleness we intend, and sooty sticks and stones break against the metal tip of the blade—fragments of desiccated, desecrated bone.

The pieces lie in a small cairn. With the end of his shoe, Durk is rolling something toward the bone-pile. He stops to retch and swear when the object splits.

"There goes the skull," he announces.

"What? You've got it? It's broken?"

"Yeah, it looked fine but when I touched it the whole thing fell to pieces right along those little cracks you see in X-rays."

"They're called sutures," Nurse Suzanne says, ever informative. "They're open when we're babies and they fill in and firm up as we get older."

The skull looks like shards of shattered cereal bowls on those Saturday mornings when my kids get their own breakfasts. My kids—Mother Suzanne breaks through for an instant, moaning out a little sorrow.

There are more than bones and ashes on the ground. Durk has collected the buckle and the wheels from May's suitcase and the long toothy snake of its zipper. As planned, her ID and cell phone didn't survive the fire. The metal notions from her purse and suitcase could have come from anyone's incinerated garbage. They aren't out of place in this party-hideout-dump-site. We will cover them in sand and leave them here.

The remains of my mother-in-law's body are chips and twigs, small and dry, as if May is not only dead and burnt but shrunken.

I let out a long breath. "I was thinking there'd be less of her left behind. I thought it'd be—you know—powdery."

Durk shakes his head. "Nope. I've heard Heather say they have to take the bones out of real crematorium ovens and use special machines to grind them up. Didn't she ever tell you that, back when she was new at work and couldn't shut up about it?"

I groan into the shovel's handle. "So when funeral homes hand out urns full of ashes it's not exactly ashes? It's more like—"

"Bone meal. And this is the end of it, Suzanne," he calls over his shoulder. "I'll bring you the cooler to stow them in but don't think I'm going to help you grind up the bones."

I prod the heap with the shovel's tip. "What am I going to do with all of this?"

Durk shrugs. "I don't know, but I'm done here. I need to go back to work. I need to go back to Ashley."

"Work," I say. Durk's work with brick and cement—it's the next step. The idea comes as a revelation from Nurse Suzanne, cold but true and inevitable. "Yes, Durk. You can come work for me."

"Suzanne—"

"No, it's real work. It's a contract. It's the last piece in this and it's ideal for both of us—for all of us."

"I am done."

"No, listen. You can start building that outdoor brick barbecue Troy's been talking about ever since you guys bought the fireplace store."

Durk stares. "You want to make this up to me with a fancy barbecue contract?"

"Just listen," I'm hurrying. "It'll be Fathers' Day in a few weeks, and I can tell Troy the barbecue is his present. I'll pay full price for the materials and the work and everything. And while we're building it, we can brick these bones inside, forever."

Durk takes the shovel from me and leans against it himself, resting his forehead on the end of the handle, rolling his head back and forth. It's vague but it's his answer. And it isn't "No."

# Ashley                    [11]

I should probably be embarrassed to be out shopping covered in dirt and concrete dust. But I'm just as short on vanity as I am short on free time. There's no chance of sneaking home for a quick shower in the middle of the day. I'm walking through a store after repairing a little old headstone by myself, without Durk, which is actually pretty cool. Something about hoisting granite all alone in a graveyard makes me mad with power, like I'm queen of the Underworld.

I am nothing like embarrassed as I call Meaghan's name through the busy drugstore. This is one of those huge, big-box pharmacies that are more like department stores. I walk through it for miles before I can see Meaghan standing next to the real pharmacist on a high platform.

Meaghan knows without looking that the voice calling her name belongs to one of her sisters, though she's not sure which one. She won't be expecting to see me here in the middle of a work day. After this morning's cemetery job I've shut down the shop for the afternoon. I figured I might as well. Nothing more was going to get done today. I sent Durk home in one of his funks again. He's been useless this week, ever since the last time he crashed for the night at Suzanne and Troy's place. He says he's still sick but—the flu my butt.

I've been leaving dusty fingerprints on everything I touch, all over the store. I'm carrying a plastic shopping basket full of paper hats, flaccid balloons, and tubs of barely edible, over-dyed candy. It's one of my girls' birthdays this weekend. I'm going to use Meaghan's employee discount to buy the party supplies. The discount is nice but Meaghan still isn't the best source in the family for this kind of thing. Everyone knows the prime place to find excess party stuff is in the back of Tina's luxury SUV—in the space beneath her hatchback window where she chucks unused pearlized balloons, metallic doilies, pastel mints tied up in tulle, and individually boxed truffles left over from the fancy charity parties she throws in the name of Martin's company.

The fact is I feel funny taking things from Tina right now, in the thick of her betrayal. It's probably dumb. She loves showering us with gifts. But even if she doesn't know anything about what Martin is up to she needs me to be giving, not taking from her right now. It wouldn't be right to raid her stash even though all I want are things she doesn't need, clutter—balloons that are going to dry out and crack, chocolate doomed to melt in the greenhouse of her vehicle.

And really, birthday party shopping is just an excuse to meet Meaghan. I have a sisters' errand that feels like it demands a team effort. Getting Meaghan to help me salvage Tina—that's the real reason I've come here today.

Meaghan is sweetness and smiles when I ask her to do me the discount party-junk favour. I get it. It's nice to have something to offer an older sister even if it is just fifteen percent off all merchandise at Quali-Drugs, excluding lottery and tobacco purchases.

In a few minutes, her shift is over and we walk through the store together, all the way to the front where the main cash registers bar the exits. Meaghan stands beside me, brushing dust from my jacket as I unpack birthday stuff and air freshener refills from my basket. In a minute, she'll show her employee card to the cashier who thinks the pharmacy staff prancing around in fake lab coats along the back wall are way too full of themselves.

Meaghan pokes at my pile of stuff. "Party time?"

"Always," I say. For large families living close together, almost every gathering doubles as someone's birthday party. There aren't enough weekends in the year to live any other way.

"And," I add, "it's also time for this." At the bottom of the basket is a photofinishing envelope. The pictures inside it are the ones Suzanne took of that idiot Martin kissing his girlfriend in public.

Meaghan knows what's in the envelope. She raises her eyebrows. "You printed the pictures?"

"Yeah. I had to do something. No one else is doing anything for Tina. But it's time to end this."

"This? End this—'this' as in Tina's marriage?"

I tug my bank card out of the machine. "Well, I can't stand it anymore. We can't keep this a secret from Tina. If it really is just a misunderstanding, then Martin needs to straighten it out—like, now."

We've finished in the store and we're sitting in the front seat of the Dash Fireplace and Monument truck, in the parking lot.

"Okay," Meaghan begins, arranging her seatbelt into her cleavage, "so we take the pictures and go to Tina's house—"

"No! We find a public computer, set up a fake throw-away email address, and send the picture from there so she can't track the IP address back to any of us."

Meaghan laughs. "Oo, so techie."

"What? Tina has her company's whole IT department at her disposal. We have to be careful or they'll know right away who sent the pictures."

"Or maybe," Meaghan interrupts, "we can handle this old-school. Look." She waves the envelope in my face. "You've already got them printed, Ashley. And it's Thursday, the day Tina goes into the office to run her community outreach committee meeting or whatever Martin's calling her charity party planning these days. Let's just drive over to their parking lot and slip this enve-lope under her windshield wiper, if you're sure you want to break it to her anonymously."

My plan is cooler but Meaghan's plan is easier—more like something that could actually happen. I'm not too proud to submit to it.

In minutes, we're deep downtown, parked on the street, walking through the asphalt lot of the building where Martin's company fills the top three floors. Tina's vehicle is barely contained in a narrow parking spot near the backdoor. Why does BMW bother to make an SUV anyways? Don't they know it'll end up packed with fancy car seats, driven by nannies most of the time, taken to drive-thru restaurants until the new car smell gives way to the reek of the old French fries?

Meaghan and I are standing on the pavement beside Tina's fancy, dirty driving machine. I've just pried its windshield wiper away from the glass when Meaghan's hand covers mine.

"Ashley, wait. This is serious now. Let's just go. Let's take the envelope and go home for today. Let's talk to the rest of the girls before we do anything rash."

We've each got a hand on the envelope, leaning together over the hood of Tina's vehicle like a pair of squeegee kids. "What? Why?" I say. "We can't wuss out on this now. It's not like this doesn't hurt Tina just because she hasn't seen it for herself."

"Maybe, I don't know, but I—I'm just not sure this is the best way—"

And that's when we hear it: a man announcing, "Look, Peaches! It's your sisters!"

That voice—as usual, it sparks an invisible wincing reflex, not on my face but deep in my guts.

"Girls! What're you doing here?"

It's Tina and Martin.

I let the windshield wiper snap against the glass, with-drawing with the envelope still in my hand. Meaghan and I are both flushed and breathless when we turn to meet Tina with expressions she'll recognize as copies of her own smile when it's totally phony.

She's wearing her phony smile too. Martin has taken her arm to escort her back to her vehicle at the end of her meeting. They are playing perfect business-couple for the office. At least, that's what they think they're doing. They're actually more like perfect-business-couple's monster, basted together with scavenged, lifeless, mismatched pieces of what they imagine such a creature should look like.

Martin doesn't have any idea how to behave in a marriage or in a family, so he's beaming at Meaghan and me like he always does, like we're valued clients, VIPs, like he's hard at work, punched into some sort of in-law time clock.

"Hey, you guys," Meaghan greets them. "We were just passing by, on our way to my place, and now we're— leaving."

Tina blows at the dust in my hair. "Yeah, good. Ashley needs a bath. Look at you."

I force a laugh.

"Hey, what's that?" Tina notices the envelope. "Did I get another parking ticket? They keep ticketing me here as if I don't own the damn lot."

I'm wussing out myself, folding the envelope in half so it can vanish into my jacket pocket. I never meant for Tina to find the pictures while she had Martin on her arm. "Oh, no ticket here. It's just—"

"Pictures," Meaghan says. "We were going to leave you with some pictures from—from the last birthday party. But it looks like it might rain and ruin them. There's no rush anyways. We can all look at them together, some other time."

"Hey, don't fold them. You're wrecking them," Tina says, snatching the envelope from where it juts out of my pocket. "Sheesh, Ashley."

"Just—wait, Tina—"

For Tina, if there can be a "now" then there is no such thing as "later." She's opening the envelope right away, right here. Tina is bringing the pictures into the daylight to see if I've creased and damaged them. She's finding out they've got nothing to do with a family birthday party.

I clamp one hand around Meaghan's arm. In front of us, Tina is turning a stupefied face up at Martin.

"We'll let you guys talk," I say.

I'm dragging Meaghan away. She's hissing at me as we strain against each other, stumbling in a jagged line across the parking lot. "We can't just leave them there like that," she says. "What if it gets crazy?"

Behind us, Tina is waving her arms. Her voice is getting loud. The truth is even when times are good, everything involving Tina is a bit crazy—not brooding crazy but blaring crazy. That's why she's so much fun. That's why she's everyone's pet sister. But when she married Martin, Tina broke one of the cardinal rules of crazy—the rule I follow every day, the one that lets Durk and me live in harmony. In a keeper-marriage, only one person can be actively crazy at a time. There isn't room in a marriage for more than one mad or bad spouse. Martin and Tina don't seem to know anything about rules like this. Or maybe they just don't care. Whatever it is, they are two full-time insane people locked together in one marriage. Sometimes, it's terrifying. Right now, it's terrifying.

Meaghan wrestles her arm out of my grip. "We can't go. There's nothing for them to smash on the ground so they might take it out on each other this time. We have to keep an eye on them at least. We don't know what might happen."

Martin's voice is loud enough to hear from a distance too. Perfect business-couple hours are over. This is not what I wanted—to take Tina by surprise and set her off, exploding with shock and confusion right in Martin's face.

Meaghan's complexion is mirroring my own again, changing from florid pink to sickening white. Maybe we're both remembering that time Tina had too much red wine and told us, "You know what, girls? I have never successfully denied Martin sex."

Meaghan and I were young and dumb and had never thought through what a statement like Tina's could mean somewhere as supposedly safe and staid as married life. At first we didn't get it, not until Suzanne choked on her drink and Heather slammed the heavy bottom of her tumbler against the tabletop.

Heather spoke in that low, bossy voice she uses when she's angry and scared at the same time. "What do you mean, 'successfully?'"

At the edge of the parking lot where Tina is arguing with the serial rapist she's been sleeping with for thirteen years, I blink deeply. Meaghan is right. We can't leave. But simply staying here might not be enough either. I am covered in cement dust. I am as strong and tough as any mason. But Martin is not a brick wall. He's something worse. He is a violent husband.

"I should get Durk," I say, even though I hate it. "He's at home with the girls, and he might not be up for driving but—"

Meaghan shoves me toward my truck, clapping me so hard a grey dust cloud rises from my jacket. "I'll keep watch," she says. "You go get Durk. Hurry."

# Meaghan [12]

If there's one thing we're all terrible at, it's waiting. Tina says it means I'll be just as miserable at pregnancy as the rest of my sisters. I don't need anyone to tell me that.

Anxiety pricks at the backs of my calves as I watch Tina and Martin cursing each other in their parking lot. I'm peeking around the corner of a building, watching my sister scream at her bad husband, the man with a secret history of domestic sexual violence against her. He won't attack her like that here in the street, in broad daylight, away from the treacherous privacy of their bedroom but—I don't know what he'll do, what she'll do. By now, I know enough people with enough intimacy to understand there's no way to predict for sure how anyone is going to behave.

Ashley will bring Durk as quickly as she can, lurching through traffic in her pickup truck, merging onto bridges, braking through school zones. At this time of day, it could take her an hour to get back here.

Down the avenue, Riker is probably sitting in his store, hunched over a comic book, useless, when he might be able to help us. Honestly, I think I'd have a better chance fighting Martin off Tina than Riker would if things got physical. People from large sibling groups are skilled grapplers. No one ever got a picture of the Dionne quints cleanin' one anothers' clocks, but I bet they were experts at it.

Riker can't fight Martin, but he could probably settle him down without touching him. Everyone knows men act out hypocritical chivalry for each other—fakers, pathetic. The sight of Riker's bearded face might be enough to convince Martin to get into his own car, drive away, and try talking to Tina later, when she's no longer a live bomb but a field of burnt out shrapnel. I don't know. But being here alone when Riker is so close by seems stupid.

I bolt down the sidewalk.

The door bangs past the stopper and into the wall. I tumble into Riker's store, grabbing him by the placket of his shirt.

"We need you," I say.

"Meaghan?"

"Come on. Tina might be in trouble."

"Who's Tina?"

I speak to him in language he'll understand, in the esoteric passwords he's taught me. "Cécile," I say, giving him the name of the middle-born Dionne quintuplet. "My sister."

He pulls the key from around his neck, locks the door, and chases me up the avenue.

# Tina [13]

The way my sisters go on, no one would believe I can speak for myself, even when it comes to Martin. They're all touchy and skittish with me, like I'm a badly made bomb smack in the middle of our birth order. Sure, maybe I picked a gold-plated loser of a husband, but I can still stand in the street and scream him down without anyone's help or protection.

Things do look bad when it first starts—when Ashley shows up with those kissy-pictures and springs them on us in the parking lot. Honestly, what the hell did she think was going to happen?

Martin is shouting, but it's not scary. I know scary. This isn't it. This is desperate. He's only loud because I'm refusing to listen.

"Tina!"

"No, Martin."

"Tina, this is stupid."

"Stupid?" I lunge to push his shoulders with both my hands. "Who's stupid, Martin?"

He staggers, not because I'm strong, but because he's

wrong.

We're both yelling. He can't hear what I'm saying, and I can't hear him. I keep hollering until there's a crack in my noise wide enough for me to hear him say one of the most potent words I know—two syllables: "Sis-ter."

"Stop!" I say. "Stop it, Martin. Sister? You're trying to blame this on my sisters? So what if they took the pictures?"

That's not what Martin said. He's shaking his head. "No—*she*—her, in the picture—*she* is my sister."

I smack at the top of his head with the photograph, right where his hair is thinnest. "This woman in the picture is your sister?"

It's ridiculous, but Martin is nodding anyway. I know Martin's sister. We all do. Constance is almost fifteen years older than him—over-dyed and blue-veined and marked with the tiny tell-tale scars of last generation's very best plastic surgeries. The woman in Ashley's photo is not her.

Martin gathers both my hands and pins them between his. "Will you listen?"

I'm confused enough to relent—or at least to pause for breath.

And then, before he says anything more, I hear one of my sisters' voices, shouting from not far away. Meaghan is back. She's running, bouncing, her momentum gathering a rampaging force. She arrives, crashing boob-first into the Coach purse I keep crammed with clean spare diapers. She's panting like someone who's in the habit of saying she's going to the gym but who hangs out in a video game store instead.

"Martin, Tina," she puffs. "It looks bad but, just stay calm."

A man I don't know—some skinny, scruffy hipster with the standard-issue wispy brown beard—has come running along with her, openly ogling my marriage, as if he knows us.

Martin lets go of my hands.

I wave the photo at Meaghan. "What the hell is this?"

"Were you guys stalking me?" Martin never knows when to shut it.

Meaghan bows her head and directs the answer to his question to me. "Stalking? Not really," she says. "Suzanne was just in the right place at the right time."

"Suzanne?" Martin says, still talking, for some reason. "How could Suzanne do that to me?"

It is strange. Conventional family wisdom says Suzanne is the least sneaky of all the sisters. Her job is to bring the sweetness not the surveillance. Still, it's a stupid thing for Martin to be saying right now.

I shove him again. "How could *Suzanne* do that to you? How could *you* do that to me, Martin? You're the one standing right out in the open, in the street, making out with a strange woman."

Every part of his face curls and wrinkles. He is genuinely disgusted. "Making out—Tina, will you listen to me? That woman in the picture—she is my sister."

"That is not Constance."

"I know. I never said it was Constance. I'm trying to

141

tell you I have another sister. My dad's mistress—"

I suck in a sharp breath. "His mistress?"

"Yes!" Martin hops toward me, grabbing each of my arms again. "My father had a child with his mistress. And that child was me. Tina, my father's wife took me in and raised me because she wanted to punish them."

"Punish him for having a mistress? I've got some sympathy for that."

"No, no. Having a mistress was pretty much expected of Dad in those days, in their circles. What his wife couldn't stand was him having a child with the mistress. So after I was born, Dad gave my real mother a bunch of money and some love letters and some gentle threats, moved her out to Toronto, and brought me home to be raised in his house, by his wife."

It's too ludicrous. "Why would she want the mistress's baby?"

"For spite, Tina. For nothing but awful, bitchy spite."

My hands grip Martin's arms. We're standing in the parking lot face to face, holding onto each other, like we're caught in the stiffest junior high dance posture ever. "So the lady—that lady who died—all miserable—in the Bentley—dead—"

"She was my step-mother." Martin's face is lit with that rising-sun smile he used to show me all the time. "I didn't know it until a few weeks ago, but that lady was my step-mother—my wicked step-mother, Tina. Won't our girls love that?"

"So the woman—kissing—in the picture—"

"That woman is the daughter my real mother—the one she had with the man she ended up married to after things ended with my dad. She's my other sister—half-sister, sister enough. She's the one who's not Constance."

Beside me, Meaghan is whispering to the bearded guy. I turn my head to see her grab a handful of his sleeve, leading him away. The bomb is not going to blow today. My sister knows it, and she's standing down.

Martin watches them leave. He twitches, remembering our surroundings—the steady march of pedestrians on the sidewalk, the busloads of people in the street, the window-walled towers all around us. He grimaces toward the top floor of his building, where anyone from the company could be standing over us, watching.

"Into the car," he says.

We duck into my Bimmer even though Martin hates being here, where so much spilled milk is hardening into a sour crust in the fibres of the floor mats.

I'm trying to finish Martin's story as he rolls down his window. "So your sister finally Googled you?"

"Right."

"And she came and found you after your real mother died?"

"Died? No, my real mother didn't die," Martin says, grinning again. When we first met, his white teeth made me think of the frosting layer in the middle of a store-bought cookie. It's a little dazzling, even now. "Being my mother doesn't mean she has to be dead, Peaches. No, my real mother is alive. My mom isn't a Socialite Suicide.

She's a retired school teacher living in Guelph."

I slug his arm. "So why did I have to find out this way? Why didn't you tell us sooner?"

He laughs. "Didn't I keep hinting I had a surprise in the works for you?"

Martin is always dropping vague hints about vaguer surprises. They're usually things like new credit cards to replace ones I've maxed-out, or spa gift certificates clients have given him that he'll never use. Sometimes, his surprises are nothing but stupid games he plays to try to keep me calm and happy and dependent upon his graces. Family life—the poor man has no idea how to live it. After the way he was raised, it's not entirely his fault.

"Martin," I say, "you found our kids a new grand-mother."

"And another aunt."

I snort. "Yeah, that's all they need."

"And I found you a mother-in-law," Martin says. "Congratulations, Peaches."

Don't start. Don't say anything. This is my messed-up marriage, and I can do what I want with it. Ashley can keep spraying air freshener over her marriage. Suzanne can keep smiling while she slurps all that fish oil or snake oil for hers. Heather can stand in that barrage of righteous ranting. Meaghan can bore herself to death with that prissy purple stuffed shirt. So everyone better stand aside as I lean across the centre console of my filthy luxury vehicle, here in our parking lot, and kiss my horrible husband on his sunny face as if he's everything I ever wanted.

# Meaghan [14]

We are retreating from the war zone of Tina's marriage, with its strange and dangerous public manoeuvres and its stranger and more dangerous private ones. I've texted Ashley with the all clear, telling her not to bother rousing Durk to hurry back to Tina's parking lot. Now, I'm following Riker to his store.

Tina has been zany for as long as I've known her. Zany is fun. It means Tina was my favourite babysitter— the one who fed me choking-hazard candies, and let me write on my arms, and spray her with the garden hose in the backyard until the sump pump backed up and the basement started to flood.

She went from zany to crazy soon after she took that job as a special event planner at a country club where she met Martin and his high society people. Sometimes, I tell myself, it's still just zany. It might be true on good days, like this one, when what's wrong between Martin and Tina turns out to be a charming misunderstanding, a cute caper, like something from the darker end of the rom-com spectrum.

And I hope Martin's new half-sister is real. Now that I know who she is, the lady in the picture does look a lot like him. But then again, Troy and Suzanne look like brother and sister too. I'm just starting to wonder about what happened to Martin's real mother—the mistress who was sent away to live out the rest of her life without him. Martin's parents would be pretty old if they hadn't died already, so there's no way the mistress could still be alive, right?

I'm saying all of this out loud to Riker as we walk. I'm saying it as my teeth chatter. The crisis is over, the afternoon is turning into evening, and I'm feeling the cold of the downtown shadow. I pull my hoodie closed as the wind blows through it. I jerk my head toward my clones' café where Riker and I usually have coffee.

"I need to warm up," I say.

Riker keeps walking. "The owners won't like me leaving my post during business hours. Trust me. I'll get you a coffee at the store."

"Ew, that instant stuff?"

Coffee quality isn't the point. I don't just need to warm up. I need to sit down and think through Tina's situation—use Riker to do the debriefing I should be doing with Ashley, or any of the girls. By refusing, he's let me down. It won't go unpunished. I poke his arm and say, "Look at you, Riker. You're not one of those gentleman types who has a jacket you could offer to lend me out here."

Riker stops walking—stops right in the middle of the sidewalk. "Are you really that cold, Meaghan, or are you just trying to get me to stand closer to you?"

I stop with a stomp.

"What?" he says. He takes my hand and pulls me to the inner edge of sidewalk, beneath an awning, against the brick wall of a bookstore. He arranges his long, thin arms around my shoulders, pressing my back into his chest as we face the traffic.

These moments—the ones where a guy breaks and shows he feels something for me—they never fail to feel surreal. No matter what's come before to warn and prepare me, I was awkward enough at age thirteen for them to always strike me as shocking. I twist in his hold, but I don't push myself away.

"I'm not trying to make you mad," he says. "I just think it's time we started saying what we actually mean when we talk to each other."

"Riker—"

"It's not easy to say what we mean," he goes on, "I get it. You're engaged to just-fine-Ian and you can't speak freely. You shouldn't speak freely. It'd be wrong. But I'm not engaged to anybody. I'll say what we mean. Let me tell you your story. I'm good at this."

I laugh and sway against him. The inevitable is happening, here in the same street where I share an apartment with Ian. I want to stay limp and quiet and watch this scene like someone seated high above it—on a balcony, maybe—looking down on herself, letting inertia drift her destiny around.

"You aren't into Ian anymore," Riker says. "He's a good guy but he's not for you, not anymore."

I hum.

"And it's not some lame issue you have with commitment or emotional maturity or readiness. It's just that you don't like him enough to stay with him your whole life. You're mismatched. And a mismatch is intolerable for a quintuplet. For you, everything has to fit together in perfect pentagonal harmony."

The Dionne quintuplets again—my body isn't limp anymore. I stiffen and pull Riker's arms apart, like a gate opening in front of me. "No." I'm shaking my head, my ponytail wagging. "No. I am single-born. And I'm mismatched everywhere, with my sisters, with everybody. I'm not sure I'll ever be able to get inside anything."

Riker waves one hand. "Okay, so I exaggerate about the quintuplet thing. Obviously. Fine. But look at you and your sisters. You start visiting my store and within a few weeks all these other women I would have never otherwise met are suddenly barging through my life. Tina, Heather, Susan—"

"Suzanne."

"Right."

"What about Ashley? You've never met Ashley."

Riker looks out at the street. "I just missed her though. And she'll be back here sooner or later. Believe me. She belongs where you are. They all do."

I scoff. "Add it up, Riker. Heather was born twelve years before me. There's a four year gap between me and Ashley."

"So?"

"So? I'm not exactly in a sister group. I'm dangling far enough off the end of the family that I might as well be an only child—an only child raised with four superfluous, terrible teenaged mothers, but with no sisters at all."

"The demographic details don't matter."

"They do." I step further away from him. "Every time I start a relationship with a man, what I'm really looking for is someone to make me into one of my sisters—marriage, babies, lawn mowers. It's trite enough for me to have figured it about myself. I go through my days trying on my sisters—their voices and personalities—like I'm some kind of psychiatric case. I'll storm in as pushy Heather. Or if you're lucky, I'm Ashley. Look out, I might lose my mind and become Tina. And sometimes I'll even be sweet, stodgy, sorry Suzanne. But it never works."

Riker runs his hands through his hair. "Meaghan, how close do you think people can get to each other? How 'one' do you think real living humans can become? Maybe you should enjoy what you have. It's a lot more family than most people get these days so—"

"I should go home—"

"Because going home to Ian will make you into your sisters?"

My shoulders fall. "Okay, this is how lunatic I am. This is proof of how desperate I am to achieve sister-Nirvana. When I met you, the very first thing I liked was how your nose is perfectly formed." I tap the tip of his nose. "And second, I liked the fact that—that your mother is dead."

Riker swallows so hard I can see it. "What? Why?"

"I'm sorry," I hurry. "It's weird. It's sick. I'm shallow and morbid. But none of my sisters has a mother-in-law. Well, except for Suzanne, but she's the exception that proves the rule, right?"

Riker is pacing down the sidewalk as if he's barely able to keep from running away from me. "My mother?" he says. "That's why you always wanted to hear gruesome details about what happened to my mother? You liked her dead?"

"I'm sorry. Don't be mad," I say. I'm snatching at his hand as he reaches for the key to unlock the shop door. "I told you, Riker. I'm messed up. I'm obsessed. I'm sorry."

He won't let me catch hold of him. He's tugging on the door handle, fumbling with the key.

Then it opens, smoothly, from the inside. Someone is standing in the doorway of the video game shop—someone with a perfectly formed nose. She's talking to Riker.

"Don't know that I like the new sales concept," the lady says, "locking up the store at rush hour, when foot traffic is heaviest."

Riker doesn't answer. He looks like he might be sick.

The woman sighs the way my dad sighed when I dropped out of university after one semester. "Go on, home, Riker. I'll cash out for you tonight," she tells him. "And I need you to run a prescription home for your father right away. His feet are acting up again, and he needs more of that antifungal ointment."

It's like I've been struck stupid. I'm standing on the

sidewalk, stunned, oscillating my gaze like my head is an electric fan moving between Riker and the lady who must be the owner of the video game store. The lady doesn't look like she's particularly old or particularly dead. And she doesn't look cremated at all.

# Heather [15]

At this stage in our process, the dead old lady on the stainless steel table looks like she's made out of phyllo pastry.

Today, it's busy and crowded in the downstairs work area so I've brought her to one of our velour and brocade upper rooms to do the final touches—the dressing and powdering and painting.

There will be one more interruption.

"Hey, your sister is here." It's the new guy, the fresh young mortuary apprentice, sticking his head into the private visitation room where I'm working.

"Great. Send her in."

He pauses. "You sure?"

"Yeah, no need to worry." I wave at the body draped with a clean white modesty sheet. "My sister is a professional."

Yes, I know right away my visitor must be Suzanne. Of the four of them, there's only one who would appear spontaneously at my workplace. It won't be Meaghan. She deplores my work—thinks it's sick and tragic, thinks it betrays me as sick and tragic. Tina is bold with births, and she did go sit in that death-car at the auto show back when she thought the woman who died in it was her mother-in-law. And I'll hand it to Ashley: not everyone can cheerfully eat lunch sitting on top of a stranger's grave waiting for quickset concrete to dry. But in a place like this, there's no earth or stone, no auto show velvet ropes or long passages of time to hide the deathliness of my work. It's here on the table.

Suzanne knows it, and she's making her way toward me anyway, silent feet in the carpeted funeral home corridor. She's outside the door, moving through the cool disinfectant-rich air. It's a lot like hospital air, actually. Only it's scented with more flowers and fewer tuna sandwiches.

"Heather?"

"Yes, come in, please," I say in my funeral voice. It's like my normal voice only spun into a single glassy thread—light and clear and strong. Its language is slightly modified too. It uses long Latin derived words when shorter, simpler ones would suffice. And it never speaks in contractions or slang, though it will slip into old fashioned idioms about brass tacks and bygones.

The door cracks open until I see Suzanne's face and she sees mine. "They said you're dressing a body."

"They are correct," I answer. "Come inside, please."

I am not trying to bully her into something terribly new and shocking. Suzanne has seen plenty of dead people. She has seen people in states that might be worse than death, for all anyone knows—wasted bodies grinding away in Intensive Care Units. After all of that, there is nothing here that should frighten Suzanne. Still, she is caught in the doorway, using the oak slab to shield her view of the body.

"Suzanne, come in," I say again. "Everything is fine. The wet-work is completed. We are just getting ready for the close-up now."

When she comes inside, Suzanne moves with panicky quickness, as if she is trying to keep a bad cat from escaping the room. She is wearing a hoodie as an overcoat and formless pastel-coloured pants with pockets sewn all over them. It means, of course, that she is going to work, about to start an evening shift at the hospital.

Suzanne clears her throat. "So who's this?"

"Someone's beloved grandmother," I say. "We acquired the remains yesterday from the Emerald Vale Retirement Community."

Suzanne nods. "Poor thing."

I cluck my tongue. "She died most auspiciously, in a nursing home dining room over cube-cut Salisbury steak."

"Uh-oh. Did she aspirate it?"

"Maybe a bit, once the heart attack was underway."

Suzanne has come to stand beside the stainless steel bier, on the opposite side from where I'm working. During other visits, she has seen me do this kind of light-duty grooming of bodies before. She has watched with elegant nurse's detachment, asking questions about the failed medical interventions comprising the first act of each final drama, aware I am a set-dresser, a stage hand, and our talk is happening behind a curtain, in the dark. We usually carry on as if we do nothing to affect the script.

Today is not the same. Suzanne's detachment is incomplete. There is tension, a drama of her own—something barely quivering in Suzanne's hands and shoulders, in her voice as she looks at the body and says, "She's beautiful."

I smile. "She is. The heart attacks clean up so nicely, do they not? I am about to slip her into this dress." The old lady's family are practical people. Instead of producing the tiny wedding dress worn when this lady was nineteen, they are content to have her buried in an enormous white mu-mu that zips closed in the front.

Dressing the body will be easier if I ask Suzanne to help—have her lift and tip the bulk away from the tabletop as I slide the fabric beneath it. She knows the mechanics, shifting deadweight at the hospital every day.

"Suze, would you mind—"

I stop, letting the body settle onto the flat of its back. There is a rustle of white fabric and a pause as I try to get my sister to look at me.

"Suzanne, what're you doing here?" My funeral voice is gone.

She startles.

"And what's wrong with you?" I continue. "You seem weird. You seem—bereaved."

Suzanne blinks, her entire head bobbing. She laughs. "Sorry, Heather. Bereaved—no, I'm fine. I just—I came to see how this is done."

This isn't true. I'm not at all modest about how this

is done. I'm like a zealot, an evangelist out to spread the good word about what invisible Western death rites truly entail. Everyone in our family has heard far more about how this is done than they ever wanted to know.

I act my part in Suzanne's drama anyway. "Okay. I guess that's pretty cool of you."

Suzanne shakes her head. "Yeah, I know I've seen you do this before. Sure. But I've never paid enough attention, not the right kind of attention anyways. I've got questions now, better questions. And lately, I have been thinking more about the future."

The future—that's one of our industry words. Suzanne is finding her funeral voice.

On the bier between us, the body's arms are bent at the elbows in soft forty-five degree angles. I've slid the mu-mu up the length of the legs, snugged it beneath the hips, and I'm rolling one of its sleeves into a cuff. "Questions?" I say. "Fine. Ask away."

Suzanne is rounding the end of the bier, standing at the head. "I read that cremation destroys one hundred percent of DNA. Is that always true?"

I slide the cuff over the wrist and ease the sleeve around the bend in the arm. "Yeah, it's true if you use one of our state-of-the-art gas-fired retorts. But those guys in the developing world who still use traditional ways, burning away on riverbanks with soggy wood fires and stuff? They could leave some genetic material intact, like, especially in the marrow of the larger bones—femurs and pelvises."

Suzanne nods toward the face on the table. The head

and neck twist against a plastic brace—nothing like a pillow—as I tug on the arms. Suzanne lays a hand on either side of the head, cradling and supporting it as if it's a patient's. It's not helpful to me, but I do admire her for handling the body without making a fuss. The dead lady's family members would probably balk at touching her body by now.

Suzanne tilts her own head. "You've done something to the eyes and mouth, haven't you? They always loll right open at the hospital."

"Yes, we took care of it," is all I say.

Suzanne presses one finger to the forehead. "They're always colder here than at the hospital too."

I nod, walking around the bier to dress the opposite arm. "Thank you, refrigerated crypt."

Suzanne taps the forehead, gently. "It feels like my own skin when I come inside from shovelling snow."

"Suz-anne," I say in the voice the girls call bossy, though I prefer the term matriarchal. "Tell me what's the matter with you. You're about to burst into tears. I'm happy to see you anytime, but maybe my workplace and my dead people aren't what you need when you're feeling glum."

She steps away from the bier, clearing her throat. I take her arm and lead her to a chair. "Just sit over here," I say. "We're almost finished. Sit right here and say nice things to me. Tell me something rosy and uplifting."

"Like what?"

"I don't know. Like—May. You haven't had much to say about her lately. So tell me: how is May doing on her mission of tooth mercy in El Salvador?"

"Guatemala."

"Guatemala, right. Tell me all about it. What could be more uplifting to talk about than charity like that?"

Suzanne coughs, hoarse and noisy, like she's sucked in a lung-full of dirty smoke. It's loud, and I twitch, jostling the body. Her racket is involuntary, not Suzanne's fault, but I'm shushing her anyway.

Her voice rattles as she finds breath to speak again. "So if someone found a big bone—like, from a body cremated in something not much better than a campfire, like you were saying, then they might be able to isolate enough DNA to tell who it belonged to?"

I furrow my forehead as I pull the mu-mu's long zipper closed under the chin. "Yeah, maybe. As long as who-ever finds it has access to their own forensics lab. Where are you going with this?"

Suzanne tries to laugh at herself. "Nowhere. It's just a morbid question."

I sigh as I wheel the cosmetics tray to the edge of the bier. No one has idle questions about death. These ques-tions are always intensely personal. Suzanne is acting. I am acting. Without a word, we will work together to preserve the illusion of her idle curiosity. I don't under-stand it but I have to respect it—her yearning for illusion, her faith in it.

No matter what the girls say about me, I am willing to play along. I'll mince through their rickety sets full of crude scenery for as long as I can—as long as they'll let me before they knock it all down themselves. The truth is I want my sisters' official messages—their pretty fictions that don't make any sense—to be their real stories. But nothing will stop them from revealing the tumult of their non-fiction to me. I can't stop them from showing me everything, daring me to tell them what it is I see.

"So what's that stuff?" Suzanne asks. She means the powder on the puff I'm using to dab the face and hands.

"It's just talc. Their skin is always terrible. It helps a bit."

"Talc? Like Mum used to get from Avon?"

"Those free gifts with purchase? Yeah, pretty much." I wave my arm through the dusty white cloud the powder puff has sloughed into the air in front of my face. "Look out. It gets everywhere."

Suzanne watches motes of powder drifting onto the plush carpet the new mortuary apprentice will have to vacuum later. "It's like when you're sanding drywall and the dust gets all over everything," she says.

I snicker. "Yeah sure, Suze. Actually, I've been fooling you guys all these years. Every time you thought I had drywall dust in my hair I was actually covered in this funeral home talcum powder."

Suzanne doesn't laugh. Even without funeral powder, her face is white, blown blank by the candour of disgust.

"Kidding, Suzanne. I'm kidding. It's always been drywall dust you've seen in my hair. Seriously. Don't look at me like you caught me embalming myself."

She sits quietly, her revulsion subsiding. She doesn't

speak again until I've moved on to colouring the lips with a brush. "So how come it's okay," Suzanne begins. "How come no one minds when you guys do creepy awful stuff to dead bodies in here?"

I snort even though I'm still dangerously close to the talc. "People do mind. They just mind it less than handling their dead themselves. Or, at least, they think they mind it less. Hardly anyone tries it for themselves so, honestly—"

"So what would you do," she interrupts, "what would you do if someone took a body home from the retirement community and let all the blood out and washed it and dressed it and made it up in their own kitchen instead of sending it here? Like—what would happen?"

"No one ever asks."

"No, of course they wouldn't ask permission," Suzanne says. "They'd never tell you. But Heather, what would happen if they did it anyway and kept it hidden?"

I'm wiping the lipstick brush clean, staring past my sister to the canned landscape painting hung above her head—a mountain reflected in a lake. Her weird hypothetical is not a funeral question. It's a legal question, a criminal question. "Ewan would know," I say.

Suzanne recoils like she's been hit in the stomach. She bends forward in her chair until her long hair hangs over her knees. "Ewan? You mean it's illegal—to do what you do anyplace but here is a crime? If we were doing this outside Ewan would take us away and have us punished for it?"

"What? Ewan?" I drop the brush back into the

cosmetics tray. "Suzanne—"

She's coughing again, deep, clenching spasms. A hacking crescendo is building. Suzanne is gagging as if she's going to vomit. And in this place, vomiting—getting sick in the presence of a dead body—is everything weak and incompetent.

I can't have it. I hoist Suzanne to her feet. "Okay, that's enough. You're done here."

We are moving down the hall, not reverently silent at all. Suzanne is bent over, stumbling as I push her along. I am nodding, almost bowing at my colleagues who have come to stand gravely in their office doorways.

"Bronchitis," I am calling over Suzanne's noise. "She is fine."

I am pounding on her back, driving her toward the doorway, forcing her, choking, out into the sunlight.

# Suzanne [16]

The house is dark except for the greasy light bulb glowing inside the kitchen range hood. My shift at the hospital just ended. The kids will be up for school in three hours. I should go to bed, to sleep next to May's son.

It'd be nice if I was the sort of pensive person who stays up alone at nights to enjoy the quiet. I'm enjoying nothing. I'm a criminal fixated on May's bones—the last repositories of any of her intact, incriminating DNA. They're stashed in their temporary hiding place, waiting for Durk to tessellate the stack of bricks in my backyard into a barbecue-shaped columbarium.

Alone in my dim kitchen, at the end of my shift, I soak my sore feet in Doctor Troy's new ionizing foot bath. The clear tap water I originally poured into its basin is now deeply orange, like a fancy tea. Troy admits colour changes in the footbath water don't actually reflect any health effects. If some know-it-all doofus were to come to the clinic for a footbath and then pull his feet out of the water as soon as Troy's assistant left the room, the water would still change colour. That doesn't mean the therapy is a sham. All it means is the machine doesn't work like people expect it to. The change in the water's colour is a coincidence, not a placebo. That's what Troy says. That'll work.

I'm sleepier than I realize. I sway in my chair, half-dreaming this orange water is the colour of my soul, seeping out of my feet.

All souls are stained, right? What colours would my sisters' souls be if I could see them suspended in warm water? I do this with everything: find a category of items or attributes and divide them between my sisters. When I did it with punctuation, I decided Meaghan was a comma—adding and adding, unfinished. Tina was a period, a full, jarring stop. Ashley was parentheses—this but that but this. Heather was a colon—the hard pause before the proclamation. And I must have been—I don't know—question marks, ellipses, it doesn't matter.

I'm doing it again, with the soul colours. I'm not sure what makes me decide Ashley's would be aqua blue, like the minerals in glacier water, up in the mountains. Tina's would be lavender-pink, like new baby's flesh. Heather's would be clear and golden brown, like her topaz ring. Meaghan, I'll let her have the verdant green she would have chosen herself. There they are, a little like the colour-coded hair ribbons of the Dionne quintuplets Meaghan's been talking about all spring—the colours of my sisters' souls.

I look into the orange water at my feet. Whatever colour a perfect daughter-in-law's soul may be, it's too late for me to find out. I admit it. Hiding May's death has saved nothing for me. I failed her, defiled her, destroyed the final traces of the faith she once had in my perfection—the faith that made perfection viable and real for me. It's over. Daughter-in-law Suzanne is over. Troy and the kids believe May is alive, but for me, she's gone—worse than gone. The smoke from May's pyre is the only thing left inside me, wafting through the vessels where my blood used to flow. I've dried up—my mouth, throat, my eyes. I cough and cough but the smoke stays inside. I can't hack it out. And there are no grey traces of it in the detoxifying water at my feet.

I didn't kill May. That much is true. Accidents are awful but they aren't always crimes. That's what I've been told. May's fall was not a crime. What came after May's fall was a crime. Heather didn't finish telling me exactly how or why it's illegal. She must know. Crimes against the dead fall into the area where her professional world overlaps Ewan's. She'd probably know the precise, technical names of all those crimes along with their section numbers in the Criminal Code and appropriate sentences for them—jail, fines, probation, all of it served with a well-deserved dose of grisly notoriety.

I am a criminal, a deceiver, an orphan-in-law, a perfect nothing. And I don't know how to reckon with any of it. Everything went wrong when I went to see Heather at the funeral home. That stupid mortuary talcum powder, light and dry like insecticidal diatomaceous earth, abrading and desiccating my already smoke-infused insides. I'm fairly sure I never intended to confess the whole thing to Heather, but I did want to start telling someone something—open a dialogue, like the Nurses' Union leaders say. I tried to be subtle, but Heather is the enemy of subtlety—except when she's its master, wielding it. The funeral home should have been the ideal setting for our first post mortem conversation about May. Private, and if we were overheard talking about disposing of a body it would've sounded like harmless shop-talk.

I've set up the footbath where I can rest my head on the breakfast table while the water does its magical, detoxifying, definitely-not-a-placebo work on my immune system. My arms are folded like a pillow under my cheek and my face is turned to the sliding glass doors that lead to our patio. In the quiet, over the hum and bubble of—ions, I guess, moving through the footbath, I hear a noise. It's like a rattling sound slowed down enough to make it more like a wave. I sit up straight in my chair.

Something flashes outside the house, reflecting back the light from the bulb burning over the stove. It flares, small and white, against the glass of the patio doors. Something about the size of my hand has pressed itself to the pane for an instant. I wait, pulling the power cord of the footbath out of the outlet.

There it is again, the white on the glass. It's not just the size of a woman's hand. It is a woman's hand.

I stand, my feet still inside the footbath even though the instruction booklet has told me never to do that. I'm watching as one of the glass doors tips back and out of its frame, opening the wall of my house to whatever's outside.

Durk isn't the only person who knows how to gain

entry through a poorly secured patio door. I'm stumbling backward on my wet feet, feeling for the doorway behind me. Outside, on my patio, someone is coughing. I hear talking and wheezy laughter. And then he tumbles through the gap in the wall and onto the floor—a man falling like a rolled up camping mattress dropped into my kitchen. He's lying on his side with hanks of long brown hair veiling his face. A woman is leaning into the kitchen, over his body.

She's speaking to me. "You Ashley?"

I should refuse to tell her anything, demand she explain herself. But I don't. "No, I'm Suzanne."

"No? Durk, you son of a bitch, you sent us to the wrong house."

Of course, the man on the floor is Durk. I'm kneeling, pushing his hair away from his face, pulling his eyelids open. "Ashley is my sister," I say as I shush the woman.

She's covering her mouth with one hand. She has a raspy voice that can't drop into a whisper without disappearing into a wheeze. "Excuse my French," she says from behind her hand.

I flick a glare at her. "Just be quiet."

Durk reeks of booze and pot and probably a few substances I don't recognize. I'm getting used to finding him here, crashed out and self-poisoned. He usually arrives in better condition than this—more like a party, less like a suicide attempt.

Who is this lady who got my brother-in-law messed up and then brought him over here, thinking she was bringing him home to Ashley? She's way too old to be partying with Durk, though until I got close to her, it was hard to tell. She's dressed like a 1980s teenager, one so thin her once skinny jeans have been stretched out around the sharpness of her bony knees and hips. Her black leather jacket is scuffed grey, ratty with long, tangled fringes across the shoulder blades and down each arm. It's hard to tell where the fringes begin and her over-dyed black hair ends. She might be an escort Durk hired just to make sure he made it home.

"Sorry," she rasps at me. "It must sound awful for me to talk like that to him. But I'm not hurting no one's feelings when I call this boy a son of a bitch. If anyone has the right to call him that, it's me."

I gape at her. She can't be saying—

"Because if he's the son, that makes me none other than the bitch herself." She grins all over her face, heavy makeup folding and cracking.

I can't hide the tension in my upper lip, the revulsion that shows on my face.

"Oh, and sorry about taking your door apart," she continues. "Popping it out takes the breaking out of breaking and entering. I learned that trick from an old man of mine. Don't ask."

I don't. In her thigh-high boots, she straddles Durk's legs and bends, boring her hands underneath his arms, talking to him. "Come on, baby. Up ya get."

She tugs and fusses, trying to scrape him over the threshold, into my house. She is Durk's mother—his blood-mother. That's why she's old but still so young. That's why her body is bone-thin and flint-hard. That's why even when she's breaking into my house in the middle of the night I can't be mad at her, shoving Durk through the back door, looking like a computer-aged police poster of one of my little nieces.

"Here, let me help."

We get Durk through the doorway and onto the couch. His mother smooths the fringes of her jacket before she goes to the opening in my kitchen wall to reinstall the patio door. She doesn't look like she should be strong enough to lift it, but I know she will be.

"You must be some kind of crazy good sister to put up with this," she says, easing the glass into the doorframe.

"And you're—"

"Bio-mom, like I said. My name's Danielle. And I do get it. I got no right to know Durk now but—you must be a mom. You must get it, right? I poked around until I found him, and once I knew he was so close, I couldn't stop myself from taking a look at him in person—even though, back in the day, the adoption people told me never to do that. 'Closed adoption'—yeah right. They never seen the Internet coming, did they. Good thing I spelled his first name so weird and he was too old for them to change it on us when I gave him up. Good thing for me, anyways."

She sits on the arm of the couch where her son is sleeping on his face. She looks up at the ceiling, as if she's got an audience with the heavens opening above her head.

"God, he's beautiful."

"What was he taking tonight?" I ask. "He looks awful."

She touches him, smoothing his hair. "Mostly booze, nothing new. Nothing I didn't take myself, right along with him, and I'm just fine. Funny thing is, it helps me figure out which of the two contenders is probably bio-dad. I was with this one guy who could party for days—a dumb guy with a wicked car, massive shoulders, played on the offensive line. And then there was the other guy— the one who talked big but always flamed out and fell over around two in the morning. And by the looks of things, he's probably the winner of the daddy sweepstakes here. I liked him. He could have played quarterback if he had a daddy of his own to bully the coaches into it. No pedigree, no shoulders, but light and fast, kind of a smart guy too. Is Durk here smart?"

I nod. "Sure, in his way."

"Well," she says, "don't go thinking I set this up as some crazy, quick and dirty paternity test. Honestly, it was just that Durk needed all kinds of loosening up before he could talk to me tonight. Guess I freaked him out a bit. Just imagine: some old skank follows you from your work all the way to a happy little pub and then corners you while you're trying to watch the Outdoor Life Network and tells you she's your mom. I'd say that'd make any guy tense right up."

She traces his nose with one finger. Durk's mom— this Danielle person—is rough but not stupid. She's got that same sheepish self-awareness Durk carries with him.

Tonight, there in a booth in the bar and then later in her car with the windows rolled up—did she tell him why she let him be poisoned and burned, scarred and abandoned?

She's standing up. "Well. It's pretty obvious he didn't want me showing up at his place if he had me bring him to his in-laws' instead."

"He usually doesn't go home when he's like this."

She smirks. "Home is where he keeps my grandkids and my daughter-in-law—my bio-daughter-in-law, if that expression makes any sense." She laces her fingers through Durk's hair. "I went through his wallet while he was blitzed and found pictures of them. Cute kids. Your sister's really beautiful. The two of you could be twins, for all I know."

"We're not, but thank you."

Danielle is nodding. "Beautiful. Yeah, it's all my own fault. And it's a shame."

She lifts Durk's hand, flips it over on her palm like it's a pancake. I hear his skin smack against hers. I can't tell if she's looking for his old scars—if she understands they're still there to be seen.

Feet shuffle on the stairs behind me. Troy is coming to investigate the noise—something faintly chivalrous and much too late. "Suzanne, what the—?"

"Troy, Durk's here again."

He shakes his head at the floor. "Great." His voice is flat with duty. "How much do you need to cover the fare?"

He's talking to Danielle.

She drops Durk's hand. "Huh?"

"For the cab. You're the driver, right?"

Danielle is laughing at him, though it sounds more like there's a pinecone caught in her throat.

I step between them. "No," I say. "No, Troy. This— lady—this is—Ashley's mother-in-law."

Troy doesn't flinch. "Sorry. Hi."

"Yeah, hi," Danielle says. "There's no charge. No worries. Hey, you probably just want me to go out the way I came in."

I shake my head. "It's okay. I'll let you out the front door."

Walking on the balls of her feet, she keeps her high heels from clicking on our hard floors. She is leaving, moving past May's stairwell, toward the door.

"Don't tell no one you seen me," she says. "Just pretend I was a ghost or a bad dream or whatever you gotta do."

"Sure," I say.

She's waving, standing in the dark of the open doorway, orange streetlight behind her, illuminating the frizz of her hair, the worst halo ever.

He'll be thrust into horrifying flashbacks if I lean over the couch and wake Durk exactly the way I did the morning May fell down the stairs. My kids wake him instead— wholesome sunshine and pink exuberance. They turn on the television as loudly as they like it and frolic all around him, chattering about sleepovers, sliding plastic tiaras onto his head, piling stuffed animal toys around him. There's preliminary talk of giving him a makeover before Uncle Durk finally sits up, rubbing his forehead, trying to smile at them, more unable than usual to reciprocate the shrill friendliness of my daughters. The best he can do is leave the tiara where they put it, dangling from his party-matted hair by the teeth of a broken comb.

In the kitchen, I'm making him another cup of lemon-fish-oil tea.

"Is she still here?" he asks after I chase the kids upstairs to get dressed for school. "That woman—you know."

I almost smile. "No. She's gone. She left while it was still dark—told me to think of her as nothing but a bad dream."

He hums into his teacup. "Still no coffee around here?"

"Never. Coffee is a diuretic anyways," I say. "It makes you eliminate water faster. And you need your essential waters replenished right now, not chemically removed."

He murmurs as he sips.

"Durk," I begin. "I hate to ask but I really need you to help me finish."

"Suzanne, no."

"Come on. Not everyone's mother is a bad dream, Durk. Some are real and they won't just wander off into oblivion on their own."

He sets his teacup on the coffee table and exhales from the depths of his guts. "You still haven't found a good place to keep—her."

I shake my hair out of my face. May is not buried yet. I bought a metal toolbox from the hardware store, one big enough for everything, even the largest fragments—bits like the ball joints of her hips and shoulders. Right now, the box is tucked inside the rim of the access hole of our rough, uninhabitable attic. It's a decent hiding place, but not a perfect one. The truth is Troy won't find anything in this house that I haven't deliberately laid out for him. The kids are just as bad. The truth is if I hid May's charred bones in the mass of shoes in the front hall closet, no one would ever find her there but me.

It's still not good enough. Everything I see—everywhere—is immediately sorted into three categories: an impossible hiding place for May, a possible hiding place for May, and the only hiding place for May. There's just one place I've imagined that fits the third category. And I can't get May anywhere near it without Durk's help.

"Durk, you remember what I said about building a barbecue mausoleum and making it a Fathers' Day gift to Troy."

He sighs again. "I remember."

"I have the supplies ready," I say. "The bricks are out in the yard, and the rest of the stuff is in the garage. I got a few tools, too, so you wouldn't have to corrupt your own with something as nasty as this. Fathers' Day is this weekend, but we can probably finish it in a couple days if we get started on it as soon as the kids are gone."

If Durk keeps sighing this deeply, he's going to pass out. "No way. It's not that easy, Suzanne. That much finished brick work will be really heavy. It needs to be built on a sturdy foundation, like a concrete pad, or it'll sink and break apart. I'd have to excavate and backfill and compact it and pour the foundation and leave it to cure for a few days before I could come back and lay the bricks."

"Yeah, I researched it already," I say. "And luckily for us there's already a small concrete pad in the back yard, just sitting there. It's by the fence. The people who owned the house before us had a shed there that they ended up tearing down, or something."

Durk leans forward, letting his forehead roll against the low tabletop in front of the couch. By now I recognize the meaning of it. It's surrender—his signal that he's going to give me whatever gruesome thing I need.

Ashley must know him with near perfection to have been able to tell which line of work Durk had to be in, years ago when she borrowed that money from Dad and bought the masonry shop. Brickwork's order—the straight lines, the plumb pull of the centre of the earth, the fitting and fitting and fitting together—it's what an overly simplistic Westerner like me might call Zen.

Brick by brick, Durk seals May away. And this time, I'm the one who's hypnotized, standing behind him, caught in the scrape and squash rhythm of his work. It's as entrancing as those geometric stop-animation films from the old kids' shows my sisters and I used to watch on public television when we were little.

I'd expected the connections between the bricks and

the mortar to be something like the bonds between gum-drops and icing on a gingerbread house. It isn't like that. It's like the mortar is the ideal sand for sandcastles, and Durk is building the best sandcastle ever, one that will harden into something that could last forever.

"I can still see the bricks going into place when I close my eyes," I say. "It must be like that for you too."

He draws a long breath through his nose. At the depths of his exhale he answers, "All the time." After the cremation of Troy's mother and the resurrection of his own mom, Durk needs ritual. Maybe that's exactly what building the barbecue is for him. Despite his initial dread, the work seems to have—I don't know—a purifying effect.

It's the Taj Mahal of barbecues—a beautiful, sturdy thing, the opening above its grill curving in an elegant arch. The lines of its chimney are perfectly square, as if we built it under the direction of ancient space travellers, or freemasons, or something.

Troy doesn't know his barbecue is memorial architecture. Even though he'd already seen it through the kitchen window, our little girls drape a bed-sheet over it and unveil it like it's an art installation in the fancy Fathers' Day ceremony they've devised. Thanks to the ossuary chamber built inside it, the barbecue is a little over-sized. But its inflated proportions enlarge Troy's love for it.

The unveiling is over, and the bricks and mortar are cured, sooty, and a little sticky with barbecue sauce by the time the man with the clipboard comes knocking on our front door. At first sight, I assume he's selling household security systems. Everyone knows I can't have a security system if Durk and his family are going to keep arriving through the patio doors in the night. I'm about to close the door when he manages to pass me his business card, pinched between two of his fingers like chopsticks. He's not a salesman but a building inspector from the city's municipal compliance department.

"I've got to take a quick look at your new barbecue," he tells me.

My nervous system fires a blast of panic signals. My fingertips prickle with electricity. I repeat the word, "Barbecue?"

"Yes," the inspector says. He's leaning and straining, trying to see past me, through a rear window, into the backyard. "Some residents in the area have expressed concerns that it might be built on an easement."

I step in front of him. "Easement?"

The inspector leans back, openly disgusted. "Yes, there's a legally significant invisible perimeter inside everyone's fence-line, all the way around." He draws a square in the air with a corner of his clipboard. "And it needs to be kept free of any major, permanent structures."

"Major structure—it's just a barbecue."

He's nodding. "Well, you may be right. But we need to take some measurements—the kinds of measurements that should have been noted on the building permit application in the first place."

"Building permit." I'm that echo again—that stupid

echo.

"You didn't pull a building permit, did you." It's not a question.

"For a barbecue? No."

"Thought the husband would do it for you?"

"No." I stop myself from saying, "It's just a barbecue," one more time.

The inspector ducks past me, hopping over the threshold, moving through the kitchen to the patio doors. I stand in my open front door, my face and feet pointed toward to the empty street. Maybe this is the part of the story where I run away and never come back to Troy, or my kids, or my sisters, or May's bones, or anything.

I follow the inspector into the yard.

"All-righty," he says. He pushes against the new brickwork, shoving hard with his knee and shoulder. "Installed on a concrete foundation. Rock solid. Definitely a permanent structure." He walks all around it, humming and frowning. "Really nice workmanship here, by the way."

"Thanks."

"Looks like something from a slick design magazine."

"Thanks."

"You have this professionally built?"

"Sort of."

"Expensive?"

"Sort of."

"That's probably a shame. Let's get the height." He unclips the tape measure from his belt like he's drawing a pistol. "Yup, it's easily over twenty inches high."

"Is that bad?" I ask.

"Well, it's not good. If it was under twenty inches tall, it would have been exempt from the by-laws, but as it is ..." He shakes his head. "One more thing to check."

He's moving to the fence, the tape measure clicking out the distance from the property line to the edge of the barbecue. And it all makes sense. The empty concrete pad—the last owners must have had to tear down the shed that stood here because it violated the same rules about structures being built on easements. We have gone and done what the last owners had undone years before.

Behind and above us, drapes are pulled closed over the windows of the neighbours whose backyards share the property line with us. Why would they do this? Who cares how tall their neighbours' barbecues are or how far they are from the fence? Or maybe the call to city hall was made by someone spooked to see me slip the toolbox urn into the ossuary. It's possible, but odds are no one but Durk saw me do it. The barbecue was built during the day, in the empty, deserted hours of the suburban lifecycle. Maybe, no matter what time it is, anyone looking out those upper windows can tell there's something grim about our barbecue and understand it has to be destroyed.

"You're in clear breach of the easement by-laws," the inspector says. "And we haven't even begun to talk about the fire code you might have broken by building what amounts to a furnace so close to this dry wooden fence."

He makes no pretence of being sorry. He promises me an official letter from the compliance department, and leaves, closing the gate behind himself. I turn to look at the barbecue again—the ultimate resting place for my mother-in-law, now in contempt of city hall.

There's a sledgehammer hanging on the wall of the garage. I can see it in my mind. I'm not sure anyone's ever used it, but it's hanging there anyway. If I took it down I could desecrate May's grave and disinter her right now. It might be better for me to do it myself than for Troy to come home and get mad enough to start smashing up the barbecue himself just to deprive the city of the satisfaction of ordering him to do it.

The garage smells like sawdust and vulcanized rubber. It's dim and dusty, especially in the corner where I find the hammer. The handle is long and the tempered steel head is so heavy I drag it along the grass behind me as I walk across the yard. My kids are following, heaping questions on me in that suffocating way of theirs. I don't answer. Instead, I give each of them an ice cream sandwich on the condition they eat on the patio, away from where Mummy needs to work on the barbecue.

Glancing at the time on my watch, I take it off and put it in my pocket. I've never demolished anything. The brickwork may be as strong as it is exquisite. It might take longer to smash it up than the time I have left before Troy will be home. If the traffic on the High Level Bridge is moving smoothly, Troy will arrive in time to find his wife—the one who's supposed to be the good sister, the one who's not morbid or crazy or deluded or self-destructive—standing in a cloud of demolition dust, clutching his mother's bones.

Somehow, right now, I don't care. It's time to end this—all of it.

I close in on the barbecue, dragging the hammerhead. When I'm near enough, I lift the sledgehammer over my shoulder, hoisting it so high its weight pulls me backward. I stumble sideways and the hammer thuds against the grass. I lift it again, more carefully, with stronger, stiffer arms. This time, I understand its momentum well enough to bring the black cylinder crashing into the corner of the barbecue. The impact rings up the handle, jolting through the fluid in my arms. Crumbly mortar and chips of brick spray into the air around me. Reflexes in my eyelids snap them closed. Without opening them, I raise the hammer again.

The clatter of steel on masonry tells me I've connected with the barbecue. My lashes are full of debris. I've breached May's tomb. Between the ragged edges of broken brick there's a dark, black space about the size of my youngest daughter's fist. I'm stooping, peering into the inner chamber. Even in the daylight, the hollow is a black void. But if someone were to shine a flashlight into the space, the beam of light would glint off the wall of the metal toolbox-urn buried inside.

I raise the hammer again. The sound of metal on brick is the same pitch as a man yelling. I know it when I hear Troy hollering from the patio. "Su-zanne!"

The hammer falls from my hands, onto the grass. Troy is threading through May's grandchildren, where they stand stunned, dripping with melting ice cream on the patio. In shiny leather shoes, Troy is skidding across the lawn, cursing the damage I've done, demanding the explanation he's owed.

I've sunk to sitting on the grass, on the green space between my husband's feet and the broken brick wall. I hate it, but I'm starting to cry.

"Look what you—what were you thinking?" he asks.

"Troy, there was a man here," I stammer, "from the city ..."

As I tell the story of the building inspector's visit, Troy bends to sit beside me in the grass, quiet. He isn't filled with rebellious rage against The Man. It was unfair of me to think he would be. He listens, leaning against the side of the barbecue, his shoulder inches below the fissure I've bashed into the brick.

He's feeling for the acupressure point between my eyes. There was a special aromatherapy promotion at the clinic today, and he smells like spice bottles and flower petals and peppermint.

"Aw, Sue," he says. "There's no need to overreact like this. It's bad news, all right. It was a really nice present and everything. But it's still just a barbecue." He curls an arm around my shoulders. The crush of his kindness wrings a sob out of me.

"Listen," he says, flawless Sears model mouth speaking against the side of my head. "There's a whole whack of official processes that have to take place before the city can legally oblige us to knock this thing down. They have to file papers, and get them approved, and everything has to move back and forth through the snail mail. And then there's an appeal period and all sorts of other stuff that will take months to sort out."

"Yeah?"

"Yeah. We can't beat city hall but we can stall it." He's smiling at me. He reaches into the grass and picks up a fragment of brick, tossing it up and down with one hand as he speaks. "By the time the city gets its ducks in a row, we'll have been out here eating ribs off this thing for a whole summer, and maybe the next summer too. How do you think these whiny neighbours would like that?"

He pantomimes throwing the brick chunk at the upstairs windows on the other side of the fence.

"Ducks in a row," I say. And I laugh a little because saying "I love you" right now would sound forced and wishful, and because it's funny—the resilience of the normal equilibrium of daily life. The hammer, the inspector, the barbecue, the bones—normalcy is already settling down over this absurdity.

Troy presses his thumb between my eyes, like a button on a remote control that needs its batteries changed. "We'll stall the city, Sue. Don't worry. And don't break anything else."

Stalling—that's all any of us ever does, isn't it? Living and dying—it's only a matter of delay.

# Ashley [17]

At our masonry shop, Durk is grooving on brickwork, light meditation, and a few discreet puffs of his favourite herbal remedy. He's in the loading bay at the back of the shop. The overhead door is open to the hot, dry alleyway outside as he's rolling the forklift back into its alcove more slowly than he realizes.

I'm in the office with a paper cup of convenience store coffee, a fan blasting in my face. It's buffeting strands of hair out of my ponytail and into my eyes and mouth. The desk is covered with invoices weighted down with damaged bits of the synthetic dry-stack stone that's going to date everything we're building right now as early twenty-first century construction.

I don't know exactly when someone steps out of the alley and rasps a greeting at my half-naked, half-baked husband. When I look through the window of my office, Durk's visitor is already standing in the bay. He's dismounting the forklift to speak to her.

I can't hear anything. But I see her craning her neck, like she's trying to see into the office to get a look at me. I know what I look like, okay. I'm used to people trying to get a better view of me. Still, it's distracting—and a little threatening.

Durk glances over his shoulder, toward me, and I drop my eyes. I'm stabbing at a calculator with the eraser end of a pencil, like I don't have anything to worry about when Durk whispers with strangers in back alleys.

I can't hold the pose for long. The smoky languor is gone from Durk's movements and posture. His happy cloud is blown away. His motions are quicker, more clipped as he pulls his T-shirt over his head.

The woman is louder now, "'Cause you never introduced me to her, that's how come," she's saying. She actually touches Durk—pushes her fingertips against his chest. "And I get that," she says. "But it don't mean I'm not curious. Who wouldn't be?"

Durk scrubs his face with his hands. He knows how loud he'd have to speak for me to hear him from where I sit, and he deliberately speaks below that threshold. I read his pantomime instead. He extends his hand toward the woman like he's presenting her to an audience, and then he lets the same hand fall against his thigh. It's a rehearsal of an impossible introduction—the one he cannot make between this woman and me.

I'm walking into the loading bay, frowning.

"You want me to hoof it?" the woman asks Durk as I approach.

He groans above the threshold of my hearing now. "Nah, it's too late. She's already seen you. She'll send her sisters. They'll be watching you when you don't know it."

I'm standing next to the forklift, leaning against it with one hand, because it's mine. "Hey, are you the new sales rep from the cultured stone supplier?" I ask her, acting a part to get this drama started. "Because in the last shipment—"

"No, Ash," Durk says. "No, this is—a relative of mine. I wasn't expecting to see her here. She's just passing by."

I let my hand drop away from the forklift. "A relative? Durk's relative? No way!"

"Yeah. I'm Danielle," she says, grabbing at my hand, greedy, kind of like a striking snake. Her palm and fingers are dry and rough, as if she's been lifting bricks all this time too. "And you're Ashley. It's great to meet you, Mrs. Durk. So great. You seem—really—special."

I'm smiling. "Yeah? Aw, thanks. Don't stand out in the alley, Danielle. Come in. I've never met a single soul from Durk's family—except our own kids, I mean. Come in."

Danielle covers her mouth, as if she knows what the cigarettes have done to her teeth and gums. She grins into her hand. "No, I can't stay. Like Durk says, I was just passing by."

There are clunky, tittering good-byes, like we're both seven years old, and she's gone. I watch her go, spiky high-heeled boots even though it's summertime and the back-street pavement is full of tiny, dangerous pits. She's getting into a low, gold-coloured car parked in the alleyway.

"How weird is that?" is all I say as the lights beneath the spoiler of her old sports car flare red.

Durk doesn't say anything about the relative-lady until the day is over, the shop closed, and we're headed to the monument factory to pick up the headstone we'll need for tomorrow morning's installation. We're in the pickup truck with the Dash Fireplace and Monument logo stamped on its doors.

"So I guess I should have something to say—about Danielle," he begins.

"Danielle—yeah, I knew there was more. Let me guess: she's not really a relative, she's an old girlfriend."

"What the hell, Ashley?"

"I'm kidding."

He won't laugh with me. "Can you spare me the suspicious sister-talk?"

"Sorry. I am kidding."

"Well, don't," he says. "Danielle is so a relative. She's my mother."

I cluck my tongue. "Wow. Holy—Durk."

"Yeah."

I cock my head. "I thought your mom would be an old lady."

"No, she's not my social worker mom. She's my mother. Danielle is my real, blood-mother."

I've seen Danielle myself. The claim feels real. It fits. She doesn't look quite like I've been imagining her all these years. I thought she'd look—I don't know—more motherly, more like Tina. It's dumb, but whenever I'm reading a book or hearing a story, every mother I have to imagine out of nothing looks like Tina.

I believe him, but Durk keeps explaining anyway. It's a habit brought on by the way everyone insists on evidence and proof whenever he tries to tell them anything. What's that line people keep quoting on the Internet to piss each other off? It comes from that 1980s TV science guy, with the hair and the "extraordinary claims require extraordinary evidence"—something like that. It's catchy and tidy but shaky when you get right down to it.

Durk is shaken, alright. He's nodding hard at the windshield. "It's definitely for real, Ash. She showed me a copy of my original birth certificate and everything—the one with her name on it. And if you can see through her burnt-out party-chick vibe, she looks like our girls. It's all for real."

I blow out my breath. "Yeah. Wow—your mother. Half of your genetic code walked right into our shop today, Durk. What're we supposed to do now?"

"I don't know."

"What do you want to do?"

"I do not know."

He's squinting as we drive along the Henday Freeway, west, into the low sunlight. He's troubled. That's easy to see. I'll have to look longer and harder to tell if he's hurting.

It's difficult. I turn away from him, just for a second, glancing through my window at the smaller cars darting around our truck in the rush hour traffic.

"Hey," I say. "Is that her? Is that Danielle driving in the vintage Trans Am right there? It looks like the same car as the one in the alley."

Durk shifts his field of vision to include the lane be-side ours. "Yeah, that's her car."

"Wow. Eagle paintjob on the hood and everything."

His head droops toward the steering wheel. "It's just a decal. She got the car from some guy in a separation agreement."

"How do you know all that? How do you know anything about her? How long has it been since you met her—again?"

His head rolls from shoulder to shoulder. "Remember the last time—the very last time—when I spent the night crashed at Suzanne's place? That was the night Danielle found me. She came and sat down, almost right on top of me, while I was watching cable in a pub after work. I had no idea how to cope with her, so I just got blitzed. And she went right along with me. It was totally stupid, I know that. Anyways, she did manage to get me to Suzanne's."

At the edge of my vision, sideways sunlight glints on dusty gold enamel. In the lane beside us, Danielle's car is picking up speed, manoeuvring as if she's tracking us. "I think she's trying her hardest to come home with us. She's following way too close."

"Everyone has to use the freeway. She'll split off and go her own way soon."

Durk hasn't finished saying it before Danielle's car shifts gears and jumps ahead of our truck, cutting into our lane of traffic. The Trans Am has gone from driving next to us to braking in front of us.

Durk slams his foot down to keep from colliding with

its rear bumper.

I grab the handle on the ceiling above my window as my seatbelt locks across my sternum. "What is she doing?"

Danielle's car stays in front of us, moving slowly for a few seconds. It's long enough for us to get a good look at the black louvers of her rear window, long enough for her to be sure we understand who she is. We hear her engine over the sound of our air conditioning as she sprints ahead again, speeding away, veering in and out of the dense traffic.

"What is she *doing*?"

Durk speeds up to follow her. He's more careful than she is, as he moves around the slower cars, but he needs to be quick to keep her in sight.

"Is she trying to get herself killed?" I ask.

Durk accelerates into a gap just barely large enough for the truck. The cars behind him are braking, screeching, honking.

"Is she trying to get us killed?"

I haven't heard Durk swear like this in a long time. He adds, "They've had that speed trap set up in the construction zone under the overpass all week. There've been at least two cop cars sitting there every time I've driven through it. Danielle won't make it past them, the way she's driving. They'll stop her for sure."

I rise to my knees on the passenger seat, trying to see over the tops of the cars ahead without giving up the protection of my seatbelt. "Not if she guns right through the pylons," I say.

Heat rising from the asphalt bends the view into waves. It's hard to see the Trans Am in the shiny smear of traffic.

"There she is," I say. "She's just about at the speed trap."

"Is she stopping?"

I yell something. It's not a word. I catch my breath and call, "She rammed right through it!"

Under the overpass, plastic flares are smashed and strewn all over the road. The police are abandoning the drivers they've got pulled over, climbing into their cruisers with half-written tickets in their notepads. There are lights and sirens. The police follow Danielle down the freeway, not exactly chasing her, but shepherding her away from the rest of traffic, toward other officers, waiting at the next exit to stop her.

Durk tromps the gas pedal into the floor and launches the truck into the open path of the shoulder lane. He throws the truck into four-wheel drive as I grip my seatbelt with both hands like the idiot token woman flailing from the sidelines in every TV crime show. The passenger-side wheels beneath me slide through gravel and weeds and shredded tire rubber on the shoulder of the road.

"Sorry, Ash!" Durk calls as I ricochet between my seatbelt and the truck's upholstery. No one ever says sorry to the token woman. This isn't primetime network television. This is a marriage on a Wednesday night commute.

We're driving off-road, following noise and red and blue lights, when I see the cars we're passing aren't moving anymore.

"Traffic's stopped." I say it like I'm terrified.

Durk keeps the truck off-road, closing in on the section of the freeway where flashing lights are spinning, cars parked, jumbled around—something.

"Close enough," he says, jamming the truck into park and vaulting out the driver's-side door.

He runs—that tense, trotting sprint of his, hands up, fingers spread, hopping and skirting the parked police cars. There's a spike belt on the road, and past it is Danielle's crippled Trans Am. The sirens are quiet now. We hear voices from her car. A policeman is stooping into the open doorway yelling in peace officer dialect, "Remain seated ma'am. Your vehicle stopped at a high rate of speed and you may have sustained an injury. You must wait for medical personnel who will subsequently attend you."

There's another officer—a lady in a ponytail and body armour—crouched on bent knees, leaning into Danielle's face hollering questions.

Above both these voices, we hear Danielle. She's loud, like she's arguing, but desperate and sadder than she can stand. Her words don't make any sense until we hear her shout Durk's name.

"Danielle!" Durk calls back to her.

He's close enough to come up against the whole "Sir, you need to keep back" bit from the police officers, just like you'd expect from watching TV. By now, I've caught up to him at the barricade. My hand grips Durk's arm. I'm pulling at him, trying to get him to stand behind me as I shout at the officers, yelling about being their deputy superintendent's family and needing to be let through the line.

Over the epaulettes of the uniforms in front of him, Durk sees Danielle's hand—flashing small and white—reaching through the open car door. Through the chaos, she knows he's here. She's reaching past the lady police officer who's still calling out a list of slang names for cocaine.

"Durk, baby. Baby—you got to be quiet when Mommy's old man is here sleeping it off. And stay away from him when he's got a hot cigarette. And—oh God—I'm sorry."

# Heather [18]

Mum is not speaking to me.

I can hear her talking to Tina. Mum has called her on the phone, which is strange. Everyone knows Mum doesn't initiate phone contact with us. She doesn't have to. At least one of us calls her, every single day, while she manages us—peeved and distracted—like a switchboard operator.

I imagine Tina in her big noisy house, answering Mum's call like an alarm, pressing the phone against her ear so hard it hurts, terrified someone is dead or maimed or sick enough to make our mother use her switchboard to dial out.

"Yes, Tina. Hello," Mum says.

Mum's tone is more like a whine than a knell. She doesn't sound poised to tell Tina Dad has finally had the heart attack, driving between jobsites, collapsed against the wheel of his pick-up truck, idling in the drive-thru of a roadside Tim Hortons, Stan Rogers singing "Northwest Passage" out of the stereo. It hasn't happened yet but I've seen it in my mind, over and over.

Mum says nothing like this, but Tina is asking after death and disaster anyway. It's plain from the way Mum clucks and says. "Of course we're okay. But I need someone to come over here to deal with Heather."

There's a pause in her talk. Unseen by my mother, I tighten my jaw and brace for the punch I learned how to take when I was still a teenager.

"No. No, Tina, nothing happened to Heather. Nothing happened to anyone. The thing is, your father mentioned he wanted more light in the bedroom. So, of course, Heather hopped up into the ceiling, right up in the rafters like some giant rodent, and she's hanging a hideous new light fixture while he's out of town."

Yes, I'm in my parents' attic, above the ceiling of the bedroom where my mother is complaining to Tina about my filial good deeds.

It must have been back in the seventies when designers decided it would be sexy to wire master bedroom light switches to nothing but the wall outlets. I'm old enough to remember the enormous, urn-like table lamps that lit up the grownups' bedrooms of my childhood—voluptuous lamps with three-way bulbs for sophisticated, sensual free-spirits. No more of those hard-wired ceiling-mounted fixtures glaring down like dour, parental, post-war oppression. But now, the sexy seventies crowd, our parents' crowd, have reached an age where muted mood lighting isn't working well with their multi-focal eyeglasses.

I am helping. Natural age-related vision loss—that's the reason I volunteered to wire a new bedroom light fixture for Dad. Mum makes it sound like a home invasion, but she gave grudging consent for this project weeks ago.

"I can't handle Heather when she's like this," Mum is telling Tina. "She keeps sticking her head out of the attic and yelling at me."

It's an exaggeration. Mum and I aren't passing the most pleasant morning together, but I'm not yelling. That's just how my voice always sounds to her. I get it. Mum can't be good to me because Dad is far too good to me. It's not personal. It's the tariff I pay for being beloved. Mum doesn't approve of the way Ewan treats me either. Ask her. She'll say I shouldn't get away with treating men the way I do—like I am also precious.

Staying hidden in the ceiling, or somewhere like it, is the best way to cope with her at times like this. I'm out of her sight, hammering cable straps to the roof trusses, waiting for Tina to arrive at our parents' adults-only condominium community—the row of tall, narrow houses fighting from renovation to renovation to stay upscale as time passes, the ones with exclusive bylaws that keep the grandkids from ever staying overnight.

My hair is full of fibreglass, I've probably inhaled something that has doomed me to lung cancer, and I'm cutting a hole over my parents' bed. The pointy tip of a drywall saw bobs up and down, in and out of my mother's view, its triangular teeth chewing an opening.

Mum is slapping at the bedspread, flicking drywall dust off the fabric, when Tina arrives.

Tina steps into the room, scolding, "Mum, you can't

keep leaving heaps of stuff piled up on the stairs like that. It's dangerous. Someone's going to—"

"Tina, finally," Mum interrupts. "Say something to Heather. She's up there sulking about the wire I bought."

A roughly octagonal piece of the ceiling falls onto the bed. "I'm not sulking." My voice comes through the newly cut hole.

Tina laughs at us.

Mum scoffs. "Heather won't use any of the wire I bought."

"I *can't* use it. You got the wrong kind."

"You said to get fourteen gauge household electrical cable. I wrote it down."

"Mum, I said to get fourteen gauge, three-wire cable. And then you went and brought me two-wire cable."

"So?"

"So? Mum, do you want the light switch to work or not?"

Mum answers with another slap at the dusty bed-spread. "Well, the switch for your father's new light might be working by the time she's finished," she tells Tina, "but the wall outlets for everything I care about are all dead."

"No, they're not. Sheesh, Mum."

Mum stands up, her footsteps padding to the doorway.

Tina is calling her back. "Come on, Mum. Heather did the lights in my girls' room with no problems. I'm sure everything will work out fine here too."

"Oh really? Look at that alarm clock over there,"

Mum says, stopping just inside the threshold of the bedroom. "It's plugged into a wall outlet, but none of the numbers will light up. Not even when I do this."

Click.

Tina screams. "Heather!"

"What?"

"Are you okay?"

I'm crawling toward the attic access opening, moving over the rafters and the sister boards strapped to them to reinforce the roof when the original asphalt shingles were upgraded to fake hacienda clay ones. I look out of the ceiling, blinking into the bedroom. "Yeah, I'm fine. Why? Did she try to turn on the light switch again?"

Tina is simultaneously so relieved and so frustrated she can only laugh.

I have survived. Of course I have. I don't take shortcuts when I'm working with electricity. Before I climbed up here, I'd already taken precautions to avoid the electrocution accident my mother still doesn't realize she could have caused with her light switch.

My survival means my sisters can go on living a little longer too. They all believe, somewhere in their minds, that I'll be the first of us to die. None of them has ever told me so, but I know it. It's like we're shut up together in a single room, and I've got my back pressed to the door while death tries to force its way inside to start carrying us off. Until I lose the strength to keep leaning against the closed door, everyone else in the room is safe. I have to be the first of us to die, the same way I was the first to be born, the first to give birth. Don't think I fail to feel the burden of it. And don't think I'd allow anyone else to stand here.

A disruption in the accepted order of the predictable timelines of our lives—that's what scares me most. I don't want to be in the flesh at any of my sisters' funerals. But Suzanne got her period a few months before mine started, proof we can't presume to know the order of anything.

Tina and Mum can see my face now—dust stuck to the sweat on my nose and cheekbones. This dust is denser and greyer than mortuary talcum. I'm powdered like Marie Antoinette—thick and toxic.

"Don't worry, Teens," I say. "I turned the circuit off at the main board before I got started. You don't even know where the main circuit board is in this house, do you Mum?"

She's still flipping the light switch up and down.

Tina grabs her hand. "You have to stop that."

Mum leaves the switch, trudges back to the bed, drops herself onto it.

I almost laugh. "It's okay, Mum. The wall outlets will work just fine once I've—oh, never mind. I'll spare you the lecture on electrical contracting. Just trust me. They'll work."

Before things get any worse, Tina takes hold of the shrink-wrapped coil of bone-coloured wire sitting at the base of my step ladder. "Okay. So this cable needs to go back to the hardware store. Is that it?" she asks. "Is that the emergency that forced me to call my nanny in on her day off and rush over here?"

"Yes," I answer. "Exchange it for exactly the same thing only in three-wire cable—three-wire. As in, having three wires. Three—white, black, and red. Red."

"Red."

The badly chosen cable has stalled my project. Not knowing how long the delay will be, I risk descending from the ceiling. There are limits to my endurance for lying on reinforced trusses, sweating under a trouble light, chanting the mantra well-known to daughters unfavoured by their mothers but well past being miserable about it: "She doesn't owe me anything, she doesn't owe me anything …"

My clothes, hair, everything about me is filthy as I reappear in the civilized levels of my parents' house. I stand at the bottom of the ladder, blowing dust from the stone in my big yellow ring.

Mum sits on the bed like a hostage. Tina is shaking her head as she turns to leave, like she might chide us, reminding us to play nicely while she's gone. It's a remark that would guarantee a fight.

"Here, you two." Tina shoves Mum's big cherry wood jewellery box across the dresser. "Instead of plotting how to make each other's deaths look accidental, why don't you cooperate and untangle all the chains in the jewellery box until I get back?"

Mum is offended. "Why would anyone assume my chains are tangled?"

"It's not personal, Mum," I say as Tina flees. "Everyone's jewellery gets snarled in storage. Look."

I open the lid. A music box melody starts to play—tinny and delicately plucked out of a metal comb. "Hey, the music still works. I haven't heard this thing play its song in ages."

Mum sniffs.

I'm humming along. "What's the tune called again?"

Mum was never any good at the silent treatment. "It's 'The Anniversary Waltz'."

I laugh. "It's a song celebrating an anniversary? Really? It's so gloomy and serious I always thought it was supposed to be spooky music." I'm raking my hand through Mum's beads and chains, lifting the upper tray to see to the bottom of the box. "Whoa, what a head-trip, Mum. I remember everything in here. It's like a museum."

Mum flinches. "A mausoleum?"

"No, a mus-e-um. Sheesh, Mum. Even with me it's not always about death," I say—though it may not be true. I'm fingering a row of earrings. "How come I never see you wearing any of these? Have your piercings grown over?"

Mum pinches her earlobe. She pulls her hand away, examining her fingertips, as if she's looking for traces of the old wound, something still oozing from her head.

I grin into the jewellery box. "Didn't you tell us your roommates pierced your ears over a kitchen sink using nothing but an ice cube and a darning needle?"

Mum smiles a little. "Yes. That's one way it used to be done."

"Gruesome," I say. "Anyways, it looks like most of

these earrings are made out of nickel compounds. If you tried to wear them they'd probably make you go into ana-phylactic shock."

The music box winds down—slow ticking and then nothing.

"Hey. It's one of those old camera film canisters." I lift a black, plastic cylinder out of the box. "I forgot about these. They used to be everywhere."

Mum sniffs again. "It's funny, the stuff that can turn into antiques if you give it time."

"So what're you keeping inside this one?" I ask.

Mum doesn't answer quickly enough. I snap my wrist, giving the canister a quick, sharp shake. It makes a noise like a baby's rattle.

At the sound, Mum is on her feet.

"Don't."

She looks ready to snatch it out of my hand. But she knows it's too much of an escalation. She opens with a warning instead. "You can't shake it like that or they'll break."

I narrow my eyes. "They? What's in here?"

"Nothing much."

"Come on, Mum. Don't make me open it," I say. I'm smiling like it's all a game and I'm just teasing.

"Don't," Mum says. "It's full of your teeth."

"My teeth?"

"No, not just your teeth, Heather. All the baby teeth I ever made—yours and your sisters' too."

I hold my stomach and pretend to retch. "Gross, Mum.

Do you have our fingernail clippings stashed in here too?" I'm peering at the outside of the canister like I'm trying to activate my X-ray vision while I do some math inside my head. "So you had five babies, and we each would have had—what is it?—twenty deciduous teeth per head. That means there are one hundred tiny human teeth in here?"

Mum shrugs. "I've never spread them out and counted."

I'm awful but I shake the canister one more time, wanting to hear the sound again, now I know what's making it.

Mum can't stand it. She's lunging toward me. "Stop it. I told you, they are going to break."

"They can't break. They're rocky little teeth."

"Yes, they can break. They do. When they get dry enough they split right in half, like firewood."

"I'll stop, I'll stop," I promise, holding the canister away from her. "One hundred tiny little girl teeth."

Mum sits down on the bed.

Then I remember. "No, it's just ninety-nine teeth. There was that one tooth we lost for good. Remember when Ashley was brushing her teeth and she accidentally spat her loose tooth into the sink and rinsed it right down the drain with her toothpaste? Poor little Ashley."

Mum smiles. "Yes, she was heartbroken."

"But then," I go on, "you came up with that brilliant idea of giving her an un-popped popcorn kernel to put under her pillow for the Tooth Fairy instead. That was great, Mum."

Mum is looking out the window. It's hard for her to

know what to do when I'm loving her, carefully, distantly, from across the room, through a thick coat of dust.

Mum faces the window as she tells me the part of the story I never knew. "But we didn't have to go through with the popcorn song and dance. When your father came home, I had him wrench open the p-trap under the sink. We got the tooth out of the drain—that and a bunch of Barbie shoes."

"What? Why would you do that? The popcorn scam was good enough for Ashley."

"Maybe. But not for me."

I blow upward, lifting dust and my bangs off my forehead. "So what are you saving our teeth for?"

"I don't know."

"Were you planning on giving them back to us someday?"

It's starting to get painful again. My prolonged presence here—my voice, my talk, my critique of sacred family legends—it's a familiar, awful tide rising around my mother. She doesn't want to panic at the high water, but she's starting to thrash. She says, "I can't give them back to you. They're all mixed together now. How could I possibly know which teeth went to which daughter?"

"Right," I say. "It's too bad."

Mum's head jerks from side to side. "No, it's not too bad. I never meant to give them back. How could I hand them over after I waited all those years and went to all that trouble to get them from you?"

I frown. "Huh?"

"I will not argue about this. The teeth are mine, Heather. They were always mine. You girls only borrowed them. All the calcium in those teeth—every last crystal of it—was sucked out of these bones." Mum grabs her left forearm in her right hand.

I fold my arms. "Well, then tell me this, Mum. What am I supposed to do with our baby teeth after you're dead?"

The tide closes over Mum's head.

I need to say this anyway. "Mum, you are looking at the girl who is going to bury you and paw through everything you own after you die. I'm sorry but it's true. I've already done it for Ewan's mom. So tell me what you want me to do with these teeth while you still can. People leave instructions like that all the time. You'd be surprised. Don't think of it as morbid. Are you going to leave the teeth here in the jewellery box where I can find them? And then I'll tuck them into your coffin with you before we close it up for good? Would you like that?"

"It is none of your business, Heather."

My voice is cool and dark. "It is precisely my business. Someone is going to reckon with your tooth collection someday. You are not going to be here to guard it forever. You want to be noble and donate them to dentistry—give them to Troy's dental school?"

"No! Stop it. I'll just start swallowing them back into myself, where they came from. Maybe I'll swallow one tooth every day—at breakfast along with my iron supplement—until they're all gone, a hundred days from now."

I won't have it. My sisters are right about me. I am a monster—the monster this family will not stop demanding. I flick my thumb against the canister's lid. The vault is open. Mum is clamping her hand over the top, making herself the lid, tearing the canister away from me. She holds it tightly against her chest.

It's too late. A smell has escaped the canister and drifted into my face. I inhale it through my nose and mouth. The air passes into me and I taste it—the entire planet, saliva, gums and plaque, all the sugar and salts that were never quite swallowed away. It's our dead-taste—mine and my sisters'.

My knee buckles and I stagger backward, catching myself with both hands on the rim of Mum's dresser.

"Do you know?" I begin. "Mum, do you know what that smell is—what that taste is?"

Mum snaps the plastic lid back into place over our baby teeth. The tide is receding. She is stashing our teeth in the bottom of her jewellery box. "What taste? What are you talking about?"

I don't tell Mum what I've discovered inside the canister. I push myself away from the dresser and start up the ladder though I still don't have any wire. "Fine, Mum. You go ahead and swallow the baby teeth. It's your calcium, like you said. Fair enough. Take them with plenty of water."

Tina is fumbling with the latch on the front door, coming back into the house. She's at the top of the stairs now, stepping into our parents' bedroom as I pull my feet into the ceiling.

"Okay, here we go," she begins, "The guy in the orange shirt said this has got to be the right stuff."

She's speaking into a terrible quiet. Neither Mum nor I will look at her.

I reach through the ceiling to take the coil of wire from her, nodding as I read the label. "Great."

I disappear.

Below, Mum closes the box.

# Tina [19]

No matter how grown-up Ashley is, I can't stand seeing my little sister's mouth full of pins. These are dressmaker's pins with oversized rainbow-coloured heads like beads. Their cuteness doesn't make them any less scary.

I'm begging Ashley, "Hon, let me get you a pin cushion."

"As if you own a pin cushion, Tina," she answers through one corner of her mouth. "Doesn't Martin get everything professionally tailored?"

"Of course," I say, "and I can tell you real tailors always use proper pin cushions."

Ashley is starting to talk again, the pins slipping over each other between her lips.

"Never mind," I say to keep her quiet. "Go ahead and use your mucus membranes as pin cushions. Just don't risk talking anymore until you're done."

Daredevil Ashley is tacking up the hemlines of Meaghan's latest round of bridesmaid dresses—the caterpillar green ones. They could be worse. Heather and Suzanne insisted the dresses be ordered with tiny cap-sleeves instead of those corset-y tube tops everyone's wearing to formals these days. It keeps our bridesmaid quartet from looking too much like a troupe of back-up singers from a Las Vegas show.

Through the sticky little handprints on our enormous front window, my neighbours can see Suzanne standing barefoot on the marble top of the coffee table in the middle of my living room. Don't tell me they aren't watching. Everyone knows Martin and the kids and I make for—well—flamboyant neighbours. It's hard to look away, especially since the kids keep stealing the batteries out of the remote that closes the fancy, automated window blinds to use in their wireless video game controllers.

Suzanne stands perfectly postured in her stiff, shiny cocktail dress. It's a more boring show than the neighbours are used to, but it's a pretty one. Everyone knows Suzanne's got the best legs of any of us. Still, she's leaning forward, trying to see her hemline, nervous Ashley might pin it across the widest point of her calves and make her look dumpy.

I just had a baby. I'd hate to know how Suzanne thinks this dress makes me look.

Ashley plucks pins out of her mouth, one by one, as Suzanne slowly turns in a circle. "Go put it on, Heather," Ashley says.

I shush her again.

"I will." Heather's dress is still zipped into its garment bag, right where it's been since I tossed it across her lap.

"Come on," I cheer. "You can't look any more seasick

in your dress than I do in mine." I'm frowning at myself in the mirror hanging over our spectacular, custom-built fireplace. We paid Durk a fortune to build it into our living room a few years ago, when their masonry business was new and about to go broke already.

This sheet of fancy framed glass was expensive enough, and it may have been a solid design choice, but having to look at it all the time does not make me happy. I should have hung that oil painting of a schooner over the mantel, like Mum suggested. I get stuck here at the mirror sometimes, looking at my face in the horrible natural light coming through the window. There are two bloodless scars between my eyes—marks of all the scowling I've done. I hate getting shots, but it might be time for some Botox. Maybe I'll ask Suzanne to come with me. There are always resources set aside in their household budget to be spent on looking fabulous. And someone needs to get her in private and have a talk with her anyways. Something about Suzanne is off. She looks kind of awful lately—awful for Suzanne, I mean. Nobody would notice but us.

Here's the scene in my living room. Meaghan is late. Heather, rightly paranoid about the neighbourhood's armchair voyeurs, is changing into her dress in the bathroom. Suzanne and Ashley have reversed roles, and now Suzanne is on the rug pinning Ashley's hemline, kneeling on the metal points sticking out of her own dress like it's mortifying medieval penance. I am standing in front of the mirror, smoothing my forehead with my fingertips.

Bathroom, table, mirror, rug—that's how we're po-sitioned when Meaghan bursts through my front door. Heather hears the noise and trots out of the bathroom, groping for the zipper lost between her shoulder blades. Meaghan skids to a stop on my new hickory flooring and scans the room as if she's counting us, making sure we're all present.

Cue the drama.

"Stop," she says. "If we leave the tags on and stop the alterations right now, we might still be able to return the dresses."

"You're going to cancel another wedding? As if, Meaghan."

"What? Not again."

"Honey, what happened?"

Heather is talking louder than anyone. "Nothing. Nothing ever happens. I'm sure if we keep calm we can work it out this time."

Meaghan takes three steps backward, retreating be-tween the balustrades of the curved stairwell behind her, as if we've chased her there. "What is the matter with me? What did you guys do to me?"

What did we do to Meaghan? No one says a word in our defence. Ashley takes Meaghan by the hand, carefully tugging her down the stairs. "It's okay, sweetie. Come sit on the couch and tell us what he did."

Meaghan won't hold Ashley's hand. "Ian? He didn't do anything. It's not Ian's fault I want out of it. Ian is fine."

I cluck my tongue. "Then it's the fault of your new boyfriend—the guy you brought with you to the parking lot the day you showed me and Martin the pictures?"

Suzanne has seen him too. "The guy with the beard?"

Ashley has missed this development. She's squinting. "New boyfriend?"

"Huh? No," Meaghan says. "No, this is not about a man—any man."

"Then cancelling the wedding is all about you?" I say, because on Mom's 1980s soap operas, that was the line that usually went along with a dumb declaration like the one Meaghan's made.

She raises both of her hands and shakes them at us, the angriest jazz-hands ever. "No. It's not me either. It's you. It's all of you."

Heather is bossing. "Meaghan, sit down."

"Look at you," Meaghan says, stepping through the four of us, moving to stand against the fireplace. "Look at all of you in your matching dresses and your matching everything. Don't any of you realize why I've wanted to get married so badly, ever since I was a tiny little girl? It has nothing to do with men. I wanted to get married so I could be one of you. On my own, you keep me outside. You keep me out. I need to find a man so you'll let me in."

Heather reaches behind her own back, finds the pull of her zipper, and lets her dress split apart and fall to the ground, crumpling like a shed green skin at her feet. She's standing in my living room, in front of us and the neighbours, in her slip—yes, in a slip. Leave it to Heather to be fully dressed even after stripping off her clothes.

"Oh, so you don't want us in the matching dresses you ordered anymore?" she says, stepping out of the ring of green fabric, advancing. "Fine. What's the problem, Meaghan? Is it your birth order? Don't like being last? Well, try being the one flying off the front of the birth order. Try being the one left to hold the door closed."

The last bit doesn't make sense. Ashley tries to laugh it off. "What?"

Heather won't laugh back at her. She waves her bare arm to where Suzanne and Ashley and I stand, our dresses still zipped around our torsos. "There's the inner three. They're the core sisters, the *real* sisters. In every way, I am just as off-centre as you, Meaghan."

"Yeah, right."

"You don't remember," Heather continues. It turns out it's fairly easy for someone wearing nothing but her underwear to keep the floor in a heated discussion. "You don't remember my university holidays, when instead of hanging out with me, the three of them would take off together with whatever bunch of boys they were into at the time. They'd leave you and me at home. They wouldn't bother to make excuses for it. They'd just go."

It's ridiculous. "Whatever, Heather. Meaghan was way too young to go out with us," I say.

"Hear that?" Heather asks Meaghan. "You were too young. And me—I was just too much."

I've had enough. I keep my clothes on but I say, "Heather, don't act like you wanted to hang out with a bunch of high school kids."

She shakes her head. "It's just one example. I spent years on the outside as the only married one, the one with kids—"

"You didn't have to. Those were your choices," I say.

Meaghan huffs. "Hey, why is this about Heather?"

"Yeah. What about me?" Ashley says, not laughing anymore. "You guys all went to college after high school. You're all married to professionals. Sure, you dabble in working, when you feel like it. But you're all living pretty much as kept women while I work my ass off lifting bricks all day."

I snort. "Yes, I agree with Ashley. There is a class distinction in the family—only it's not her problem. It's mine."

Heather sneers. "You and old-money Martin are unhappy with your class, Tina? Aw, I think I might burst into tears."

"Cry your eyes out, Heather. But there is a class distinction here, and it works to keep me isolated. I mean, look at the way you guys won't come to any of the corporate charity events I work so hard to plan."

Ashley throws her head back, laughing again, but uncharacteristically ugly and obnoxious. "You mean, your parties at the Hotel Macdonald? I can just see me and Durk there. Which pair of shoes should Durk wear to your high society charity events, Tina? His steel-toed boots or his fair-trade handwoven flip-flops?"

This might be the very worst kind of sisters' meeting—the kind where everyone is telling the truth. I hate them when we're like this. I hate me when we're like this. I hate the sound of my own voice saying, "Who said anything about high society? They're *my* parties and you guys totally boycott them, like it shouldn't matter to me—like it doesn't kill me to be left alone in that fussy hotel trying to please all those horrible, horrible people pretending to be Martin's friends."

Meaghan is going back to the beginning. "I'm not talking about being left at home. And it's not the differences in our schooling or work or class or anything like that. None of you will have thought of this." Everyone waits while Meaghan takes a breath. "I knew being married wasn't going to be enough. I wanted to be married the same way all of you are married. I want to be married, but without a mother-in-law."

Suzanne groans.

"Except for Suzanne," Meaghan hurries to say. "We all know Suzanne is the exception that proves the rule."

Suzanne is quiet now, but she looks sick and trapped, cradling her stomach. Something about her reaction is ominous enough to make me feel it in my own gut. Either she's working up some disgusting, excruciating digestive condition, or something else has gone wrong.

Now is not the time to ask if Suzanne is okay. Her problems fade into the queue. "Wait. Meaghan, wait," I say. "The day you and Ashley showed Martin the kissy pictures—I'm sorry, I don't think I ever explained the rest of it. Martin's mother isn't—"

It's not the right time for me to mention this either. Meaghan interrupts. "So making sure I didn't have a mother-in-law meant I couldn't stay with Ian, a mama's boy. And then I met Riker—"

"Oh, Riker," Heather bawls. "Riker the sci-fi, orphan shop-keeper—that's your new boyfriend?"

Meaghan is sniffling now. "No. But he told me the first day I met him that his mother was dead. And I fell for it. And then I let myself get involved with him—emotionally, I mean. I didn't cheat on Ian, not really."

Ashley is handing her a tissue, pushing Meaghan's hair away from her eyes. "Aw, honey."

"Only, you were right, Heather," Meaghan says. "Riker's mom isn't dead. Of course she's not. He made that up because I said his real life story must be lame and clichéd—which it is. And then I saw her, his mom, someone's future mother-in-law. I heard her voice. She's alive."

Though she's right about Riker's mother, Heather's only movement toward gloating is a faint shake of her head. I'll say one thing for her, she takes no pleasure in calling us out. She never does.

There's no need for Meaghan to cry. Ashley and I both know it. We're talking at the same time, cooing like a pair of pigeons. We drape ourselves around Meaghan. Behind us, Heather is stepping back into the closest clothes at hand, her green dress. Suzanne doesn't move to help her with the zipper.

"Sweetheart," Ashley says. "You don't know this but I do have a mother-in-law. Durk's bio-mom showed up a few weeks ago. It's a long, painful story, so we haven't been talking about it. She's a total mess. She got herself arrested after crashing her car on the Henday, and now she's doing a court-ordered stay in a residential addictions recovery programme."

I get it. "Rehab?"

"I guess," Ashley says. "Durk has been visiting her at the facility. We've agreed to let her come to dinner on his birthday, after she gets out."

It's the first I've heard of Ashley's mother-in-law. Heather seems to know all about it. The traffic cops at the car accident must have told Ewan the details. There's no way Ashley went through that ordeal without mentioning her family connection to Ewan.

I like stories like the one about Durk and his mom—stories where people give each other chances they don't deserve. I've seen the scars on his hands. In a world that's fair, Ashley's mother-in-law shouldn't get to see Durk ever again. But when it comes to family, what does what we deserve have to do with anything?

"And," I'm saying when Ashley's done, "it turns out I have a mother-in-law too."

Meaghan already knows the real connection between Martin and the socialite who died in the Bentley. But she's made the same mistake I made, assuming Martin's real mom must be just as dead as his wicked stepmother. When I tell her Martin's mom is alive, Meaghan trips backward. "So suddenly, both of you have mothers-in-law. And Suzanne still has May, of course."

Suzanne drops to sitting on my couch, bending over her churning stomach.

"So what about you?" Meaghan asks Heather. "How are you going to resurrect your mother-in-law? I was at the funeral after Ewan's mom died. I saw her urn. I saw Ewan crying and saluting in his fancy police uniform."

Heather flicks her Smurfette hair, saunters to the fireplace, pauses. When she stops at the centre of the hearth, she wrenches the big topaz ring from her right hand.

"I have no mother-in-law? Well, what about *that*?" Heather clinks the topaz onto the mantel.

"Did your mother-in-law give you that?" Ashley ventures. "I thought she died broke."

Heather tosses her head again. "Oh, she contributed to it alright."

Heather's gaudy ring—it's been a puzzle to me. It's not Ewan's taste and it's too big and ostentatious for everything Heather does, yet it's on her finger all the time. I've been wanting to take a good look at it for ages. I lift the ring from the mantel, holding it in the all-seeing afternoon sunlight of my big dirty window. Martin is good for some things. He's taught me about gems, making sure I understand the value of the gifts of affection and apology ordered for me in his name by his secretaries. Heather's ring is unlike any of those. It's perfect, symmetrical, glassy clear.

"This is a synthetic stone," I say.

"Yep."

"Where are we going with this?" Ashley asks, though

this is Heather's story and she should know all Heather's stories end up in a graveyard.

Heather resumes. "None of you has ever run a funeral before. Right? So odds are none of you has ever seen those glitzy brochures from companies that transform cremated human remains into gemstones." Heather says it like it should explain everything.

Maybe it does. I tilt the ring, flashing its stone in the sunlight. "This rock is your mother-in-law?"

"Yes."

Meaghan cringes. "Gross."

Ashley pounces. "Let me see it!"

Heather rolls her eyes. "It's just a tiny bit of her. We buried the rest. I charmed Ewan into waiting in the car with the kids while I went into the funeral home to sign the release form for the cremains—the cremated remains, the ashes, whatever laypeople are calling them these days."

"Cremains." I repeat the word. It sounds like a cute cheesy trade-name Martin would invent.

"Anyways," Heather says, "on my way out of the funeral home, I sneaked into the ladies' room, pried the urn open with a nail file, and skimmed off the tablespoon I knew they'd need to make the ring."

"You went right inside the urn?" As the girl who sat in the Bentley of death, I need to know.

Heather shrugs. "I had to. And then I mailed the tablespoon of cremains to some company in Arizona. A few months later Carol's memorial diamond was couriered to our front door while Ewan was at work."

Suzanne speaks. Her voice is weak, like I expect it to be after seeing her looking so sick to her stomach. It's also ragged, like her throat is sore. "You never told Ewan about it? You kept it from him?"

Heather frowns. "It doesn't concern him. In the end, it does not concern him. I always wanted Carol and me to have a relationship of our own, without him—not always a triangle, just a straight line."

Suzanne coughs, cupping her hands over her face.

Heather looks hard at the top of Suzanne's bowed head, speaking over the coughing. "Oh, don't act like I'm a bad person," Heather scolds. "It's not like I didn't stand back and let Ewan have his own grief. He had access to all of Carol's death rites he could stand. I wanted a little more. I wanted this. Maybe someday I'll slip over to the cemetery and bury the ring under the sod with her. But not yet."

Ashley and I have finished inspecting the ring. Meaghan is holding it at arm's length, pinched between two fingertips like a snotty tissue.

"Stop it. She's perfectly sanitary," Heather assures us. "Everyone's much cleaner after cremation than we ever were before it. And remember the gem's not a topaz. It's a diamond—you know, hard, sparkly carbon. They say everyone's memorial diamond comes out a slightly different colour, usually somewhere in the yellow-orange family. If people don't like it they can pay extra to have it treated so it comes out blue or green or something that looks a little less like urine crystals."

It's classic Heather—telling us how clean and sensible something is long enough for it to get filthy again.

"So how did you explain where the ring came from to Ewan?" I ask. I didn't think Heather and Ewan kept secrets. Maybe Ewan doesn't.

She grins at me. "I told him it's a present from you, Tina. You gave it to me on my thirtieth birthday. Okay?"

I nod. "Sure."

"Look, I didn't mean to freak anyone out," Heather says as she puts her mother-in-law back onto her finger. "I just wanted to explain that, yes, I've kept my mother-in-law in my life for my own reasons and in my own way."

Meaghan doesn't know what to say anymore. So she laughs, no happiness in it.

It's sad and prompts Ashley to start gathering Meaghan's hair like she's about to braid it, talking sweetly over her shoulder. "It's okay, honey. See, it's easy to be one of us. And it's a big relief for us to hear this was about something silly like mothers-in-law. Heather had us worried it was serious. She had us thinking you felt left out of our sisterhood because you're scarred from your abortion."

Our tidal wave of truth-telling breaks and crashes. The room is doused cold.

"My *what*?"

Ashley drops Meaghan's hair.

Everyone looks at Heather. She's a monster so she doesn't back down but steps out in front of everything. She speaks softly, as if she means to be tender. But she still says, "Come on, Meaghan. You're standing here telling us you've never had an abortion?"

We each stay rooted to wherever we were when Ashley first said "abortion"—a word none of us has ever spoken in Meaghan's presence. We're locked in our tableau so long the neighbours might get bored and go back to their Sudoku. It's so quiet in my living room we hear the little girls in the upstairs bedrooms talking to their dolls about dating and weddings. It's so quiet we hear the click in Meaghan's throat as she starts to speak.

"I was only seventeen. Mum said it would be better."

Heather turns away in something like a slow, tortured pirouette. "I knew it."

"I can't believe Mum told you guys."

"Mum didn't have to tell us anything," Heather says. "We are your sisters, Meaghan—the sisters you're so much a part of you can't hide things from us. At least, not something as big as a pregnancy, terminated or not. No one told us. But we *knew*. We've been mourning with you all along." The monster's voice cracks. "And you must have known that."

Suzanne lets go of her stomach. She stands and folds her arms around Meaghan's neck. "Oh, my girl ..."

Meaghan bows her face into Suzanne's shoulder, and sobs. It's grief and pain, and it's relief too—relief that this news isn't the shock Meaghan dreaded it would be. We have known. She has not revealed herself to us. We have revealed ourselves to her.

Like I keep telling Martin, part of what makes secrets so bad is that they don't curb any hurt. Whatever we think our secrets are holding back, someday it'll go flooding off in every direction—forward and backward like fruit punch spilled on a tabletop. It'll spread out from the moment it's shared, filling up the past with every ounce of red sticky agony that belonged there in the first place.

Arms and tears and a little more quiet time are called for here. Pacing is vital in everything, our sisterhood too. We take our time until a slow, careful pace tugs us forward.

With the heel of my hand, I swipe at my eyes and nose. I am going to speak into this quiet. I am not going to tell Meaghan that what happened to her when she was seventeen doesn't matter. That would be cruel. I am not going to say we don't feel the pain of it ourselves. That would be more cruel.

All I say is, "Okay, okay." I kiss Meaghan on the face. "Let's fix what we can fix. Something easy, like, what are we going to do about the bridesmaid dresses?"

Meaghan blows her nose and slides her smeared glasses back onto her face. "Dresses? I don't want to talk about dresses. I want to talk about Riker. I think I might really have something with him, even though his mom is alive—"

"Stop," I say. "Stop playing dumb in-law games and go find the beard-guy, if that's what you really want. Tell him you need a man with a real, living mother so you can be like your nasty old sisters after all."

"Or go back to mama's-boy Ian," Ashley says. "They're both exactly the same when it comes to their moms. You can pick whichever one you want. Right, Suzanne?"

Suzanne clears her throat. "Sure."

"But I'm having dinner with Ian's mom tonight," Meaghan says. "I'm supposed to be there in forty minutes. I have to decide."

"No, you don't," I interrupt. "We've given each other a hell of a lot to think about today and none of us is in any condition to be making big decisions."

Ashley's nodding. "Yeah, just let it ride for a few days."

"But get away from these dresses. Your love of lime green is confounding your judgment," Heather says. She spins Meaghan around, shoving her toward my front door as I mash Meaghan's purse into her arms. It's an awful handbag—cheap, wrinkly, pink like a goat's stomach, and I'm always happy to get it out of my house.

"Just go to Ian's mom and act normal for now. Don't promise them anything." That's what Heather says as she pushes Meaghan through the door and leans against it to close it.

"She should stay with Ian," Ashley says.

I'm reaching for my zipper. "The fully-employed computer tech guy with the sweet high-rise condo? Oh, definitely."

"Ian, Riker, a single life," Heather says, "whatever gets me out of this dress."

# Meaghan [20]

Ian's mother is tall for a woman. She verges on a height that would be tall for a man. She might be taller than Ian himself. I've never stood them back-to-back and measured. It may take a few years, but his mom will outgrow Ian eventually.

These are crazy thoughts, and I wobble my head to clear them away. Still, it's true that somewhere in her late middle age, Ian's mom surrendered her secondary female sex characteristics. They slipped away, leaving her voice low, her skin rough and fuzzy, her clothes hanging from her shoulders, skimming her body as if she's made of coat hangers and pipe cleaners. She's let them go without a defiant show of copper lipstick or dangly earrings or converting her whole wardrobe to floral prints. Right now, she's dressed in a huge, un-dyed hemp blouse, and she's standing with me, her future daughter-in-law, in the wet heat of an immaculate backyard greenhouse.

I am exhausted. The dress fitting at Tina's house was as draining as it was doomed. In this day of revelations, maybe Ian's mom will pull the bobbed grey wig off her head, flip the last of the Kleenex out of her bra, and show me she's actually Ian's dad now, not his mother at all. It could happen. If it did, I'd have to pretend to be shocked.

It's possible that I will never be shocked again. Look at what just happened at Tina's house. My sisters and I could confess anything to each other and none of us would ever say, "No, I can't believe she did that—not her." I could hear them accused of anything and I'd never throw myself in front of them saying, "No, she wouldn't do that. She's not capable of that. She's not that kind of person."

Don't misunderstand. I'd still throw myself in front of them. I'd just do it without a word.

Anyways, evidence like that—character evidence— doesn't mean much at the police station or in court or anywhere. I've never been to court or a police station, but that's what Ewan tells us. Technically, good character evidence is supposed to help when people are in trouble, but practically, it doesn't. And it shouldn't. How could anyone give that kind of evidence in good faith? It's when we get closest to each other that we see the tiny pores, the little gaps, the micro-chinks in our characters where anything could seep inside or leak right out—where anyone could shrink or swell to anything.

None of this is what I want to be thinking as I stand in a tiny suburban greenhouse, pinching oregano leaves off twiggy plants and dropping them into an ice cube tray. Thoughts of my sisters will sap my strength, and thoughts of Kleenex in my future mother-in-law's bra are just weird. What if this is the beginning of the obsession

I need to cultivate if I want to be a good daughter-in-law, like Suzanne?

But wait—my sisters say they're all daughters-in-law now. They've ruined the game, trumped everything, flipped the board.

"Get the bottom of each section covered with leaves," Ian's mom instructs me, "and we'll fill the rest with olive oil and put them in the freezer. Then we'll have fresh-frozen, pre-portioned herbs at our disposal all winter long."

"It's perfect," I say. And I mean it. I might like to grow up to be a tall, clean, brilliant man like Ian's mom someday.

My fingertips smell like oregano—casseroles and spaghetti sauces. When I sniff them I wish it was closer to dinnertime. Being hungry makes me think of Riker. Even inside the greenhouse, I wish I knew what my face looked like that afternoon at the video game store when Riker acknowledged his mom, right in front of me.

"Are you tired today, dear?" Ian's mom asks.

I try to shake my head but the movement gets cramped in my neck, more like a twitch. "No—I mean, yes."

Ian's mom laughs, but not unkindly. My awkwardness has always been darling to her.

"I guess I'm hungry, more than anything," I say.

She is happy to explain that a good greenhouse is the very best place for hungry people. She plucks a pickle-sized cucumber off a vine covered in bristles almost like thorns. "Here," she says. "Rub the little spines off the skin with the palm of your hand and eat this up. Go on.

It's delicious. Think of it as a juicy green candy bar. And it's organic, so we don't have to wash it."

"Perfect," I say again. I bite into the fruit, remembering her telling me that, in the orthodox botanical sense, cucumbers are fruit, from the melon family to be precise.

"Perfect," Ian's mom agrees. Something moves on the other side of the Plexiglas wall. "Oh, here comes our boy."

The view of him is warped and cloudy, but a man in a purple dress shirt and white tie is strolling across the lush, green lawn. Even through the plastic, I can tell his face, as always, is shorn smooth and red. It's Ian.

My stomach clenches against the warm cucumber. It's no longer a vegetable or a melon. It's not food at all. I can't swallow any more of it without being sick all over the greenhouse.

Ian's mom is watching me. "Meaghan?"

I have to get it out. I cup my hand around my mouth, bending over, spitting a mouthful of half-eaten cucumber into my palm. "I am so sorry."

I can be inside something, part of something, someone. I know that now. But it can't happen here. I'm clawing at the metal clasp on the door, panicking, frantic to get out of the greenhouse before Ian comes in. "I'm sorry. Tell Ian—I'm sorry about everything."

He has come close enough to be standing right outside the greenhouse door. I shoulder past him, into the yard where I chuck the watery green mess from my hand into the long, thick grass growing against the plastic wall.

Ian sees it fly. It's disappeared into the grass. He keeps his eyes turned to where it's landed.

I stand panting, my arms folded, still spitting onto the ground. My saliva is thick, hanging in unbreakable elastic strings from my lower lip, like I'm a rare, evolutionarily ridiculous spider who coughs and dribbles out her web.

I'm within arm's reach of Ian, but he knows not to touch me anymore. His profile is all I can see of his face when I wipe my mouth and lift my head. And I can tell. I can tell he already knows.


Riker must be startled when I come banging on his front door. I bash the wood with the fleshy heel of my hand. I mean for the knock to sound aggressive—not the kind of sound that could be ignored as the approach of fundraisers or white-shirted missionaries out after curfew. I wait on the concrete front step in a street full of split-level houses until Riker throws the deadbolt and flings open the door. There I am—wide-eyed, freaked out, speechless in a suburb.

I don't know it yet but Riker's mom and his dad (who is also alive and well) are out at a junior league football game. They're reliving his dad's glory days, when he played for Scona in high school—tight pants and shoulder pads, sauntering across fields lumpy with night crawler mounds. I've heard Riker's theory about how sports are just sweaty macho cosplay. Maybe he hasn't explained it to his dad yet.

Riker is home alone, exactly as I'd hoped, standing

in the doorway with a can of his mom's awful American light beer in his hand, holding it clumsily, as if she asked him to hang onto it while she went to the bathroom.

He's standing tall instead of slouching toward me, like he usually does. He plants his sock feet in the centre of the doorway. He wants to be cold to me. We're enough alike for me to know there's no way he'll be able to maintain it. What he can do is be drunk, even if he's just started his first beer of the night. I can't tell how much he's had. There's an open can in his hand, his breath smells like alcohol, and he can invent the rest—the levity, the candour—if he needs to, he can exaggerate it. Don't act like we haven't all done it.

"Meaghan, come on in," he bawls. "Your timing is right on. My mom's already out for the night, so we won't have to go through our farce routine this time. You know, the one where I hide my mom from you, and you hide me from your fiancé, and—"

"Riker," I begin as I slip past him, coming into the house, closing the door behind myself.

"But I'll kind of miss the farce. You know what I mean? All that pretending—it was invigorating. You know, like we were actually important to each other— worth lying and shame and stuff." He steps backward, slumps against the banister until he's sitting on the bottom stair, gazing into the can in his hand.

I make a funny, phony coughing sound and twist the doorknob against the small of my back. "Maybe I should come back another time."

"No. No, it's awesome timing, like I said. Stay and tell me why you came."

Nothing I was thinking of saying to him while I was rooting through the Internet for his street address seems right now that he's so loud and loose. Instead, I say, "I've almost beat the dance challenges from the game you sold Ian."

Riker sneers. "No you haven't."

"Yes, I have," I say, taking a step forward, clearing a space around myself. "Watch me."

Of course he'll watch. I start to dance—jerky, stompy, bouncy—like a kid on one of those flashy, dance pad amusement park games. Everyone knows the only way to get through something as embarrassing as this is to own to it. I'm half-singing, half-humming a song while I hop and lurch in the front entryway of Riker's mom's house. All I really know of the words to the song is, "Pop that thang."

Riker mimes taking another swig from the beer can before he sets it down on the stairs and lolls to his feet. "Oh, I get it. It's para-para," he says. "Everybody loves para-para."

I stop dancing when he starts to sing. It doesn't sound like English, except for the way he keeps saying "Party time" and "Feel the power." The song gathers momentum, and he starts to dance along with it. His footwork is simple and clunky, like mine. He keeps his head motionless, his arms bending and unbending at the elbows, chopping through his personal space like he's signalling a ship.

I'm laughing. "You look like a cheerleader."

"Do I?"

"No, actually."

"It's just para-para. The point is precision and synchronization. Don't you know para-para, Meaghan?"

I've pressed myself against the wall, trying to stay clear of his choreography.

He scoffs. "It's Japanese nightclub line dancing. They do it in South Korea too."

"Oh. Of course."

"It doesn't make any sense when just one person does it. You're supposed to do para-para as a team, a perfectly harmonized team." He's starting the routine over again with a hearty, English "Party time!"

"Okay, Riker. I get it."

He doesn't stop. "Seriously, you should get your sisters together and form your own para-para team. Five is the perfect number for it. You'd need short skirts and some matching boots and a cute, catchy name for yourselves like 'Everlastingly Girls' or 'Go Team Happies.'"

He's starting to sound like one of my brothers-in-law. It makes me comfortable and brave. I've watched Riker dance until I'm able to decode the rhythm well enough to safely cut into it. I hop forward, like a little girl joining a skipping game, pinning his arms to his sides with my own. He's strong enough to break away, but he doesn't.

"No more," I say. "Shh. No more bearded hipster para-para, okay?"

"Huh?" he says as he stops moving between the margins of my arms.

"No more dancing—please. I need to talk to you, Riker."

This close to him, I can see there's no alcohol in his pupils. He knows it and stops pretending, starting to look scared instead. I keep my arms clamped around him as I begin to speak. "Your mom isn't dead."

"Clearly."

"And your major in school wasn't creative writing, was it?"

He shakes his head. "No, it wasn't. It's Canadian History, the interwar period."

That explains the Dionne quintuplets trivia. "But, Riker," I say, timidly now. "Like, your real name is Riker, isn't it?"

He smirks. "Yes. The weirdest parts of the story are always the true parts. I was really born in 1987, the year Jonathan Frakes got his big break on television. Riker was the name of his character—"

"I know," I interrupt. "Everyone knows. And Ian and I, we're over." I speak with my face so close to his my bottom lip touches the short, brown hair growing over his jaw as I form the final phoneme.

It's too much. He bends and kisses me.

I hate first kisses. I've never told anyone, but it's true. Every time, with every new person, I'm as clumsy and stupid as I was when I was fifteen. But Riker is careful and slow. He's slightly afraid, greatly awed, and he's worried I might taste too much of his mother's bad beer in his mouth. So when his kiss comes, it arrives as a question, not an answer.

I tip my face away from him. I want to make my answer with my voice. My hands cradle the back of his neck. And I tell him, "Yes."

# Suzanne [21]

We're a bit sad when Meaghan moves out of Ian's high-rise condo and into our parents' place. The engagement is broken not only for her, but for all of us. Ian was supposed to have been our normal brother-in-law. He was going to be our boring brother-in-law—not the sound-bite speaking crime fighter, or the pretty-boy detoxifying dentist, or the slippery millionaire, or the craftsman hippie. He was going to be the brother-in-law with a happy childhood and a stuffy job none of us understood very well.

Meaghan hasn't been staying in the spare bedroom of Mum and Dad's place for very long when Troy comes home from a Saturday afternoon of golfing and notices my phone vibrating on the kitchen counter.

I'm outside, standing on the lawn, my back bent in an awkward sweeping stoop as I finish the last of the grass clipping with a noisy electric trimmer. It's not hot anymore, but the grass is still growing. It's important to me to keep the tall, seedy stalks sprouting around the condemned barbecue cut low and neat and out of Troy's notice.

I don't see him crossing the lawn, waving my phone.

I can't hear anything over the high, hungry whine of the grass trimmer's motor. As I work, I'm playing my sister classification game again—not with soul colours or punctuation this time. Today, it's parts of speech, grammar, conjunctions. Meaghan would be "and," Ashley would be "but," Tina is "so," and Heather is "because." I'm just deciding I must be "if" when Troy taps my shoulder.

I squeal and twitch, whipping the trimmer's nylon flail against the brick-face. "Troy!" I exhale when I recognize him.

"Sheesh, Sue. Sorry. You've got a text from Meaghan," he tells me. "Looks important. She says your mom fell down the stairs and they're all gathering at the hospital."

My face blanches so quickly it hurts. "Mum? Is she okay?"

Troy sees I'm scared. In truth, he doesn't have anything to offer to reassure me, but he still says, "I sent back a message asking for details. No one's replied yet. But no one said she's not okay so—"

"It doesn't say she is okay either." I'm talking too loudly, dropping the trimmer onto the lawn, snatching my phone.

"Sue, you need to calm down," Troy tells me as I read Meaghan's message. "People fall down the stairs all the time without getting badly injured."

"At her age?"

"Sure. And then they head to the chiropractor in the clinic next door to mine, he fixes them up, and that's the end of it."

"And sometimes ladies like her fall down the stairs and wind up paralysed or—dead."

Troy catches my arm as I'm rushing past him. "Suzanne, calm down. Your mom didn't paralyse or kill herself."

He's feeling for an acupressure point in my wrist but I tear my arm out of his hold. "You would say that, wouldn't you Troy?"

"Suzanne," he calls after me. "Let me drive you to the hospital. You shouldn't go out into traffic when you're upset like this."

"I am not upset," I yell to him, over my shoulder. "At least, I won't be as soon as I see for myself she's okay. You need to stay here and watch the kids for me while I'm gone."

My pulse is crashing behind my temples as I drive to the hospital. I'm still able to navigate the complicated exchanges, in and out of fast, dense traffic. Maybe Nurse Suzanne has surfaced to take the wheel.

As she drives, my memory is working, flipping pages, skimming records, scanning for references to my mother—some testament of her strength or hardiness. I find something—not quite my mother's image but close. It's Tina, in her own house, between pregnancies, pink-faced, punishing Martin for something she won't fully explain to us. He's away on a business trip again, and she's determined to drink an entire bottle of his best, most expensive Scotch before he gets home.

"Hey, you don't give whisky to the baby sisters,"

Heather scolds as Tina pours shots for Ashley and Meaghan. "What's the matter with you? If the point is to mortify Martin, just flush it down the toilet."

The three of them laugh, hissing fumes into our faces. It's goofy enough for Heather and me to be standing to leave when Tina stops us, clawing at our sleeves, ranting about Mum.

"Girls, wait. It's important. My kids discovered that show—that old cartoon about the giant robot."

Heather yawns. "Sweetie, all cartoons are about giant robots."

Tina shushes her. "Do you guys know it? It looks like it's from Japan, I think. It's got that look. And it's about a giant robot made out of five other robots all stuck together. Five. It's the most powerful machine ever."

Meaghan knows the show and hums something that must be its theme song. "Defender of the universe!" she sings.

Tina flaps her hands. "Ssh. Yeah, this robot takes care of the whole universe. It's, like, the ultimate mother of everything—fix you, help you, save you." Tina stops to nod at us. "Get it? Do you get it, Heather?"

Heather piles both of Tina's hands between her own. "Tina, honey, it's late and you reek and you're—"

Tina extracts her hands. "We are that robot. All us girls—we're five things stuck together to make one super-thing."

Ashley throws her arms around Tina. "Aw, nice."

Tina is reaching, gripping my wrist and Heather's

in each of her hands. "No, it's not nice," she says. "You know why we have to make the super-thing out of ourselves? You know, Suzanne. Tell them. Tell everybody."

She blinks at me, slow and drunk, no mascara, light brown eyelashes soft and straight like little-girl Tina's. I don't drink but that doesn't mean I can't understand why other people do. Sometimes, they do it hoping to be treated like children again. They want other adults to handle them with the same tender bemusement, sympathy, and pity normally reserved for noisy, naughty children. They want someone to take responsibility for them the way no one will when they're sober. They want the same thing they always want. They want love.

I turn up the palm of my free hand to show my drunk sister it's empty. "Sorry, sweetheart. I got nothing."

"Tell them, Suzanne," Tina insists. "Tell them it's because there's no super-thing in our universe. There's nothing much to mother us. Our mother—no, she always says it wrong, makes us lonely, takes us apart."

Ashley seems to understand. She keeps one arm around Tina as she grabs at Meaghan, pulling her to where the rest of us are crowded together, hands and arms fitting in and around each other like plugs in sockets. I give in, cupping the crown of Tina's head with my palm. Heather plays along too, patting Meaghan's back, adding percussion to the cartoon robot's theme song the girl won't stop humming.

"We have to build it out of ourselves," Tina calls over the humming and thumping, "because there's too much space and she can't come near us."

Outside the Grey Nuns Hospital today, Nurse Suzanne finds a place to park in the crowded lot, moves through the motions of paying at the meter, like a good citizen.

Nurse Suzanne looks like every other woman walking through the hospital atrium to the information desk. She doesn't storm the clerk and demand to see Mum. She smiles, waits patiently to be told where to find her. When the clerk doesn't say, "In the morgue," she doesn't let out a huge sigh or anything so dramatic. She just says thank you and heads for the elevators.

Maybe Nurse Suzanne can't exist when there's no one around to see her. Even if it's just the other drivers on the Whitemud Freeway, someone has to be able to see her or she can't be real. There's no one else in the elevator when it lands on the main floor. When Nurse Suzanne steps inside and its doors slide closed, she is cut off from her audience. She dissolves even in this small, brief bit of solitude and I fall into the elevator's wall. I slide downward until I'm squatting on the dirty floor. Against the wall, my breathing is loud and heavy. My hands have nothing to hold but each other.

# Tina [22]

There's no point freaking out when I find Suzanne down on the floor inside the hospital elevator. The doors clatter open, and there she is, head bowed into her knees. I see her before she sees me standing at the vending machines.

"Suzanne? Suze, honey, get up."

I step into the elevator to tug her to her feet. We don't clear the doors before they start to close, banging against me and bouncing back into the sides of the box.

"Hey, you look like you could use some juice," I say. "Take this."

"How is Mum?"

Suzanne is stunned, flattened and single-minded. I laugh—not because her fear is funny but because laughing will fight it off. "Mum is fine," I answer, latching my arm through Suzanne's. She is older than me, but not by much, born in the frenzy of the oh-so fruitful middle of our parents' reproductive career. It's weird for me to be guiding her along the hospital corridor like she's an old lady crossing the street in a 1950s Boy Scout manual. "Mum is fine," I say again. "But she did break her ankle."

Suzanne hands my bottle of juice back to me, un-opened.

I keep talking. "They say it looks pretty good for a break, but there's still a chance they might have to oper-ate. They're keeping her in here until she can bear weight on it, just to be sure."

Suzanne isn't saying anything, so I speak for her. "I know. I kind of spazzed out when I got Meaghan's text too. She's not the greatest communicator sometimes—sending out a vague, scary message like that."

"Yeah."

There, I finally got Suzanne to agree to something.

"Where is she now?" she wants to know.

"Mum? She's here, in room four. Dad's out of town, of course. Heather already phoned him. Don't worry. He's heading back—not that there'll be anything he can do once he gets here."

There's a nurse coming out of room four. He's a young, cute guy with fuzzy blond hair all over his bare forearms. He's carrying a capped, empty syringe. "Hey, look at you," he greets me. "You went and found another sister?"

I grin at him. "Yup. This is the last of us. All five ac-counted for."

"What? There are only five of you? That's a shame." He laughs and waves the empty syringe. "Well, you'd bet-ter hop inside and say 'hi' to Mom quick, before she falls asleep. We gave her a hand managing her pain, and it's already making her mighty drowsy."

None of us appreciates cute guys more than Suzanne, but she doesn't say anything to the nurse—doesn't even identify herself as a fellow member of their nursing sister—er—siblinghood.

I tow her through the doorway. Mum is in bed—safe, drugged, dozing. Heather is leaning into her face, way too close to Mum's closed mouth and eyes. "I think she's asleep already," Heather says.

"It's not just the drugs," I add. "She's probably exhausted from being in shock from her injuries, right Suze?"

We always defer to Suzanne's professional medical experience at times like this. She never gets uppity about it. She's smart, but she's still Suzanne, all sweet and modest. It's weird that she's got nothing helpful or reassuring to offer us today. Instead, she's got questions.

"How did it happen?"

Meaghan sighs. "You guys have heard me explain it three times already. Why doesn't one of you tell her?"

Heather sighs right back. "Because that would be a hearsay account, and it's not as good as an eyewitness report."

"What the hell happened?"

It's Suzanne—or, some kind of crazy version of Suzanne, yelling over their voices in the hospital room like an idiot. It's loud, but Mum doesn't twitch in her sleep, under the flannel blanket.

I've had enough. "Okay, Suzanne. You know how Mum always piles stuff on the stairs, so she won't forget to take it up with her?"

"Yes."

"Well, she forgot she'd left a stack of clean towels—"

"Actually, it was a pair of sandals," Meaghan interjects.

"Whatever. She'd left something on the stairs and then she forgot it was there and ended up tripping on it. It was a fall sixty years in the making."

"So anyways," Heather interrupts, as if I'm not telling it right. "Mum hyper-extended her right ankle and broke it trying to catch herself on her feet at the bottom of the stairs."

"I heard the crack all the way from the kitchen," Meaghan adds. "I'm just glad she didn't tumble down head over heels. It was really more of a slip with a bad landing than an actual fall."

"Yes," Ashley says. "Yes, it's a good thing Mum landed on her ankle and not on her neck. Isn't that right, Suzanne?"

Suzanne looks up from where she's been watching Mum revving up her snoring engines in the hospital bed. Across the room, Ashley is leaning against the wall. Her chin is tucked and her eyes are slightly narrowed as she watches Suzanne. I'm pretty sure that's considered glaring.

And I feel it—I think we all do. Ashley and Suzanne are the edges of two tectonic plates about to slip against each other. Something is shifting.

We can't stay like this. I'm talking again. "So, yeah, the ankle is in a cast under the blankets there. Maybe you want to take a look at it, Suzanne. They say operation or not, she should be totally fine in a few weeks."

Suzanne stares into the hospital bed.

"Smile, Suzanne," Meaghan says. She bats Suzanne lightly on the arm. "Mum is going to be fine."

"Be happy for her," Heather adds. "We've all heard her say she loves being in the hospital. It means she doesn't have to get dressed, or cook, or clean, or answer the phone."

Suzanne starts to cry. She's not crying with her breath but with her voice, sobbing like a kid.

"Hey, hey. It's alright." I put an arm around her but she hops away, retreating into the corner between the oxygen port and the window, raising a racket from the plastic vertical blinds.

"Okay, what is going on with you, Suzanne?" Heather moves to stand in front of her, taking that wide stance.

In the opposite corner of the room, Ashley is shaking her head. "It's time to tell everyone, Suze."

Suzanne raises her head, burbles, speaking through a sob, talking to Ashley as if the rest of us aren't here. "You know. Durk told you."

"Of course he told me. How could he stop himself from telling me?"

"When did he—?"

"Right away—the same day you did it."

Meaghan looks like she might puke. "Suzanne and Durk *did it*?"

"No!" Ashley and Suzanne answer in unison.

I'm shaking my head. "What are we talking about?"

Heather pounces. "Is this it? Is someone finally going to explain why Suzanne has been in mourning all summer?"

"Yeah, Heather says you're acting bereaved." Meaghan tells Suzanne. "And I think she could be right. But I can't imagine how it'd be true. My theory is you killed someone's pet. But Tina accidentally killed the cat that was sleeping in the guts of her car last winter and she says you'd be over that by now."

I did say that.

"So she figures it's got to be something worse—like a secret unreported car accident, maybe."

I gasp. "What? I never said that! I never meant it seriously, anyways. Sheesh, Meaghan. Shut up."

I can't face Suzanne. I look at Ashley instead—this strange seething, glaring Ashley. I've never seen her and Suzanne look so little alike.

"See," Ashley says, "they've been waiting for months, Suzanne. No one has any secrets—not for real and not for long. So how about I get your story started for you? Girls, this isn't the first time this year a lady we know has taken a bad fall down some stairs."

We wait.

Ashley scoffs. "Oh, come on. You're still not going to tell them, Suzanne? Fine. Girls, last spring—"

"Wait," Suzanne blurts. "Ashley—just—wait."

Suzanne is panting, struggling to breathe. "My mother-in-law—May—she fell down the stairs and landed on her neck. And she died."

"Seriously?"

"Yes."

"In Guatemala?"

Suzanne gulps at the hospital air. "No. She fell and died in my house, while Troy was at work, about four months ago."

# Suzanne                              [23]

I am braced against an onslaught that is not coming. Huffing, denouncing, swearing, slapping—that isn't it at all. My sisters' response to the news that my mother-in-law is secretly dead is restraint—cautious, slow, almost dense.

As always, Tina is the first to risk speaking. "Wait, Suzanne. If May is dead, how come we never heard anything about it? Are you sure—"

"She is dead. It's true. The only reason no one knows is because I purposely postponed telling anyone about it. Troy himself doesn't even know."

Ashley yells out a humourless laugh. "Postponed? You hid it."

"Shh." Heather leans forward. She's sorting through the archives of the criminology degree lodged in her head. She's in the abnormal psychology section, under "d" for delusional. "Suzanne, you're very close to your mother-in-law, and you haven't seen her for a long time now. That's got to be scary and stressful but—"

"She's dead," I interrupt. "She really is. It was an accident. And it wasn't my fault. It was even more innocent than what's happened to Mum today. It's not like I left tripping hazards all over the stairs. May just—slipped."

Heather taps her forehead. "You're trying to tell us May fell, died, and then, since no one else was in the house at the time—"

"What do you mean, 'no one else?'" Ashley tears in. "What about Durk? Go ahead, Suzanne, tell them what you put Durk through."

My head droops. I can't speak.

Ashley is talking, not speaking for me but against me. "Durk was crashed on Suzanne's couch that morning. He was still lying there when May fell. So Suzanne got him to help her move the body out of the house and drive it into the country to cremate it."

Tina snaps. "Oh, come on. The corroborating witness is Durk? So Durk told Ashley another crazy story. So what?"

There's an awful pause.

I break it before Ashley has to do it herself. It's the least I can do after all I owe her and Durk. "No. Believe him this time. Believe Durk. And I'm not deluded. I understand perfectly. May is dead. She's cremated. I did it myself. I made Durk help."

Heather pulls the hair at her own temples. "Oh, for the love of—I never should have let you visit me at work, Suzanne. I should have never told you about my mother-in-law's ring either."

"No," I say. "No, it all happened way before I knew there was anything strange about the ring. And it wasn't neat and sterile. There was no talc or lipstick. It was nothing like what you do at work."

"Yeah, Durk said they made the fire at a bush-party site, in the old gravel pit, with gasoline and pallets in the dirt," Ashley finishes.

"So why?" Heather says in a whisper-yell. "Why wouldn't you call the ambulance as soon as she hit the ground? The paramedics and the police would have come. Ewan could have been there. *I* could have been there handling everything properly, legally. Instead you're telling us you went mucking around committing indictable offences with Durk."

They're still talking like this isn't quite real, like it's still negotiable—"would have, could have."

I tighten my hands into fists. "This was my mother-in-law. This was the lifeblood of Daughter-in-law Suzanne. This was perfection. Perfection—I had it between me and May. I had it. I couldn't lose it."

Tina shakes her head. "Lifeblood—metaphors. Every time Suzanne's in a panic—"

"What she means," Meaghan takes up my explanation. "Is that Suzanne did—what she did—for the reason exactly opposite to why I imploded my engagement to Ian."

Tina scoffs. "Suzanne did it because she fell *out* of love with a video game store clerk?"

Meaghan swallows a calming breath. "Remember? I wanted to make sure I never had a mother-in-law so I could become just like the rest of you. But Suzanne—Suzanne wanted to make sure she kept her mother-in-law forever, no matter what, so she wouldn't ever have to be just like—"

There's no need to finish it.

Heather looks like she wants to hit me.

Tina is kinder. She takes my hand. She says, "Sweetheart, the five of us are not all the same just because we are all the same."

I sniff. "You're about to start with the giant cartoon robot again."

"Robot? What?" Our family's connection to the defender of the universe must have left Tina's mind when she threw up Martin's whisky in her kitchen sink. She doesn't remember—not in those terms, anyway.

She laces her fingers through mine and raises our hands, holding them between my face and hers. "Look. We're like five fingers on one hand. Separate but inseparable, all fused together at the roots—and better that way. See? It's okay. It's good."

I look where she tells me. I examine our clasped hands, turning them on the ends of our wrists. My sister's hand is whiter than mine, and rosier. But the symmetry in our hands' shapes is unmistakeable. Each finger, the palms and knuckles—the hands are not perfect, but the way they fit together, there's something sublime about it anyway. It's the fit that's perfect. It always has been.

My body is losing its rigidity. I sag at all my joints. My movement drags my hand out of Tina's grip. I'm slumping onto the hospital bed, falling next to Mum's casted ankle as she sleeps her deep, codeine sleep.

I hear Heather speaking as I crumple. "Okay, Suzanne, we get it. Your mother-in-law is dead. Troy thinks she's cleaning teeth in Guatemala but in reality, May is dead."

And with that, May is indeed more dead than she has ever been before.

My range of vision has shrunk. The blinds in the window, the signs taped to the walls, every one of my sisters has drifted out of scope. The only thing I have left to see is my body against this blanket, my thighs in mottled grey faux-ga pants with grass-stained knees, my hands empty and clenched.

There are arms around my shoulders. I am propped up, sitting. Meaghan's cheek is pressed to mine. She's saying something vague and sweet like, "Oh, my girl ..."

My sisters' hands smooth my hair, wipe tears from the sides of my nose. This time it's me. I am the one with the catastrophe that disrupts and devastates everyone. Birth, death, botched birth, botched death—anger is never my sisters' answer, never our answer to something so vast. This is our answer—a closed circle, arms and tears, time.

When I can see the rest of the room again, Ashley is still standing in the corner, arms folded. Heather is holding one of my hands. Meaghan is finger-combing my hair. Tina is settling a box of tissues into my lap.

She remembers her lines. "Okay," Tina says, "let's fix what we can fix."

"Right. First, the practical problems," Heather agrees. She is actually rolling up her sleeves. "Suzanne, where are

251

May's cremains right now?"

Ashley snickers. "You're going to love this. You know Troy's new barbecue, the one Durk built right where Suzanne told him to? The one the city condemned?"

"She's in there," I say. "May is packed inside a toolbox and bricked up in the barbecue."

"I don't get why Durk went along with it." Tina is addressing Ashley, not me.

Ashley snorts. "Suzanne got him to drink some kind of witch-doctor tea."

"I did not."

"It was yellow and fishy and unholy."

"It was a detoxifying infusion. Troy developed it himself. It's a cleansing, rehydrating, completely legal herbal remedy." This protest is a mistake. The witch-doctor tea story is a less bizarre explanation for Durk's cooperation than the real one—the one where I manipulate him, blending and shading the already smudged lines between Ashley and myself, tapping into that needy obedience he uses to redeem himself whenever he's let her down.

Heather is rubbing my hand between both of hers. "We need to figure something out. We can't erase this, but we can edit it—fix it up. Right, Suze? We'll find a way."

I'm pulling my hand from hers. "If you mean Ewan's way, the one where I walk into the police station with May's bones under my arm—"

"No, of course I don't mean Ewan's way," Heather calls over my voice. "There's got to be something else we can do."

There's another pause. And then, finally, someone says it. "Poor old May."

Yes, it's taken too long for someone to say it. But it's not because my sisters are without sympathy for May—the grandmother of their nieces, the noble humanitarian who fell to a quick, secret death on a set of wooden stairs she'd probably cleaned and polished herself out of love for me. Any sorrow, any grief my sisters have for May is crushed beneath something more pressing in their hierarchies of compassion. Everyone has a ranked order in which we're able to feel for people. It's the reason no one for thousands of miles was on the news talking about children in refugee camps the morning the World Trade Center collapsed. The toxic dust cloud that obscured my sisters from the pity they eventually found for May was their concern for stupid, sneaky me.

Tina raises one finger. "Suzanne's mother-in-law is supposed to be in Guatemala, right? And that's the country next to Belize, isn't it?"

None of us knows.

"Sure it is," she continues. "Now, Martin has been saying he wants to take his new mom on a reunion vacation. It's all garbage. He doesn't mean it, of course. But I can call his bluff anyways. I'll go ahead and book the trip. And I'll book it for Belize. Vacationing in Guatemala would be a stretch, but there's nothing suspicious about traveling to Belize."

Meaghan is figuring it out. "You could take May's remains with you on vacation to Central America. And then leave her right where she's supposed to be. So if someone finds her, so what?"

"Wait." I shake my head. "You can't just pack her up in your suitcase and walk past the sniffer dogs at the airport. You'll get busted."

"No, silly." Tina pushes my knee. "While I'm on vacation, I'll open a post office box in Belize. And then you can mail her to the box."

I gasp. "Can we do that? Can we mail charred human remains across international borders?"

"You mean, the same way I mailed my mother-in-law's ashes to the gemstone people in Arizona?" Heather reminds us. "Sure you can."

Dead stuff in the mail—it does happen. Troy tells about working in a university zoology lab as a summer student when a parcel arrived labelled "most of a mole."

Tina looks at her hands. "But it will be tricky for me to get away from Martin and his mom long enough to—handle things."

"Then take me and Durk with you," Ashley is saying. She may have been angry, but she's always intended to help rescue me anyway. "Suzanne can watch our kids while we're gone. Durk and I will make up some excuse to go off on our own in Belize, get as close to the Guatemalan border as we safely can, and then—"

"Bury her in the jungle?" I finish.

"But don't bury her too well," Heather says. "It's alright if someone finds her. If they do, Troy can have his 'closure' and a funeral. Things go wrong and people go missing in Central America sometimes—more often than they do way up here, anyways."

I'm still stammering protests. "What about the forensic stuff they can do with human remains now? Won't they examine her with microscopes and test her for pollens and dig out the last of the DNA in her big bones and find out who she is and discover she didn't really die in Guatemala?"

Heather rolls her eyes. "Forensics? I've told you this before, Suzanne. It's fiction. Those dark, blue-lit labs in TV shows where beautiful people agonize over one case at a time until they've unravelled it all and fooled the perpetrator into confessing everything in the interview room—it's not real life. That's not real police work. In real life, forensics labs are the same old understaffed government departments you see everywhere. They've got fluorescent light bulbs and staff in hairnets trained to be more concerned with closing files than solving mysteries. I mean, it can take Ewan months to hear back from the forensics lab on something as simple as a rape kit."

There is a list of horrifying words Heather and Ewan say more than any other people I know. "Rape" is on that list.

"But," I begin again, "but what if Troy goes to some Foreign Affairs department and demands a full-scale investigation?"

"Then he'll be working from inside Canada to get an investigation started in Guatemala on a body found in Belize. It'll be a dead end. The other governments will freeze up, juggle responsibility between them, offer some pat answers, and do everything they can to never talk about it again." Heather says it the way she says everything, like she's completely sure of it. She rotates her wrist to see her watch. "Honey, your mother-in-law is due at home in a couple months, right? When she doesn't come back, Troy is going to start asking questions. We need to take control while we still can."

"Is Mum really sleeping through this?" Ashley asks.

Everyone jumps. Tina leans close to Mum's face but Heather shoulders her out of the way. "Oh, for Pete's sake. Here's the test," she says. "Hey Mum, Dad says my lasagna tastes way better than the crap you make."

We brace ourselves. Mum doesn't stir.

Heather stands up, arms folded. "Oh yeah. She's asleep."

"Okay, so we mail—the package?" Meaghan says.

I shudder. "No. No, we can't be sure she won't go missing in the mail. And we can't very well write my return address on the parcel. Mail won't work. It's the worst combination of too unreliable and too traceable."

Ashley is getting mad again. "Come on, Suzanne—"

Tina raises a hand to stop her. "There is one route left," she says. "The sea."

# Tina [24]

Look, we are not sailors.

But we can pilot our big, dumb husbands. At first, Martin acts happy when he hears I've invited his new mother, the humble former mistress now retired to the suburbs of Guelph, on a reunion cruise to Belize. I get a big smile and a "Nice one, Peaches."

Then little by little, he realizes there's no way to escape coming along himself. Only after he agrees to come do I tell him the rest. It will be a private cruise on a chartered yacht with just the family and a small crew on board—no kids, not even our bottle-sucking baby. Martin cheers up a bit when he hears that. He starts to scowl again when I tell him the yacht sails out of Halifax, five thousand miles away.

"Tina, why in the world—"

Things get worse when I tell him I mean to drive with Ashley and Durk to southern Ontario to pick up my mother-in-law myself.

"Don't worry, Martin, I certainly don't expect you to slum it on a long car ride," I say. "You can fly to Halifax and meet us there right before we ship out."

It isn't enough. I have to spin some crazy story about postpartum depression recovery and instructions from my therapist and indulging my nostalgia for those long cross-country car rides Mum and Dad used to take us on when we were kids. I tell him road trips build relationships—say it's a reason my sisters and I are still so close despite the spying and squabbling and everything.

Martin keeps trying to squirm out of the trip right up until I mention how much he owes me after spending the winter having an affair with his sister.

"Well, it's cheaper than divorce court, right?" he laughs when he tells his downtown fat-cat cronies about our trip. That's how he describes everything important to me: cheaper than divorce court.

I know. The trip will probably go more smoothly if I don't force Martin to come along. It might be safer to reward him for paying for the yacht and its crew and the resort and all the drinks by granting his wish to stay home. But not everything is about Suzanne's bag of bones. Maybe I'd genuinely like to go on a vacation with my husband.

Before we leave, we all go to Suzanne's house while Troy is at the clinic. Durk comes with us. We are a demolition crew with sledge hammers, crow bars, a wheelbarrow, masks, and big plastic goggles to keep brick shrapnel out of our eyes.

In the weeks his mother was entombed there, Troy never looked closely inside the hole Suzanne bashed in the barbecue. He left it alone, and the hole stayed small and dark. The one time I looked into it a little spider with a spotty grey exoskeleton the same colour as the mortar had spun a cobweb over the open space.

The day of the demolition is in autumn, almost cold. The brick and cement are brittle and shatter on impact. We haul the barbecue down in one morning. We have to. Troy can't know about the demolition phase of the plan until it's finished. He is one of the more difficult of our husbands to pilot. There is no guarantee Suzanne could get him to agree through civilized marital negotiation channels, or the currency of sexual favours, or anything. Headlong destruction—it's an old family trick of ours, a way to avoid arguments and move right to asking for forgiveness. If Troy is angry about the barbecue, Suzanne won't lose much by apologizing for destroying it.

When the cleft in the bricks is barely large enough, Suzanne pulls the metal toolbox urn out of the barbecue, gingerly, like a live explosive.

Inside the house, she spreads a sheet of plastic on her bed and opens the toolbox. It's May like I've never seen her before—a few curved pieces of cranium, the knobs of hips and shoulders, ash, and some sand from the gravel pit where they cremated her. Suzanne empties all of it into an oversized plastic freezer bag and seals it shut.

Ashley and I kneel on the floor and tamper with the big green suitcase Ashley is going to be using as her luggage all the way to Belize. We sew the cremains—Heather's got us calling them that now—into the space between the suitcase's silky nylon lining and its thick, woven outer shell.

"You know, it's a good thing she's not broken up any finer or she'd look like cocaine," I say.

"You think being caught at a border crossing with cocaine would be worse than being caught with a burned up human body?" Ashley asks.

I smirk. "Probably depends on which border."

Hurricane season is over, Mum's ankle is healed, and our plan for taking care of Suzanne's mother-in-law is underway. Ashley and I have left to cross the continent, driving to the ocean, getting as close as we can to the Guatemala-Belize border.

Ashley's daughters are staying at Suzanne's house. No one's said so, but it's part of the penance Suzanne is doing for making Durk help her in the first place. The little girls' stay started as a giddy cousin sleepover but degenerated into a complicated system of alliances and power struggles, like a tedious reality television show that cannot be edited. Troy can hardly stand it.

"It wouldn't be so bad if there weren't so many girls." That's what he says, according to what Suzanne's written to us.

I fall in and out of sisterly love with Troy, over and over again. All in-laws spin in that cycle. This is one of the moments when I am in no way in love with him. But I do know what he means. Troy doesn't mind the girls fighting nearly as much as he minds them running to tell him about it all the time. The problem with raising boys is they don't pay enough attention to their caregivers. The problem with raising girls is they pay way too much attention to their caregivers. I'm not sure how we end up programming them to act that way, but there it is.

My kids are with our lazy nanny, snug and filthy in their own home. Mum is supposed to stop in once a day. She feels bad for me, being married to Martin, so she'll do favours like this sometimes.

Since we left, Ashley and I have been keeping in contact with the sisters at home through some superficially typical travelogue emails and the pictures we post on the Internet. Our messages are the same kinds of lame posts anyone would make, except for one thing. Somewhere, in every set of photos, Ashley's forest green suitcase has to be visible—safe and secure—included as a sign everything is still alright.

The first email postcard we send from May's secret funeral cortege comes from the Terry Fox Memorial in Thunder Bay, Ontario. The monument stands along the Trans-Canada Highway, a life-sized statue of a young man running on an artificial, metal leg.

"It's kind of gorgeous," I write. "The base he's standing on is all decorated in chunks of raw amethyst. The bronze statue looks impressive but they say the metal is actually mixed with a bunch of sawdust and stuff. Maybe that's just a rumour they spread to discourage anyone from stealing it to sell for scrap. Who knows?"

Jet-set Martin holds me to the promise of not making him leave with the rest of us in a rented SUV to dawdle through thousands of miles of wilderness. We drive to

Toronto without him. A few days into the trip, a grey-haired lady appears in the online photos with us and the suitcase. She shines out of the screen with the same sunrise smile as Martin's.

From Guelph, the four of us drive to the Atlantic coast through a blur of bad French, expensive gas, and roadside sandwiches.

When we arrive in Halifax, Ashley writes to the sisters at home. "They call this stretch of water the Northwest Arm, and it's basically a liquid parking lot for yachts. On the shore overlooking the whole thing there's this old, stone tower with two bronze lions sitting on either side of its entrance. At least, I think they're bronze. Tina says they must be mostly copper. She says you can tell because they're green now and not copper coloured at all. What kind of sense does that make?"

The sisters at home don't hear much from us once Martin joins us and we head out to sea. It's safer to stay away from land until we've got well beyond the United States with its rabid border security. They hate freezer bags. This quiet interval must've been hard for Suzanne.

"I wonder what they're doing," she'll be asking Heather, as if Heather knows.

And Heather will answer, as if she knows.

We hide from the cold spray for the first few days at sea. When we reach the lower latitudes we lie in the still, open air trying not to get sunburnt and fat. Ewan sent along books for us to study on the voyage—typical Ewan books, really gripping stuff about the native flora and fauna and fungi of Belize.

Finally, we veer close enough to land to post a picture from my phone. The entire frame is full of water—a whole horizon of water.

"This is the Bermuda Triangle," I write to my sisters. "Remember when Dad went to that convention in Bermuda when we were kids? Nothing here looks supernatural to me. I mean, I assume we're still on the same planet we started from, but really, looking out at a view like this, would we be able to tell?"

# Heather                           [25]

While Tina and Ashley take to their boat, the three of us left behind on the plains stay closely connected. We haven't spent this much time together since before I grew up and moved out of Mum and Dad's house. Today, we're gathered at Suzanne's house for dinner, in the middle of the week.

We need to talk. Out of a long taut silence, a new photo has appeared on our screens in Canada. It's of Tina, her mother-in-law, Martin, Ashley, and Durk waving from a sunny Caribbean pier by a marina full of white boats. They are in Belize. Ashley poses sitting right on top of the coffin-suitcase.

We sisters are not the only ones at Suzanne's dinner party thinking about the travellers. "Boy, I bet the weather on the equator today doesn't compare to this," Troy says to Ewan as they look out the living room window at the cold non-Caribbean sky sulking over our northern Alberta suburb. Poor old Troy. After what happened with his dad taking off with that Australian lady, he's got to be a bit touchy when it comes to family members sailing away without him.

Our excuse for having dinner together tonight is that Suzanne and I are trying to get better acquainted with Riker—the man so beguiling Meaghan trashed her engagement to be with him. Everyone knows a gathering of all five sisters at once is overwhelming for new boyfriends. I usually enjoy being part of something overwhelming, but I've settled for a quieter dinner with just two sisters instead of the full complement.

"Don't mind him if he tries to call you Yvonne and Annette after the oldest of the Dionne sisters," Meaghan has warned us. There's that slightly morbid quintuplet fetish again. I don't get it. Ewan and I looked up the quintuplets' story and it just seemed miserable to us.

Sitting in Suzanne's living room, balancing a plate of Meaghan's homemade, sloppy cheesecake that didn't set properly, Riker isn't calling us anything. He can hardly talk at all. This casual dinner party atmosphere is loose and unpredictable. Even while he's eating, Riker leaves one hand planted on Meaghan's body at all times—her shoulder or knee, the nape of her neck.

I don't believe in indulging shy people. Being shy doesn't make them happy. It doesn't make me happy either. So I interview them like I'm a talk show host, trying to get them to relax and say something charming. Everyone needs to learn how to hack out their own charm, and I am here to help.

Thanks to my kids, I can interview Riker about video games and Pokémon. I can add conventional old lady questions about where he went to high school, ask after any food sensitivities—because who doesn't love to disclose their food sensitivities these days?

Suzanne sucks at this, so she asks if he has a pet. Nope. He doesn't.

We're as polite and warm as we can be, and when Riker finally makes a little joke, we both simultaneously flick on our phony laughter. Our fake laughs are identical in pitch and timing and voice. It's creepy even to us. Meaghan shudders, probably contemplating throwing Riker over her shoulder and fleeing into the night. I can't let them leave yet.

"We'll be back in a sec," is all I offer as an explanation for dragging Suzanne away from her hostess chores and Meaghan away from her boyfriend's social angst. I clamp my hands around my sisters' wrists and retreat to the privacy of Suzanne's bedroom.

"I've thought of something," I begin as I shut the door, "something we need for things to unfold in a more natural way."

Meaghan groans. "Natural? He's really cool once you get to know him."

"No, I don't mean with Riker. I mean with—May."

They wince.

"No. No, everything's going well in Belize," Meaghan argues. "You saw the pictures of the suitcase. I know it's hard for you, but try to trust other people to get things done in their own way. Stay out of it, Heather."

I turn to Suzanne. "I've been living with a law-man

for ages. I can anticipate the questions that are going to be asked when May doesn't come home in a few weeks."

I can tell from the pink flares in Suzanne's skin that she knows she has to listen to me.

I say, "Troy needs to start worrying about why his mother has been out of contact for the last few months. His lack of interest is moving out of the realm of neglectful son behaviour and into the realm of suspicious son behaviour. And the remedy is for him to start asking questions, right now."

"But—but he doesn't have any questions," Suzanne argues. "He asks if we've heard from her every once in a while and I always tell him 'no.' And he just leaves it at that."

"You can't let him leave it. Pick it up and throw it back at him every time he tries to leave it. He has to look into what's happened to his mother before the officials do. If he doesn't, he'll seem like a brat at best and a criminal at worst."

She's accepting it. "So I have to get him to call someone—like, the Canadian Consulate in Belize."

"No!" Meaghan and I yell.

"It's the Canadian Consulate in Guatemala," I correct Suzanne. "No one has any idea there's a connection between May and Belize. As far as anyone knows, she never went farther than Guatemala."

"Gua-te-ma-la," Meaghan repeats.

Suzanne scrubs her face with her hands. "How am I ever going to do this?"

Meaghan grips her by both of her arms. "Think, Suzanne. You've already hauled your mother-in-law's dead body out to the woods and burned it up. The hard part is definitely over."

"Relax. I'll get you started, Suzanne," I say. "We'll go back in there and I'll help you get Troy to start thinking about something other than himself."

I shouldn't have said it that way. I know that. I always know. It's like that time I told Meaghan's high school boyfriend to get out of some of the shots when we were snapping photos on her graduation day. "Just so we can have some of Meaghan by herself for after you break up." I knew it was cruel, but he was no one's destiny and—that boy, he's lucky I never chased him down, spread his legs, and scraped his insides out.

Suzanne isn't mad. She's nodding and nodding.

"All you have to do is agree with whatever I say and look worried." I check Suzanne's face. "Yeah, exactly like that."

She catches my arm as I reach for the doorknob. "We're going to do it now?"

I push her toward the door so she can open it herself. "Yes. Think, Suzanne. We probably should have done it the minute Tina and Ashley docked that yacht. Go on."

I herd my sisters downstairs, driving them from behind. In the living room, I tackle Ewan into a chair so I can sit in his lap, right next to Troy.

"So how's your mom doing?" I ask Troy, interviewer-style. "Cleaning teeth in—it's Guatemala she's in this time, right?" I add, because it's not Belize.

Troy cocks his head. "Yeah, Guatemala."

"Gua-te-ma-la."

He shrugs. "It's going good, I guess. She loves it down there with the heat and the lizards and the poor people. Hey, we haven't heard anything from Mom lately have we, Sue?"

Once Suzanne starts talking, the things she needs to say come easily. And why not? They make sense and they're all true. "I told you, Troy," she says in a voice like the ones I've heard in hospitals, when someone's waking me up to give me a shot, "we haven't heard anything from her since she left. Not one word."

I sit up straighter in Ewan's lap. "Really? Nothing at all? How long has it been?"

My questioning sounds scripted and calculated, like our chorus of phony sister-laughter a few minutes ago. But in-laws talk to each other like this all the time. It's what happens in relationships where both candour and company manners are demanded at once. It's a paradox. And it's working.

Troy squints at Suzanne. "Mom's been gone for just about six months, right?"

"Yes. She's been gone since late last spring. But she'll be home for Christmas."

"Wow," I say. "No contact with her for half a year. You've got nerves of steel, Troy. I'd be worried sick by now."

Troy knows the long, silent absence should worry

him. He also knows it doesn't. "I don't know. No news is good news, right?" he ventures. "Mom's been down there twice before, so she knows where she's going and how it's supposed to work. Besides, no one's called here looking for her, right Suzanne?"

"Well, no," she says. "But May might not have given anyone our phone number. There might be hundreds of calls looking for her at her home number."

Troy strains against the upholstery of his chair. "No, there wouldn't be any calls at her place. She doesn't keep a landline anymore. Remember? She just uses that old pink flip-phone for everything. And I'm not sure what she did with it when she left the country. She could have it with her right now."

"I'm sure she's fine," Meaghan says. "Our mom never calls us either."

Troy is pulling his cell phone out of his pocket, flicking through his list of contacts, looking for his mother's number. The phone he's calling has been taken to a gravel pit and scorched and melted into the litter of broken glass and pallet staples. No one will answer. We know that. Yet my sisters and I wait, tense, as a recording is activated to offer Troy excuses.

"Voicemail box is full," he says.

"Well, there you go," I say. "The number is still in service, anyways. Now you know she's well enough to be paying the phone bill. Unless, she's arranged for the bank to withdraw the payment automatically."

Troy lowers his phone.

"Like you said, Troy," Meaghan goes on. "Your mom is an experienced Central American traveller and everything. She'll get her phone sorted out eventually. But just to be sure, if you really couldn't get a hold of her, who could you call to find out how she's doing—if you were concerned about it?"

"You'd call the aid agency she's working with," Ewan says, fingering the ends of a lock of my hair. "And if she hasn't checked in with them then you'd want the Canadian embassy in Guatemala."

"Right. Hey, why don't you make a few of those calls tomorrow, Sue? I'm booked solid at the clinic."

"Inquiries like that are always better coming from next of kin," Ewan says, weaving my hair between his fingers. His voice is calm and lazy, but the words are deathly. Only dead people have "next of kin." Ewan is acclimatized to function best in a heavy, doom-ridden atmosphere like this one, but all the extra gravity is pulling Troy into the floor.

"Alright, alright," Troy says, low in his chair. "I'll call them myself, first thing in the morning. But I wish I knew some Spanish. Do they speak any English at the Consulate?"

"Oh, for sure. English *and* French." It's the first spontaneous thing Riker has said all night.

# Ashley                                    [26]

How can it be this hot when there's still so much cold outer space between us and the sun? This is inland Belize, jungle Belize. It's drenched in thick, humid heat. I'm sheltered from it in a luxurious rented pickup truck, an air-conditioned glass and metal bubble riding over an engine and wheels.

"I don't want to go back out there," I say to Durk. "So hot. Maybe we could just roll down a window and empty it on the side of the road. People must scatter ashes like that sometimes. And Heather said to be sure not to hide her too well, right?"

Durk knows I'm joking but he explains anyway. "This is the main highway through here. It's no good."

I lean toward the windshield. "Highway? This is a track through a tunnel of trees."

Durk smiles. "Welcome to Central America, Ash."

I sit back in my seat. "Try not to call me 'Ash' today, would ya?"

"Right, sorry." He glances into the backseat. "I think I'm nervous. And not just because—you know. I want to do a good job of this, the same way we always set the headstones so nicely back home. I've been with the grey lady a long time now."

I hum. "No matter what happens, we can call this our most memorable wedding anniversary ever."

He hums too. "The year we disposed of the body."

"Hey, Durk, you know those charts inside the pocket calendars they used to give out free in greeting card stores?"

"Uh—no."

"Well, they'd tell you what material your anniversary gift should be made out of, every year. You know, like, silver for the twenty-fifth anniversary and that kind of thing."

Durk is nodding. "Right. So what kind of gift should we be giving each other for our eleventh anniversary today?"

"I have no idea. Though I doubt it's human bone."

"Good thing we don't need presents. Me, I'm just happy we made it here without any trouble."

He's right. No one asked any questions in the port in Belize City when Martin dismissed the yacht and its little crew. The customs officers might have met the captain later, but we and May were all gone by then.

Without May, it will be safe for us to make the return trip to Canada in a normal commercial aircraft. After she's buried here in Central America, the rest of us will clear the security checkpoints at the airports without any worries. We plan to leave my green suitcase behind and bring my things back in a brand new one to make sure the airport hound dogs don't detect traces of anything too smoky or too human.

Tina chose our resort because it's deep in the forest. It's in the eastern part of the country, not far from ancient ruins and other cool things none of us has much of an interest in, honestly. Heather and Suzanne would have liked them.

From the resort it's easy to get to this road, winding through dense forest, reaching for the Guatemalan border.

"There," Durk said this morning as he scanned the map and pointed to the Mountain Pine Ridge Forest. "We're heading through there."

It's a national park. I don't know why it surprised me that foreign countries have them too. It's nice that a park will be May's graveyard, maybe until the end of time.

Tina and Martin and Martin's new mom didn't come along for the trip into the forest. They're staying at the resort while Durk and I pretend to be off on some sappy, solitary anniversary picnic. Martin cracked a bunch of lewd jokes and handed Durk the keys to the rental truck.

It will be a quiet day at the resort, indistinguishable from yesterday. Martin will act like he's relaxing on the pool deck when really he's lobbing endless volleys of business emails. His mom will drift through the chlorinated water on a floating chair, sipping drinks and remembering what she liked best about Martin's cheating father. Tina will sit in a lounge chair looking at the same page of chick-lit for hours, fretting.

Out in the jungle, I'm wishing I knew how close we're getting to Guatemala. "Do you think we'll meet a bunch of guys with machine guns if we get too close to the border?"

Durk shrugs. "I don't know. We'll meet whatever we meet."

I watch the road go by for another minute before I look away from the windshield and say, "This is far enough now, right?"

He squints down the road. "Not yet."

I'm frowning. "I don't believe in the witch-doctor tea story, Durk. I know you did this for no one's sake but mine. Every bit of it—you did it for the part of Suzanne that overlaps me."

No one sighs as heavily as Durk. "This is far enough," is what he says.

A sign on the side of the road is marked with a yellow stickman holding a walking staff. It means there's a trail here, branching away from the road, into the forest.

Durk steers the truck as far off the highway as he can before it would have rolled into the steep ditch. When he's outside, I crawl over the centre console and out the driver's door. The unrefrigerated air hits me like steam shot out of a kettle. I'm instantly sweating as I step into the road behind Durk. He's pulling my nearly empty green suitcase from behind the front seats. He rips the lining out, exposing the bag of bone and ash.

The cremains come into plain sight, under a high, equatorial, noonday sun. The plastic shroud crackles, moving between Durk's fingers. The grit inside it is dull—no tiny flakes of quartz to reflect the sunlight, not like real inorganic sand. I hate it.

I'm staggering, sick. Maybe it's from the light, or the heat, or a blast of the same *chi* that moves through the graveyards back home—the bad energy that used to knot up Durk's stomach when we'd worked too long among the dead. It's funny. Ever since this thing with May, graveyards don't make him sick anymore. I'm the one who's sick now, doubled over in the middle of a highway next to my gutted suitcase.

Durk doesn't see me sinking toward the hot, oily surface of the road. I want to call out to him but the need to keep quiet and unseen as we finish this errand overwhelms me. I can't speak. I snatch at his free hand.

"Ashley? Hey, you okay?"

I've got him. My grip is strong and I'm moving, lunging forward, foot in front of foot, dragging Durk out of the light, out of the open roadway. I'm sick but running through the heat, toward the trees.

"Not the trees, the trail," Durk calls down the length of our arms.

I veer toward the trailhead, to the space where the trees are farther apart than in the rest of the forest. On the path, beneath the trees, it's instantly green and dark—dark enough to dilate my pupils. I halt. Durk runs into me, knocking me forward and grabbing me backward at the same time, trying to keep me upright, setting me onto my feet again. The bag of bones in his grip crunches against my back as he reaches for me. Something in me so desperate and visceral I hardly recognize it throws my body away from him. I'm on the ground, scuttling away from my husband in a crab-walk through the forest litter.

"Ashley, get up," he pleads. "There might be centipedes."

"Dump it."

"We're still too close to the road."

"Dump it out!"

"Not yet. A little longer."

I give up and sit there, on my tailbone, on the ground, looking almost exactly like Suzanne must have looked the morning they took May to the gravel pit. Only I'm crying, sobbing into the palms of both my hands. I'm telling Durk what Suzanne has never told him.

"Durk—we're all so sorry."

He's on his knees in spite of the centipedes. "I know," he says. "I know. Come on. Let's go."

He's hauling me upward. When I'm on my feet, he tucks my head under his chin. He keeps the bag of bones away from me as he bends his neck and kisses the top of my sweaty head. "You okay? You ready?"

"Yeah."

"So what kinds of animals do they have out here, anyway?" he asks, because it has nothing to do with a burned-up mother-in-law. "You spent all that time on the boat reading those books Ewan gave us. Did they say anything about monkeys?"

I sniff. "Uh, yeah. But there probably aren't any up at

this elevation. We're too close to the mountains."

"What about jaguars?"

"They're down in the lowlands too."

"Eating the monkeys?"

"Maybe."

"How about alligators? Are we in danger from alligators?"

"Only if we're near water."

"Okay, so what's the scariest animal threatening our lives right this minute?"

I stop walking and look into the green canopy over our heads. "Boa constrictors."

Durk twitches. "That'll do it."

He stops and turns in a slow circle. "Time to make a resting place for our passenger. How's right here?"

He's got a small trowel with him, like the kind we use to plant tulip bulbs in the fall. He takes it out of his pocket. Both of his hands are full. One holds the trowel, the other is holding May.

"I can take her." I'm tugging on the edge of the plastic bag. "It's not like I haven't held her before. I'll take care of her while you dig."

"Are you sure?"

"Yeah. I didn't like seeing the direct sun on you and her at the same time. But it's not so bad in the trees."

I slip the bag from his hand as he crouches to scrape a hollow out of the earth. It's about a metre away from the edge of the hiking trail. I stand behind him, gripping the edge of the bag in one fist, watching the trailhead. "Not too deep," I remind him.

It doesn't take long to prepare the shallow trench-grave. In a moment Durk is stooped beside it. I hand him the plastic bag.

"We can't leave the bag behind," he says. "We're going to have to take her out of it, scatter her inside the grave."

There's no wind in the trees, and the humidity of the place makes the light ash and grit instantly heavy and damp. May's remains fall out neatly, filling the hollow without drifting. Durk uses the trowel to pile a layer of dirt over them. With the side of my foot, I heap dead leaves and indignant insects on top of it. A cracking sound is muffled as I pack the mound with the sole of my shoe. It's not all that gross or sad. It's final, like good punctuation.

Durk tucks the trowel into his back pocket and glances up the path to where the hot metal of the pickup truck blocks the trailhead.

"Steel," I remember. "On our eleventh anniversary, we're supposed to give each other gifts made out of steel."

There's still no one here to see us. Durk finds his lighter and flicks a flame out of it. He touches the fire to a corner of the plastic, and the whole thing disappears into smoke. It happens so quickly he hardly has time to let go.

"Should we," he begins, "should we, I don't know—pray, or something, before we leave?"

I let my head droop. I haven't prayed since I was a kid, since we all used to go to church together. "What could we possibly have to say in a prayer?"

"Nothing. But talking isn't the only way to pray."

Durk closes his eyes and spreads his arms. He tips his head back, facing every boa constrictor in the canopy above. "Like this," he says.

I raise both my arms, exactly like his, leaning back so the dappled green light colours my face.

We blow all the air we can out of our bodies. And as we pull it in again, Durk speaks. He says, "Adiós."

# Suzanne [27]

From our winter-dark early morning bedroom in Canada, Troy places a phone call to Dental Vision International, the agency May volunteered with in Central America. On the edge of our unmade bed, he sits down with the phone and a pad of paper right at eight o'clock. He's been fretting all night.

"Are you sure they're in the same time zone as us?" he asks, fingering the keypad, stalling now the time has arrived.

"Positive," I say. "Mountain standard time."

"May?" says the American humanitarian on the phone in Guatemala. "When she didn't report in last spring, we figured May must have made other plans."

"Made other plans" is his polite term for "flaked out." The humanitarian on the phone is not Mother Teresa—not yet—and he's a bit cynical when it comes to good intentions.

"So you just let it go?" Troy prods. "You didn't try to find her when she didn't show up?"

"Oh no," the humanitarian rushes. "We did try. But

we couldn't contact her at either of the numbers we had on file. We did leave quite a few messages on her voice-mail." He hates the sound of his own cynicism, reverber-ating through Troy's silence. "Sorry."

"You just—gave up on her?"

"Unfortunately, we have to give up on people all the time around here. Volunteers come to us when they're dumped or grieving or flunking out of school, trying to redeem themselves. But once they start to cheer up, they can get distracted and forget about our work. And then they can't bring themselves to face us and they just ig-nore our calls. I'm not saying May is like that. But thanks to everyone who is, we don't have the resources to chase down prospective volunteers who lose touch with us. I wish we did."

Troy hangs up the phone and claps his hand on the back of his neck. I flip his notepad to the page with the number for the Canadian Consulate in Guatemala.

Embarrassed by his meek neediness with the aid orga-nization, Troy takes a different approach with the Con-sulate. He speaks to them coolly, almost disinterestedly. He's saying, "You probably get pestered by jumpy rela-tives making requests like this all the time but ..."

Of course, they haven't heard from May either. They agree to start looking for her.

The phone calls don't last long enough to cause Troy to open the clinic late. He tells the officials in Guatemala I'm authorized to speak for him for the rest of the day, and then he rushes down the stairs for his shoes.

I follow, watching as he scuffs his loafers onto his feet. Before he goes, I kiss him goodbye. I kiss him goodbye whenever he leaves the house. It's not because we have a good marriage but because we don't quite have a good one. Our kiss is a wish, or a prayer. I bow to it every morning like a ritual performed by rote. But today's parting kiss is useful. It's dry and tight and quick—so hard it knocks me slightly backward, as if Troy can't calibrate his force. He is starting to panic.

He can't work. The clinic closes early when Troy leaves at lunch. He's not coming home, but driving to May's house. "Who knows, Sue, she could be in there. She could have come back and just laid low, taking a break from everything or—or—I don't know. We shouldn't have let her work so hard when she came to visit us."

I mind our home phone while Troy goes questing for his mother, alone. If we were Heather and Ewan or Ashley and Durk, I would go with him. He wouldn't be able to stop me. But we are Suzanne and Troy. He goes. I stay. From an upstairs window, I watch him reversing into the icy street, backing away from our house with his arm thrown over the top of the vacant passenger's seat, jaw tight over straight, white, gritted teeth.

It's not until Troy is standing on his mother's front step, between two huge blue willow bushes, that he realizes he's forgotten to bring May's emergency spare key. He comes in through the patio doors, the way Durk taught him. It's okay. Breaking and entering is lawful in exigent circumstances. That's what Ewan will say when

Troy confesses to him, later.

Stomping through her empty house, Troy calls May's name, loudly but not yelling. She's not there. Nothing is there. The fridge is empty and her parakeet, her papers, her purse, her pink cell phone, her biggest suitcase are all gone.

Troy returns home, a jittery wreck. I meet him at the door. I already know he's found nothing at May's house but I listen to his report anyway, my head bowed, face hidden as I tidy the pile of boots in the front hall closet. His hair is matted where he's been rubbing at the back of his skull, a nervous habit he's hardly ever nervous enough to activate.

He's anxious, asking me for a report from the Consulate in Guatemala. I stand and close my arms around his ribcage. When the Consulate called this evening, I tried to sound confused as they told me they couldn't find any written record of May entering the country. What no one in the office wanted to admit is how un-extraordinary this is in that part of the world.

"They say she's officially missing," I tell Troy. "And they said we should keep it quiet and out of the news for a while. There are people who might hear an affluent foreigner is unaccounted for and try to extort a ransom from us whether they know anything about where she is or not."

He pulls away from me, stooping to sit on the bottom step, right where I found May.

I hate this house.

"Anything from Mexico?" he asks.

There has been word from the officials in Mexico. It's new information—and it's worked out far better than I imagined it could.

If the search for May had started in Canada, following a trail of circumstantial evidence southward, it would have been clear she never boarded a plane. She used her airline's online service to check in and printed her boarding pass on the computer at our house the morning of the fall. That's the closest thing there is to a paper trail of her trip. It's short and it ends right here, in my house.

But the search for May doesn't begin in Canada. It starts in Guatemala, working northward, traveling backward through stranger territory.

We've told the Consulates May planned to fly from Canada directly to Mexico. She meant to stop to visit the Mexican village where she did her last humanitarian mission—a homecoming for the angel of floss and fluoride. From there, she was supposed to ride a bus across the border into Guatemala.

In Mexico, bureaucrats tried to find a record of May arriving in the country. They were still looking for it when something arose that trumped a mere paper trail. Ewan says direct evidence—things like eye-witness reports—are always considered superior to circumstantial evidence like scraps of paper and electronic blips. And somewhere between the people in the little village on May's itinerary and the police officers the Consulate sent to investigate, everyone agreed they'd seen May—the tall, old, white lady with the case of shiny metal hooks for picking at teeth. They'd seen her, fed her, and sent her safely on her way. That's what they all said. No one wants their hometown to become part of an international incident involving a missing aid worker. They want her to pass through safely, even if it takes all the powers of their collective imagination to make it so.

Everything is easy—everything but the sight of Troy on the bottom stair with his elbows on his knees and his fingers laced through his hair.

I didn't do this to him. I made it stranger and more difficult than it has to be, but May would have died whether I'd been standing here to see it or not. And since then, I've given him months and months more of his mother's life than the cosmos ever intended him to have. I've kept May alive. A person's official death date isn't declared until someone living knows for sure they're gone. That's what Heather says. Remember? What was it Durk said in the gravel pit? What the eye doesn't see, the heart doesn't grieve? I don't know if it's true. I'll find out when Troy finds out.

The day we call the Consulate, my sisters post a new picture from Belize. It's a shot of Ashley and Tina beside a low, five-headed waterfall. The girls are standing on wet, dark rocks at the bottom of the falls, and at the edge of the frame, floating in a pocket of still water, is a large, green suitcase. The suitcase's zipper is undone. The flap is wide open and the whole thing is inverted, face down in the water—empty.

"Check out this crazy waterfall we found," Ashley writes. "You'll never guess what they call it. Someone who's never even met us named it The Five Sisters."

By the time Tina and Ashley and the rest of them fly home, May's disappearance has become part of supper-time television news after all. It leaked into the tiny town where Troy was raised—a town where everyone is a little bit related and a secret shared among family is the same thing as common knowledge. The news coverage comes with a grainy reproduction of a photo of herself May posted on an Internet profile ages ago.

Martin tries to lighten the funk by making up stories about May falling in love and eventually turning up happier than any of us have ever known her on a beach somewhere in the Dominican Republic. It's as typical of him as it is excruciating.

"Or maybe," he says, "she's joined the Castro brothers and she's part of the revolution now."

The scenario is goofy even for Martin. He's in full-throttle improbable happily-ever-after mode. None of us knows it yet, but it's part of his denial that his marriage to Tina is over.

The day Ashley and Durk went into the jungle to bury May, Martin fell asleep on the pool deck at the resort. As the planet moved him out of the shade to where the sun's radiation could burn him up, Tina tried to tow his wheeled lounger back into the shadows. That's when his phone slid off his chest and onto the concrete. She picked it up to see if the screen had cracked. The glass was intact and beneath it was a photo not of any long-lost sister but of a woman Tina knows well: Martin's assistant—the one with the brand new comic book breast implants—completely naked.

"It was not pretty," Tina will tell us after Martin starts sleeping in his office. "The stupid girl was splayed out like something in a medical textbook, like she was prepped for surgery."

There's no cute route around it this time. Martin is the cheating brother-in-law, the ex-brother-in-law. I suppose it was inevitable. What are the odds five sisters would all marry and stay that way for life? Not one of the Dionne quintuplets did it. Divorce, vows of celibacy, death—statistical probability will not abide a universe of well-loved girls.

While Martin is glossing over the immediate future, pretending catastrophes like May's disappearance can always be softened into charming capers, Ewan is expecting the very gloomiest outcome. Heather has kept my secret from him, but his well-developed sense of foreboding tells him May is dead. Ewan can't help being a doomsayer. If something doesn't end in carnage, no one puts it on his desk so he can make it right. He's got no faith in any happy ending but his and Heather's. There isn't much happiness at the police department, only justice—all that horrible justice.

It's still winter when the Canadian Consulate in Guatemala finds remains that might be May's. A federal police officer—not one of Ewan's city cops—comes to our house with latex gloves, a sterile bag, and a swab to rub against the inside of Troy's cheek. They're trying to match his DNA to whatever might be left in the densest part of charred human bones they've found.

"The remains in question were located near the Guatemalan border," the officer explains. "Off in the east."

"East?" Troy echoes. "There's no reason my mother would have been way over by the border."

"The remains weren't necessarily found at the site of the fatality. The area of interest is utilized by a large and mobile wildlife population and there is reason to suspect some animal involvement."

Troy drops his head into his hands.

The officer knows he's wrecked it. He's panicking. "What I mean to indicate is the area where the remains were subsequently located might not be the same as the location wherein they were first deposited."

The DNA match between Troy and the bones at the Guatemalan border comes back from the lab quickly enough to impress even jaded Ewan. He says so when he arrives at our front door with the official letter explaining the remains have been identified as May's.

The police theory tacked to the bones is that something living in the forest found and unearthed them. Eventually, they were noticed by a troupe of amateur European lepidopterists on vacation, hiking through the Mountain Pine Ridge Forest, near the Guatemalan border. By now, pictures of May's bones are probably posted in travel galleries all over the Internet alongside shots of rare, equatorial butterflies.

Despite any guidelines about conflicts of interest, Ewan is now personally involved in May's case. The "animal involvement" officer comes along with him, but only Ewan speaks to us. It's sweet but terrifying. The possibility of Ewan assuming his badger form and clamping onto May's suspicious burial has been something I've dreaded and avoided from the moment May fell.

But he seems satisfied with the story the police and the consular officials have agreed upon. He repeats it to us in our living room. "They're saying May could have just as easily suffered an accident or a natural death—like a stroke or a fall or something—as a homicide. All it would have taken would have been for whoever found her to see she was a foreigner, panic, burn her remains, and hide them in the jungle."

Troy sits through all of it leaning forward on the couch, pinching his hands between his knees, agitated but grave.

"Oh, May," I say. There's no acting, no pretending to be gutted. I thought I'd be fighting the urge to high five my sisters when we got to this point. But I'm struck with a funny nausea, not in my stomach but in my chest, around my heart itself.

I will mourn May, now it's possible for me to do so. I will miss her. I will miss what I see of her in Troy as he covers his face with both his hands and finally starts to cry.

Ewan pats him hard on the back and takes leave of us. The remains, he says, will be released for burial in a few days. There are arrangements to be made. Heather will help.

The front door clicks closed, and I go to Troy. I cradle his head in my arms. I try to smooth the knot of dark hair on the back of his head. I kiss his crown. The rote prayer of my kiss has traces of soul in it.

What the eye doesn't see, the heart doesn't grieve. I know this for what it is now. It's a lie and that's all—fantasy, delusion. Troy's sorrow for his mother isn't only for her death but for the time he carried on eating fish oil, sniffing eucalyptus, golfing, drilling teeth, living as if his mother was safe and well when she was not.

The moment Ewan arrived here to reveal the results of the DNA test was like the point in a pool of water where a stone is thrown into it. Ripples move away from the point in unbroken concentric circles, waving in all directions, the same speed and size, disturbing all the waters. In the same way, Troy's grief flows away from here—from this evening, this room, these tears—filling the immensity of his entire life. It's as if there's no such thing as time, nothing aligning and separating the events that make up our lives. His mother's death floods into every minute before and after this one. And we are left with one great waving sea of pain.

Those months I thought I spared Troy suffering are shot through with grief now. In his sobs I hear that I've spared him nothing.

The eye—what's seen with the eye is no gauge of what the heart will grieve.

The son whose mother lives, spry and happy, on and on, is gone. He joins my perfect daughter-in-law persona in a place neither Troy nor I will ever see again. Neither the son nor the daughter-in-law was meant to last forever—not as we knew them, anyway. It was madness for me to fight against their endings. But don't we all fight against our endings, every minute of our lives? I missed the signal, somehow—the sign we all acknowledge as the point where resistance must end.

I accept the endings—all of them—as Troy's arms clamp around my waist. I am horrible and wrong, but my body is here to comfort him anyway, still soft and warm, still keeping its promises. It is what I can offer—for the moment, all I can offer.

# All [28]

We are sitting the way everyone wants us to sit: lined up in the descending chronological order of our births.

At the head of the line, there's Heather: the eldest of us, loud, bossy and faded, like a tea towel someone's left hanging on the clothesline all winter long.

Suzanne comes next: tall for one of us, and the only sister who looks any good wearing a colour known as lime green. She won a poetry contest back in high school, and if she hasn't got over it by now, she never will.

Tina is next: stark mad but rosy and robust the way some ladies get when they've had a lot of children—like flowers might spring from her footprints as she walks away.

Second from the end of the line is Ashley: the pretty little sister. But she's had too much sun lately, and it's beginning to make her older, like everyone else.

Meaghan is last: arms folded, all curves and plastic and irony. Out of habit, we were about to add "sadness" but it's just not there, not today.

We're together—all of us and the husbands we've

kept—a party of nine gathered for Meaghan and Riker's wedding trip in Niagara Falls. All that water is the back-drop for a family picture. We're perched on the edge of the heavy, quarried stone and iron fence that runs along the edge of the cliff overlooking the falls. We have been here before. Mum and Dad brought us when we were kids. Meaghan doesn't remember anything about that visit. And Ashley admits what she believes she remembers might really have been planted by a Superman movie and a Travel Ontario ad campaign.

When the five of us first looked over the railing as grown women, Ashley's big, bright eyes started to tear.

"Here, honey," Heather said over the noise—water on rock, water on water. "Quick, throw a nickel into it."

Ashley took the coin. She flipped it into the river below the way Dad taught us to flip coins, working our thumbs like catapults. The silvery disc seemed to vanish before it broke the surface of the water. It hadn't sunk; it was more like it had been vaporized, scattered into infini-tesimal pieces, becoming part of the spray.

Maybe this is the kind of maelstrom where any-thing—anyone—could disappear. That's what each of us will think for the rest of our lives every time we lean out over utter destruction like this waterfall. We will think of all it could consume.

Even destruction usually leaves ruins. And ruins are found, documented, guarded like the death-defying ar-tefacts in the museums here. The museums tell us the first person to survive riding this water over the cliff was a woman wrapped in a mattress inside a barrel. She was called "Queen of the Mist"—or maybe that's just what she called the barrel. She was an old lady, like May and, more and more every day, a bit like us.

After one accidental death, one cremation, two false burials, and thousands of miles over land and sea, the remains of Suzanne's mother-in-law are where they belong. She's planted in the cemetery of the flat brown town where she was born and raised, lying within arms' reach of the bones of her homesteader ancestors.

May's funeral was a massive event. With as many third cousins as she had, it would have been a big funeral no matter how or when she died. Being found dead and incinerated after going missing in Central America elevated it to a celebrity funeral. The nearest television station sent a news crew to wait outside the chapel to film May's older brother marching toward the funeral limousine, holding her urn cradled in one arm like the most precious of all footballs.

Her final urn was a steel capsule coated in enamel and painted to look like Mexican pottery—a sign from Troy's family that they held no grudges against Latin America.

May's burial monument ("headstone" doesn't make much sense for cremated remains) is mounted flush to the ground—a granite slab the colour of cooked salmon's flesh. The death date forever carved into the stone is eight months too late.

If the extended family and the townspeople in the chapel had known what happened to May's body after she died, they might have found it ghastly when Troy broke down reading May's eulogy, and Suzanne stood up, threaded her arm through his, and held onto him until he finished speaking. As it was, she was all grace and beauty, standing beside her husband at May's funeral pulpit. It was true even for those of us who knew the real story.

Don't ever believe Suzanne was callous about May— not by the end, anyways. And in a world made possible only by forgiveness, the ending is the part that matters most.

At the luncheon, after the memorial service and the interment of May's urn, two tall, grey-haired women came toward Suzanne out of the crowd, walking arm-in-arm—Troy's aunts, Julie and March, May's sisters. Suzanne could not have them touch her, tell her how thankful they were, without crumbling into grief.

Above Niagara Falls today, the sky is stratified—fog, rainbow, sun. Mist rises from the water. Tiny airborne droplets settle into our hair, frizzy and damp. If there's one thing this family can do right, it's grow hair. It hasn't always been this way. When we were little, Mum kept us shorn. Now that we're grown up, each of us keeps our hair long, without exception.

Maybe all those shorthaired years Mum was toying with the fantasy of us ending up boys—five sons, not her image but our father's. Not that Dad ever complained to us about being sonless. He called us his lucky streak, a complete set.

Mum and Dad were here in Niagara Falls for the wedding earlier in the week. Riker's parents from the video game store were here too. Dad stayed long enough to pull his favourite feminist stunt, where he refuses to give his daughter away at her wedding. It's his chance to show his sons-in-law and anyone else that women are not goods to be traded. Dad is actually pretty cool. It's too bad he kept so far out of this story—and out of all our other stories too.

When the wedding ceremony was over, Heather bossed Mom and Dad into coming to dinner with everyone. But then they were gone. Mum hates it when we boss, and Dad hates it when we get married. They didn't stay any longer than strictly necessary. We don't know what's become of Riker's parents. Maybe they're in a casino, or on a Ferris wheel, or down on the river, draped in rented plastic ponchos, holding onto each other, ogling the falls from below.

Across the wide sidewalk from where we sit lined up on the stone wall, there are four cameras pointed at us. There isn't much hope any of them will capture a decent image of all us at once. Our family portraits are famously bad.

"Nice," Ewan says, looking through his viewfinder with his camera pulled right up to one of his eyes, like it's 1995. "The mist in your hair makes you look like a bunch of mermaids. Either that or a bunch of harpies."

He snaps a picture just as Heather is rolling her eyes. "Not harpies," she says. "You mean 'sirens.'"

"Nah, I've heard you guys sing and I've seen you eat. Harpies."

Maybe Troy means to rescue Ewan when he breaks

from the line of brothers-in-law and bounds to where we're seated. Troy is trying to squeeze into our line, between Suzanne and Tina.

"Hey," he calls to the other men, "someone take a picture of me with my five wives."

Tina jumps, shoving Troy's arm back at him as he's draping it around her. "Gross."

Heather howls, and Ashley and Meaghan hop to their feet like they've been jolted with electric currents.

Troy is laughing. "What's the problem, girls? They say natural sister groups make the very best plural wives."

"Will you get out of here, Troy?" Suzanne is pushing him away, and he goes easily, laughing and tripping back into the line of brothers-in-law. Someone got a photo of him as he was sitting down and we were recoiling from him. It will be one of his favourites for the rest of his life.

Troy's stunt must have made Ewan possessive of his own wife, and he is through teasing us. He lowers his camera and speaks with senior-brother-in-law authority. "Honestly, you're impossible to photograph en masse. In every one of my shots someone's talking or looking sideways or pulling a piece of hair out of her mouth."

Heather stands. The oldest person in a picture is usually keenest to leave it. "Yeah, let's just forget it and move on."

"No, no, no," Durk drawls. "We can do this. We just have to mellow. Take a deep breath and say it, sisters: mellow."

And someone takes a picture of us saying "mellow" together, our lips formed into five Os. It's an interesting concept, but it's not what we were hoping for in a family picture.

Troy slaps Riker on the back. "Get up there, dude. You're our last hope at getting a nice sisters shot."

"No pressure, honey." Meaghan chirps it at him, an apology for all of us.

Riker has been less nervous of our harpy troop ever since that night in the karaoke lounge. The place had the feel of somewhere meant for tourists from overseas, but everyone there was polite when we took to the stage and did some kind of Japanese cheerleader routine Meaghan and Riker tried to teach us.

Sitting on the wall over the falls, we remember a bit of the choreography and form our hands into the shapes of hearts, pulsing them toward Riker. With everyone watching and fawning at once, Riker is tensing again.

Heather knows she must make the tension worse. "Come on. Make us smile, Riker. This is very important."

"Stop it," Meaghan hisses down the line.

Riker raises his camera. "Okay, everybody. On the count of three we're all going to say one little word together as we smile."

We're nodding at him, ready for our cue.

"Everybody put your hands down, open your eyes, and say 'quints.'"

He gets a picture of us smiling, each of us charmed by his insistence, beyond all reason and mathematics, that we are quintuplets.

Tomorrow, we'll show Riker how much we want to

love him by going in search of the remains of Quintland, hours north of here.

"I already looked it up on the Internet." Heather has told us. "It's just a little old house on the side of the road."

Quintland is also a lawn, an empty space, the void left where Depression-era tourists used to queue to gawk at five little sisters. The freak show part of the original nursery complex is gone, torn down and swept away. There's no sign of the observation area where crowds used to stand behind screens made of something like gauze bandages to watch the sisters play.

That's the story, anyway. Caught in the rippling currents of history—backward and forward—everything is a story. The strangest stories are the truest ones—a barrel over the falls, five babies born at once, maybe even our story. What matters isn't always whether stories are true, but whether they could be true—whether we could rise up and live through them if we were ever called upon to do so.

When we get to Quintland, we will walk onto the grass and stand on the lawn. We don't know what we'll feel. Maybe we'll be like the other pilgrims, thinking about the real Dionne quintuplets, feeling sad and guilty about children exploited for nothing but finding their lives in the same cells.

Or we might not be thinking about the Dionne sisters at all.

Maybe we'll be thinking of Riker, worrying that the museums and shrines—the empty spaces and little wooden monuments—will be smaller and more tainted with ambivalence than he expected. Still, he'll love it anyway.

And the rest of us—my sisters and I—we'll be standing in the ruins of Quintland, on the grass, together. We'll reach out our arms, fingers splayed, until our hearts are braced open. We'll tip our faces up to the sun, not looking into each other's eyes, but out of them.

# Acknowledgements

My first thanks go to my young sons, Jonah, Samuel, Nathan, Micah, and James. If any of them ever wished I were baking cookies instead of writing books, they never said so to me. As always, my husband, Anders Quist, was indispensably supportive throughout this creative process and not just for his familiarity with the Criminal Code of Canada.

Especially in this endeavour, my family of origin must be acknowledged. This includes my parents, Lloyd and Pat MacKenzie, who are warm and caring, unlike the parents in the story. There are also my four blood sisters, the lovely non-committers of indictable offences, Amy Woolf, Sara MacKenzie, Mary Bourne, and Emily MacKenzie. It's the connections between us, not our true life stories, that were the inspirations for this book. My sisters' husbands must be thanked for what they've contributed to and tolerated in our relationships. Thank you, Curtis Woolf, Greg Bourne, and Allan Taylor.

My publisher and editor, Linda Leith, was a major factor in shaping my second novel, one written before my first book was published in the days before I was sure who I was as a novelist. With her guidance, it's gone from being a story I liked to being one that I love.

Jennifer Quist